THE RELUCTANT MATE

SHIFTERS OF THE THREE RIVERS BOOK 5

KIRA NIGHTINGALE

ÉDITIONS SPOTTISWOODE

Book Cover by 100 Covers

Edited by Brigitte Billings

Published by Éditions Spottiswoode

First edition 2025

ISBN (ebook): 978-1-998510-03-0

ISBN (paperback):978-1-998510-02-3

CONTENTS

DEDICATION AND TRIGGER WARNINGS

"The only thing necessary for the triumph of evil is for good men to do nothing." – Edmund Burke

"I'm done feeling helpless...I will not stand by and watch them tear apart everything I believe in. I fight." – Sofia Miller

Dedication

To those who feel invisible while holding everyone else's worlds together. To the ones who stay when others leave, who give when others take, who smile through the exhaustion. To everyone who's ever wondered if they're worth staying for.

You are seen. You are the strongest among us. And you deserve someone who chooses you, again and again, without hesitation.

Trigger Warnings

This book contains adult themes and lots of spice. Triggers include attempted rape; trauma and PTSD; kidnapping; violence and graphic fight scenes; torture references; and substance addiction and its effects.

CHAPTER ONE

PROLOGUE - DEREK

*T*he nightmare had changed in recent months. No longer just a vague memory of Harris dying in my arms; now, the sound of the bullets whizzing past my head and Harris's shouted warning before he lunged toward me, shielding me from the worst of the blast haunted my dreams. It smelled so real: the dust and oil, the dry sand, the adrenaline and fear leaking from my men, the metallic blood as it seeped from Harris's body.

Harris. My best friend. Human, yes, but my brother, all the same. He'd signed up at the same time as I had, and we'd gone through basic training together. He was the person who'd snuck me out of the med tent, despite a sprained wrist, so I wouldn't miss my shot at the obstacle course record I'd been chasing all year, the one I'd pulled out of a freezing lake during survival training, while he cracked jokes through trembling lips the entire time to keep my mind off how fucking cold I was as I hauled his half-frozen ass to shore. He'd been the first to congratulate me when I was promoted to Captain and the last to leave the bar we celebrated in that night. He was my brother-in-arms, and I would have done anything for him.

I'd stopped trying to wake myself up; there was no point. No matter what I did, I was stuck reliving this memory until it had all played out. I looked down at his body, the blood pumping out of him, the knowledge that he would be dead in seconds hitting me just like it did the first time.

Tonight, though, something was different. The blood pooling around Harris's body moved like oil on water, thick and goopy, creeping outward in spiraling patterns that made my eyes hurt to follow. The copper stench was overwhelming, mixed with cordite and something else—rot and decay that shouldn't be there yet. His eyes snapped open with a wet sound, milky gray turned to burning amber, and when he smiled, his teeth were stained crimson, dripping black ichor that hissed where it hit the ground.

What fresh hell is this?

My muscles locked as photographs appeared on the blood-soaked ground around his body. Sofia. Dozens of images of her. At the Bottley Bar and Coffee shop, serving customers with her bright smile; locking up the bar late at night, keys clutched in her hand. Sofia in the Three Rivers market, the sunlight making her hair flame like a beacon, unaware of the lens capturing her every move, close-ups of her laughing with Wally and Mai. These were the photos my brother Mason and I had found pinned to a cabin wall when we'd been tracking the remnants of Tristan's Pack. Hundreds of photos of her, my mate.

"You can't protect her," Harris's voice came out wet and gurgling, "just like you couldn't protect me. Just like you couldn't protect any of them."

More photos appeared, overlapping the ones of Sofia. Dead soldiers from our unit. Men who'd trusted me to have their backs. Men who'd died because I'd been too slow to catch Victor Kane, the rogue operative we'd been tracking. Too slow to protect my best friend.

"No," I growled, trying to move, to gather the photos, to do something. But my muscles were frozen in place.

Harris's head turned at an impossible angle. "You'll fail her too. And this time, the blood won't be mine."

The photos began to dissolve, red seeping through them until Sofia's images drowned in crimson. Inside, my wolf threw back his head and howled as darkness consumed everything, the sound of Harris's laughter echoing in the void—

I jolted upright, sheets tangling around my legs like restraints.

"Fuck!"

Sweat had soaked through everything—my sheets, my hair—the dampness making my skin prickle in the pre-dawn chill. The bedroom air felt too thick, too close, carrying the echoes of cordite and blood that weren't really there.

I checked my phone: 3:17 a.m.

"Fuck!" I repeated, fighting the urge to Shift, to run to Sofia's house, to circle her property until sunrise, to tear apart anything that dared come close.

"Status report," I muttered, falling back on military protocol to center myself. "Location: Three Rivers territory. Time: zero-three-seventeen. Mission: protect Sofia."

The nightmare had felt so real. I could still smell Harris's blood, still hear his voice. My stomach lurched, and I swallowed down the bile that rose into my throat.

No. I wasn't going to be sick. Not again.

It had taken four months after I left the army for me to stop vomiting when I woke from the nightmares every night. I wouldn't go back to that. I couldn't. Sofia needed me to be strong, not broken.

My hands shook as I reached for my laptop. I clenched them, taking a few deep breaths to still the trembling, then grabbed my computer.

I pulled up the security feed I'd installed around Sofia's apartment building the night Mason and I got back from the cabin in the woods. The security feed showed everything still, quiet. I pulled up the feed I'd watched before going to bed, the one of her arriving home in the early hours, dressed in her work clothes, her copper hair spilling over one shoulder. My wolf growled in my head. He saw what I saw; she was working too hard. She was tired all the time. She needed someone to look out for her. I'd been trying for months to be that person, but she refused to let me in.

At least for now, she was safe. Protected. My fingers itched to touch the screen, to somehow reach through it and brush that one wayward curl from her face. Harris's words echoed in my head: *"You can't protect her."*

My wolf snarled.

We'll protect her. We'll protect our mate.

Yes, I agreed. We would die before letting anyone hurt her.

This time would be different. It had to be.

Chapter Two

SOFIA

The Friday night crowd at the Bottley Bar pressed against the counter three-deep, their scents a dizzying mix of perfume, sweat, and the metallic tang of Shifter energy that always intensified as the moon waxed fuller. Music thumped through the speakers, audible even over the constant roar of voices demanding drinks. I could pick up every conversation, every clink of glass, every burst of laughter. Being a werewolf had a lot of advantages but on nights like this, my enhanced hearing wasn't doing me any favors; after eight straight hours on my feet, my head was throbbing.

Shannon had called in sick again, leaving me short-staffed on one of our busiest nights. I'd bet my next paycheck she was skinny-dipping in the Whispering Willow River with her latest boyfriend. The thought made my chest tight. Everyone seemed to be moving forward with their lives—Mai was pregnant with twins, Wally and Thomas were busy with Amara and Ben, the siblings they had adopted; even Shannon was doing something fun with her life with her endless stream of romances. Meanwhile, I was here, pulling another double shift.

Don't get me wrong, I freaking loved working here, loved being the manager of the Bottley Bar and Coffee Shop. This place and the people who came here meant the world to me. They were my extended family, and I had their backs when they were lost, or lonely, or just needed to see a smiling face. It was just that lately, I had been wondering more and more if there was something else out there for me. And if I didn't try to find out, would I sit in my rocking chair when I was eighty and regret it?

Out of the corner of my eye, I saw Marsha Tun, one of the new teachers at the high school, hold her hand up and wave, trying to get my attention.

"Hey, Sofia, can I get two Renegade's Iced Teas and a Lunar Eclipse?"

"Sure thing," I called back, ignoring my aching feet and forcing brightness into my voice. Renegade's Iced Tea had been my own creation and had been a huge hit with the Bottley crowd. Made with a mix of white, dark and spiced rum, orange liqueur, and cola and served with a wedge of lime, it was my favorite drink to make. For a moment, I forgot my aching feet, forgot my unruly hair was once again escaping its ponytail, and that I had another five hours until closing, and just let my hands make the magic. I loved creating new drinks, loved it when people liked them and ordered from me.

I gave Marsha her drinks as Frankie Erwee caught my eye from his usual spot at the end of the bar, his fingers wrapped around an empty bottle as he gestured for another one. I'd need to call him a cab later, make sure he got home safe.

My wolf whined, craving a run through the forest, wanting to shed this human skin that felt too tight, too confining to her. I pushed her down, like always lately, and kept moving, kept smiling because that's what I did. I was Sofia Miller, the one who held everything together, who never let anyone see what was really going on inside. But between covering for Shannon's frequent absences, helping Mrs. Patterson with her weekly groceries, and making sure my brother Jase actually ate something besides pizza, I was starting to admit to myself that I was running on fumes, and I wasn't sure how long I could keep this up.

A familiar scent cut through the chaos of my thoughts. The sharp, clean bite of pine hit me first, crisp and wild, like the air in an untouched forest after a storm. Then, underneath, something darker, richer came through—the earthy warmth of moss clinging to stone that made me think of ancient woods and untamed places. It wasn't just a scent; it was a presence, raw and alive, curling around me like a whisper of the wild he carried within.

Derek Shaw. The Beta of our Pack.

My fated mate, if you believed all that destined-to-be-together bullshit. I mean, yes, I saw that it worked for Mai and Ryan, and for Shya and Mason, for Wally and Thomas. They were meant to be together; you just had to spend thirty seconds with them to see how much in love, how devoted to their mates they were.

But that wasn't what Derek and I had. No, he'd once made it clear he didn't want that with me, ghosting me for months. And now? He might have changed his mind, but I hadn't. The image of Derek crushing my heart in his hand, sprinkling it into a whiskey, and then drinking it rose in my mind. Yeah, I wanted nothing to do with him. Of course, Derek wasn't making it easy.

This evening, he was in his usual booth, the one Wally had

nicknamed the Booth of Brooding, laptop open, pretending to work while he watched everything around him. Always watching. Always present. Always a reminder of what I couldn't have, what I'd been stupid enough to think was mine for one perfect night before he'd disappeared without a word.

The memory of that night flashed through me, as it often did these days, no matter how much I tried to put it in a box and set fire to it. His hands in my hair, his mouth on mine as the Ferris wheel carried us above the lights of Three Rivers. The way he'd whispered against my lips before making me come apart under the stars.

Then nothing.

No calls, no texts, not even a passing acknowledgment. Just silence that stretched into weeks until I got the message—I might be his fated mate, but he had a taste and didn't like it. I wasn't worth sticking around for. Just like I hadn't been worth it to my parents or to my best friend, Mai, when she'd run away for four freaking years. At least Mai had come back and apologized. Derek just pretended nothing had happened while showing up at my bar night after night, watching me with those intense gray eyes that gave away nothing.

I sighed, ignoring him for as long as I could, focusing on mixing drinks, on smiling at customers, on being the Sofia everyone expected. But my eyes kept finding him in my peripheral vision.

It wasn't just that he was tall—though, at 6'2", he was—it was the way he sat, all controlled strength and effortless power, a predator constantly assessing its surroundings. Every movement was deliberate; he was calculated, precise, but with a clear undercurrent of tightly controlled violence. You took one look at him and knew if you crossed him, he would not hesitate to end you. Not in an out-of-control-Friday-night-fight sort of way, either; no, you got the impression he was constantly assessing everyone around him to work out the most efficient way to put you down.

It was scary as hell, especially since I'd known Derek and his twin, Sam, my whole life. Had known them as teenagers, playing harmless pranks, like rigging all the lockers in the teachers' lounge to play the Imperial March from *Star Wars* whenever they were opened. But that was before Derek joined the military and came back with bulging muscles and that look in his eyes that said he was sizing you up for dinner.

Out of the corner of my eye, I saw Derek lean back in his booth, his arms flexing slightly with the motion, the fabric of his dark Henley pulling taut across his biceps, and the shirt doing nothing to hide the sculpted ridges of his torso. Damn him and his perfect body and his perfect hair, and his stupid smirk and the way he made my pulse race even after everything he'd done. Damn the Moon Goddess for making him my fated mate, for tying me to someone who could walk away so easily.

Finally, unable to ignore him any longer, and knowing if I did, he would come and find me, I made his usual order—black coffee with a shot of Aberlour whiskey—and made my way to his table. His eyes followed me, making my skin tingle in a way I refused to acknowledge.

"Your usual," I said, setting down his drink with slightly more force than necessary. "Though I don't know why you bother with the coffee. It's almost midnight."

A smirk played at the corner of his mouth—the same mouth that had kissed me senseless before he'd ignored me for months without so much as a text message to say thanks, but no thanks.

Urrrggg. I so had to get over it, over him.

"Worried about my caffeine intake?"

"Worried about my profit margins. You only have one drink every two hours. Most people here drink four times that much in the same time. If you're not here for the drinks, maybe you should find someplace else, someplace quieter, to work."

"Maybe I enjoy the view here." His voice dropped lower as his eyes bore into mine, giving me no doubt as to what view he was referring to.

"Well, *the view* has work to do. Unlike some people who apparently think looking mysterious in corners counts as a job."

His grin widened, making him look way more sexy than any man had a right to. "You know, I give a mean foot massage. In case all that running around catches up with you."

The thought of his warm hands caressing my aching feet almost made me pull up a stool and plonk my feet in his lap. But I knew if I felt his hands on me, I'd want to feel them *everywhere* on me.

I turned away quickly, needing to get out of there. "I'll be sure to let Mrs. Henderson know. She was just telling me how her arthritis is acting up."

I would, too. I heard his chuckle as I walked away, just as I felt his stare following me back to the bar. Heat crept up my neck, and I hated myself for reacting to him at all. He'd had his chance. One perfect date, one mind-blowing orgasm at the top of the Ferris wheel, and then radio silence for weeks. Derek Shaw might be my fated mate, but that didn't mean I had to like it.

Or him.

Chapter Three

SOFIA

"**S**ofia!"

I looked up to see Wally sweep in, weaving his way through the crowd with practiced ease. Wearing a crisp pink button-down that practically glowed under the bar lights, he was a spot of vibrant color in the sea of Friday night casual wear. Thomas followed, his huge 6'5" frame towering above everyone else here. Thomas was our Pack doctor, and usually, he would hunch down to try to make himself look less threatening when seeing patients. Here, though, out for date night with his mate, he stood tall and proud, allowing himself to take up all the space he needed.

Wally air-kissed both my cheeks, then pulled back to study me critically. His nose wrinkled at whatever he picked up in my scent.

"Honey, I want to tell you that you look fabulous, but I'd be lying. Your hair is a complete disaster. Did you, by any chance, stick your finger in an electrical socket?"

I self-consciously patted my wayward curls. "We're short-staffed again. Shannon called in sick."

"Mmhmm." Wally's eyes sparkled as he caught sight of something over my shoulder. "Off with Henri, no doubt. And I'm sure having Tall, Dark, and Brooding over there watching your every move has nothing to do with your disheveled state? My sources tell me he's been here every night this week."

Sources? Wally was the Pack gossip. Anything going on in Three Rivers, Wally usually knew all about it. He was also known to drive like Vin Diesel and fight like Jason Bourne, even though he had been known to come to battles armed with a tennis racket.

"I have no idea what you are talking about," I lied.

"Oh, please." Wally settled onto a barstool, Thomas taking the seat beside him. "I haven't been here five minutes, and I know that man hasn't taken his eyes off you all night. Are you ever going to get over being angry with him?"

"I'm not angry." The words came out sharper than I intended, making both men raise their eyebrows. "I'm not anything," I tried again in a calmer voice. "I'm completely over him. It. I mean it." I winced, hoping they didn't notice my slip-up. "It's just... he's just... always here. Watching. Like I'm some kind of problem he needs to solve."

"Sounds like someone's obsessed. And I don't mean Derek."

I narrowed my eyes at Wally, more annoyed at myself than him. I knew he was right. No matter how hard I tried to forget about Derek Shaw, my thoughts always circled back to him. And him being here all the time wasn't making it any easier. Maybe I needed a vacation. Maybe I needed to go someplace where Derek was not.

I turned and poured a Blood Moon Sangria—red wine, blood orange juice, brandy, and mulled dark berries, served over ice with a cinnamon stick—Wally's usual on date night, and grabbed a bottle of beer for Thomas, desperate to change the subject from Derek fucking Shaw.

"How's Mai doing? Is bed rest driving her crazy yet?"

"Oh, we are well past that. Our dear Alpha is about ready to commit murder." Wally accepted his wine with a look that said he wasn't fooled by my deflection. "Ryan's hovering is making her insane, and she's blaming Thomas for putting her on bed rest for the rest of the pregnancy."

Thomas shrugged. "She only has to do it for another two weeks. The break from everyone bugging her to make decisions for the Pack will be good for her and the pups."

Mai had been Alpha with Ryan for nearly a year now, and it was wearing on her. After the uncertainty of Jem and Hayley's years as Alphas, and then the shitshow that was Brock and Hayley, some of the Pack had grabbed onto Mai and Ryan as a stabilizing force. Maybe too much. These days, it seemed like every minor dispute ended up at the Alpha's doorstep.

Last month, Brielle Lewis pitched up at 5 a.m. demanding an audience because she claimed her night camera trap she'd set up to catch the raccoon that kept raiding her bins had picked up Larry Moore in wolf form shitting on her lawn. Ryan had ordered Brielle to go home, but the disputes just kept coming.

Then, two days ago, Mai had fainted while she and Ryan were having sex, and Ryan, whose paranoia meter was already redlining, went into full Terminator-Alpha-protector mode. He'd called Thomas in a panic, demanding a complete workup. Now Mai was on bed rest until the pups were born, with a contingent of enforcers guarding the Alpha House night and day like it was Fort Knox.

Her being on bed rest was good for her, but it was making seeing Mai tricky. I missed my best friend; between her Pack duties and now the bed rest, and me pulling double shifts, I hardly saw her anymore.

As if reading my mind, Wally leaned forward. "I'm seeing her tomorrow, if I can ninja my way past the horde of bodyguards. Want to come?"

Hell, yes, I did. But before I could answer, a crash from the other end of the bar snapped my head around. Two of our regulars, Brad and Joey, were squaring up to each other, their wolves close to the surface. The scent of their aggression filled the air as the smart people started backing away.

Damn it, this had been coming for a while now, ever since Joey had a one-night stand with Brad's sister, Daisy. I knew for a fact it was Daisy who insisted it was just a one-night thing, but Brad had been grumbling for days that Joey was a sleazy whore.

"Hey!" I called, already moving toward them. "Not in here! Take it outside!"

I couldn't afford a fight in here. I wasn't kidding when I'd told Derek I was worried about my profits. We did okay, but I'd noticed in the past month that fewer of our human customers were coming in. It was becoming a Shifter bar, and it was on my never-ending to-do list to work out why and do something about it.

Ahead of me, Brad shoved Joey back, sending him stumbling into a table and knocking glasses all across the floor.

Great, just freaking great.

Behind me, I felt more than heard Derek rise from his seat. I ignored him. I could handle this. I had to handle this.

"You're gonna apologize to Daisy!" Brad snarled.

"Apologize! For what? I gave her the best ride she's had in years."

I stepped between them. "Both of you, calm down now, or you're banned for a month."

For a moment, I thought it had worked. Joey hesitated, some of the anger leaving his face. But then Brad made a sound, half growl, half snort, and Joey's control snapped. His fist shot out toward Brad, with me still in the way.

Time slowed as I watched the punch coming. I knew how to block it, but I never had the chance to put it into action. The punch never landed. One second, I was watching Joey's fist heading straight toward my face, the next, Derek was in front of me, moving with that fluid grace that made him so lethal. His hand locked around Joey's fist, stopping the punch mid-swing with ease, and twisting, forcing Joey to his knees.

"Ow! Fuck, man! You're gonna break my hand!" Joey yelled.

Damn Derek fucking Shaw. Damn him for making it look so effortless. And damn my traitorous body for the way it immediately relaxed in his presence as his scent wrapped around me like a shield.

"Enough," Derek growled. "Brad, talk to Daisy. She wanted to have fun with Joey. Joey obliged. There was nothing more to it. Joey, give the guy a break. He doesn't want to hear who his sister slept with or how good or bad it was. Now both of you are gonna clear this up, apologize to Sofia, and are gonna work here, for free, every evening for the next month, washing dishes or doing whatever shit Sofia wants you to do. And if either of you does anything to put Sofia in a place where she could get hurt again, I'll break both of your legs. Got it?"

Joey cradled his hand and stood up on wobbly legs. "Shit, I'm... I'm sorry."

"Yeah, me too," Brad mumbled, already bending down to pick up the pieces of glass. "Won't happen again. I swear."

I put my hands on my hips, a clear sign to anyone with a brain that I was in what Wally called my "DEFCON 1 mood" and whirled to face Derek, fury building in my chest until I could taste it, bitter and metallic on my tongue.

"I had it handled!"

He ignored my hands on my hips and crossed his arms, his expression infuriatingly calm. "Had it handled? Is that what you call standing directly in the path of a werewolf's fist?"

"I was about to move."

"Really? Because from where I was standing, you were about to get a free rhinoplasty."

I stepped closer, close enough that I had to tilt my head back to meet his eyes. "Has anyone ever told you that playing the hero gets old real fast?"

"Has anyone ever told you that your self-preservation instinct is practically non-existent?" he countered, not backing down an inch.

"I don't need you to fight my battles."

The corner of his mouth twitched. "Not all of them. Just the ones where you're outnumbered and out-muscled."

Arrggghh. The man was insufferable.

I jabbed a finger at his chest. "Next time, stay in your seat."

He caught my hand before I could pull it back, his touch sending an unwelcome jolt through my system.

"Next time," he said quietly, "if I'm not here, duck."

I yanked my hand away, hating how my skin tingled where he'd touched it. "I don't need your advice. Or your help. Or your... constant hovering."

"It's not hovering. It's strategic positioning."

"Well, strategically position yourself somewhere else from now on."

A ghost of a smile touched his lips. "Can't do that, gorgeous."

"Don't call me gorgeous," I snapped. He didn't get to call me gorgeous, not after throwing me away.

"What should I call you, then?"

"Nothing. Don't call me anything. In fact, don't talk to me at all."

"That's going to make get-togethers at Ryan and Mai's awkward."

That was it; I had to get out of this conversation before I threw something at him.

I straightened up, jaw clenched, shot him one last glare, then whirled past him back to the bar. Next time, I was going to make sure I handled it. On my own. I didn't need Derek. I didn't need any man, or Shifter, or fated mate, coming in to rescue me. I was perfectly okay on my own.

Yes, perfectly, perfectly okay.

Chapter Four

SOFIA

The alarm pierced through my exhausted haze, making my wolf whine in protest.

You and me both, I thought at her.

Every muscle screamed as I ignored the overwhelming desire to throw my pillow at my alarm and go back to sleep. I had to get up; I had things I had to do today. People were counting on me, and I wasn't going to let them down.

I could do this.

I dragged myself out of bed, my feet catching on the super-soft purple rug that made me smile every time I stepped on it, the one splurge I'd allowed myself when I'd decorated my room. I nearly tripped over the stack of recipe books I'd been studying for new cocktail ideas, but—go me and my werewolf reactions—I just managed to stop myself from face-planting on the floor.

Silence filled the apartment as I made my way down the narrow hallway. Jase's bedroom door was open, his bed untouched—another all-nighter at Shaw Investigations. These days, he only came home to crash for a few hours and demolish our food supplies before heading out again.

The mirror in the bathroom reflected back my exhausted face—tangled curls desperately needing conditioning and dark circles under my eyes that even my best concealer wouldn't hide. To top it off, the faint smell of stale beer and cleaning products from the Bar still clung to my skin despite my shower last night.

I looked like a complete mess. At least the jasmine plant I kept on the windowsill was thriving, its sweet scent helping to mask the boy-bathroom smell of shaving gel and aftershave that seemed to follow my brother around. Empty shampoo bottles balanced precariously on the edge of the tub, telling me Jase had used my products without asking again. I blew out a breath. I'd have to tackle this disaster zone before my shift at the Bottley, but only after I'd had coffee. Copious amounts of coffee.

I gave myself a weak smile as I remembered my date with the spa this afternoon. At least I had that to look forward to. Wally and I had booked it a few weeks ago as a gift to Mai, so she could be pampered before the pups arrived. I don't know who'd been more disappointed when Mai was put on bed rest and had to cancel, but she'd insisted we go without her.

Then Wally had told me last night that he wasn't going to make it either. Ben had announced he was joining the football team and needed to go to the after-school training. It was the first time Ben had wanted to do any sports since he and his older sister, Amara, stopped living on the streets and moved in with Thomas and Wally. Wally thought it was a sign that Ben was feeling more settled and wanted to go and support him. Me? I'd decided after last night's debacle that I could do with some pampering, so I'd kept my booking.

I dragged myself to the kitchen, muscle memory taking over as I pulled out two mugs for coffee before catching myself. The second mug—the one Jase made when he was seven, Dad's favorite with "Howl At The Moon Responsibly" accompanied by what was either a wolf or a hairy potato drawn on it—went back in the cupboard with trembling fingers. Four years, and I still couldn't break the habit of making Dad a coffee every morning. I sighed, knowing it was probably because it was his birthday today. Jase had probably forgotten, but then, he was never good with dates.

The memory of the last time I'd seen my parents hit without warning, sharp and clear as the day it happened.

"It's just temporary, sweetheart." Mom's voice had been gentle as she packed. I'd moved out three months before, but living in a dorm house wasn't working out. I'd come over, planning to ask to move back, only to find my parents packing. My Aunt Lilith had called, saying her daughter, my half-werewolf, half-witch cousin, had decided the Wolf Council's rules about witches were unfair. So, she'd joined a guerrilla campaign to take the whole Council down. "Your aunt needs us. Once things settle down with the Wolf Council—"

"What about what we need?" The words burst out before I could stop them. Jase's door was closed, but I knew he could hear everything. "He's sixteen, Mom. How am I supposed to—?"

"You're strong, Sofia. Stronger than you know. The Pack will help—"

"The Pack?" I laughed, the sound brittle. "The same Pack that was too scared of Oliver to even glance at us just because I was friends with Mai Parker? That Pack?"

"It's different now. Jem and Hayley are good Alphas. It is safe here for you." She came closer, placed her hands on my shoulders. "You never

backed down from Oliver, never gave up your friendship with that Mai, even though we ordered, threatened, even begged you to."

I closed my eyes and said softly, "Fat lot of good that did. She's gone. I haven't heard from her in nearly two years."

Mom pulled me into a hug. "You can't control what others do, Sofia, only what you do, and you were a good friend to her. You stood up for her, even when it was dangerous to do so. I'm proud of you. We both are. I know we didn't show it at the time, but this is why your father and I have to go. You inspire us, Sofia, to do what is right, no matter the cost."

"But the cost is me and Jase!" I whined, desperate for them not to leave. "Can't we... can't we come with you?"

I felt her head shake next to mine. "Not now. Let us find your aunt. See what mess your cousin Annabella is in. Maybe after that, okay? This is just temporary. We'll be back soon, when we get things straightened out."

I shook off the memory, but my hands wouldn't stop shaking as I made my coffee. One cup, not two. My wolf paced restlessly, agitated by the remembered pain. Temporary had stretched into years, occasional phone calls growing shorter and less frequent until they felt like obligations rather than connections. My parents hadn't straightened out anything. Instead, they'd joined the cause, aiming to overthrow the Council to make a better world for werewolves and witches.

An hour later, I hefted groceries up the stairs to Mrs. Patterson's apartment, my arms trembling more from lack of sleep than the weight. Mrs. Patterson was a human who lived in the block opposite. Her son, Donald, and his wife had moved south to a human-only city two months ago, and she found getting out for food and medicines difficult these days. Takymora Delivery, where Jase used to work, would deliver, but they didn't unpack it all or stop and chat like I did.

My wolf perked up at the sound of Mrs. Patterson's shuffling steps on the other side of the door.

"Sofia! You're an absolute angel." Mrs. Patterson beamed as she opened the door, her hands clutching the frame for support.

"It's no trouble," I assured her, setting the bags on her counter and starting to unpack. "I got those sugar-free cookies you like and that special tea for your joints."

"Your brother must be proud to have a thoughtful sister like you. Speaking of which, is that boy eating properly? He looks too thin whenever I see him leaving your apartment."

I laughed. Jase ate enough for three wolves, but Mrs. Patterson had been trying to fatten him up for years.

"He's fine, I promise. I make sure he eats." He certainly went through the food in our fridge quickly enough.

"My son was the same at his age. It was like nothing could fill that belly of his!"

"How is Don doing?"

Her face darkened for a split second. "Oh, you know how he is. Still wants me to move near to him. He's coming up again this weekend to try to talk me into it. He keeps saying it's not safe here, not anymore, not with bloodlust wolves around."

My brows creased together. For a werewolf to succumb to bloodlust was incredibly rare. It signified the complete loss of control, where a Shifter couldn't be reasoned with, couldn't think logically or rationally. For a werewolf in bloodlust, there was no differentiating between allies and enemies; anyone who got close would be attacked. There was no coming back from it; the only way to stop a Shifter in bloodlust was to kill them.

"Bloodlust werewolves?" I asked, not sure now if I had heard correctly. There hadn't been a bloodlust werewolf in Three Rivers in twenty years.

Mrs. Patterson nodded. "It's all over the news these days. That drug—what do they call it? The one that affects you Shifters so badly?"

My heart skipped a beat. I'd been so busy with work lately, I hadn't been paying attention to the news. "You mean ripple?"

"Yes, that's the one. They say it causes bloodlust in some Shifters. That werewolves everywhere are losing control. Targeting humans. That you can't be trusted to live in the same places as us anymore."

She must have seen something in my face, because she patted my hand. "Not you, Sofia, not you. But Don reckons I should move closer to him, just in case."

Ripple was bad news for Shifters. It was a new, highly addictive drug that not only affected us, which was unusual in itself, but it prevented us from Shifting into our wolf forms and drove us to break our Pack bonds. Mason Shaw, one of Derek's brothers, along with his mate Shya, were the new Alphas of the Bridgetown Pack, and they'd been doing a lot of research into the effects of the drug and whether it was reversible. I'd have to ask them if this bloodlust effect was true.

"Mrs. Patterson, even if it was true about ripple causing bloodlust, Mai and Ryan shut down ripple in Three Rivers. They're keeping a close eye on it. There's no ripple getting in."

"Well, you know Don. He says we humans won't be high up on Mai and Ryan's list of priorities soon with their babies to think about. He thinks I'll be safer if I move to his human-only town." She glanced around at her apartment, her eyes glistening. "But this is my home. All my memories are here."

Don was an ass for trying to scare his mom into doing what he wanted. There was no ripple, no bloodlust werewolves, and very little criminal activity in Three Rivers; it's hard to commit a crime and get away with it when werewolves can track you all the way back to your home. I had half a mind to pop around this weekend and give Donald a piece of my mind. I reached out and squeezed her hand.

"Mrs. Patterson, you decide what's best for you, but Jase and I will always be here for you if you want to stay, you know that?"

"You and Jase have always been so good to me. Stay for coffee?" she offered hopefully. "I just made a fresh pot." Mrs. Patterson normally drank tea; if she'd made coffee, it was because she really wanted me to stay. Maybe I could rearrange the rest of my errands and do them after work this week instead.

"Sure." I smiled at her. "That sounds lovely."

Forty minutes later, I said my goodbyes and stumbled down the stairs and out into the morning air. I don't know why, but something about Mrs. Patterson showing me photos of Don and his new home had gotten to me. My hands shook as I fumbled with the buttons on my jacket. What the hell was wrong with me? I used to have a lot of these moments of desperately missing my parents after they left, but I hadn't felt the ache of their absence this strongly in months.

I shook my head. I was fine. I would be fine. I didn't need my parents to hold me and tell me everything was going to be okay.

My phone rang as I walked back to my car, and my heart sank. I didn't need to check the screen to know who it was.

"Hey, Sofia!" Shannon's voice dripped with fake sweetness. "I am *so* sorry, but I can't come in today. I'm still, like, really sick. Fever. Cough. The works. You understand, right?"

My jaw clenched. Of course I understood; this was the fourth time she'd been "sick" this month. I could practically smell the river water and Henri's cologne through the phone.

"Of course," I said tightly, already calculating how to rearrange my day. "Feel better."

As soon as I hung up, a groan of frustration escaped me. I glanced at my phone's calendar, my heart sinking at the spa appointment reminder.

Damn it.

I took a deep breath. It was okay. I'd book another one for next month. It was no big deal. I fixed a smile on my face. Because that's what Sofia Miller did. She kept going. She kept going as if everything was fine, even if nothing had been fine for a very long time.

Chapter Five

DEREK

My phone buzzed, Armeen's name flashing across it. I answered on the second ring, my eyes flicking to the dot on the screen in front of me showing the tracker I'd put on Sofia's car. She'd gone to the market this morning and then parked it outside the block opposite hers, so I knew she was delivering groceries to the Patterson apartment.

"Tell me you have something," I said.

"You know, most people answer the phone with a 'good morning,' or at the very least a 'hello,'" Armeen's familiar drawl came down the line. He'd been a contact I'd made in the Syrian army intelligence when I was in the army. After I got discharged, we'd kept in touch, hitting each other up for intel whenever the need arose.

"Have you got something?"

"Yeah, yeah, you're too busy or too much of a hard-ass for the niceties, I get it. Fine. I've been asking around about Kane. I got nothing so far, not even a whisper."

I pinched the bridge of my nose, fighting back frustration. "Keep looking. It was his scent in that cabin, Armeen. I'd stake my life on it."

"Maybe that's the problem." He paused, and I could picture him leaning back in his chair, feet up on his desk like always. "You've been chasing Kane's ghost for years. You ordered the airstrike yourself—"

"There was no body, no confirmation," I cut him off. After Harris had died in my arms, I'd called in an airstrike and pulled the rest of the team out before it hit. I'd thought at the time that we'd got him. There'd been no trace of Kane since then, not until I found his scent in the cabin, along with all those photos of Sofia. "You know better than anyone the resources Kane had. He could have survived, gone underground, created a cover."

"I do. But something's not adding up here, Shaw. You said yourself that the cabin was being used by military guys who were trafficking humans. The Pack that they were working with was rabidly anti-human. They wanted to enslave humans. So why would Kane—a human, one who hated Shifters—work with them? Why help traffic his own kind?"

It was a question I had no answer to, something that had been playing on my mind for weeks now.

"Shaw, you know I respect you, but maybe you've chased Kane's ghost long enough. Maybe it's time to move on. Live your life, man."

I couldn't accept that. Not when every instinct I had told me Kane was involved, that he was a danger to Sofia.

"This isn't about me. Kane was there; I know it. This is about making sure he can't hurt anyone else. Keep searching. Call me if you get anything."

I heard Armeen sigh before he replied, "Will do."

I hung up and pulled out everything I had on Project Dusk, the operation Kane had been running when I called in the airstrike. I overlaid them on the three screens on what had been the dining room wall. I'd installed them after Ryan moved to the Alpha House, Sam left to work for the Wolf Council, and Mason moved to the Bridgetown Pack.

Most of my work as Pack Beta was done at the enforcers' building at the entrance to what used to be the Alpha Compound. After Mai and Ryan tore down the walls of the Compound, it was more like a large cul-de-sac, with Pack members able to come and go as they pleased. Ryan and I had been skeptical at first, but Mai was right; the whole Pack felt more connected now that there wasn't a physical separation between those safe in the Compound and those outside of it.

Now, when I walked the two hundred meters to work each day, I'd be just as likely to pass enforcers training as the bakery owner bringing her six-year-old daughter to see Mai and Ryan's kitten before school. Even though I worked elsewhere, here, in the house I used to share with my three brothers, was where I kept my research on Kane.

I stared at the screens, flicking through documents I'd read a hundred times. I knew the answer had to be in here, somewhere. I just couldn't see it.

Yet, my wolf nudged.

Yet, I agreed. We'd get him. We had to. Failure was not an option.

I got up, stretched, and headed to the kitchen to make some coffee. The coffee maker hummed, the only sound besides my breathing in the room that at this time of the day should have had Ryan's tapping at his laptop, Mason's constant phone calls, and Sam's running commentary on everything.

Coffee in hand, I walked back to the dining room. I stood in the doorway, staring at the screens. Victor Kane had been a promising human officer in army intelligence. A rising star who could have made it to Major General, if the rumors were to be believed. He was charismatic, smart, and commanded respect and unwavering loyalty among those he served with, in particular the humans under his command. That should have been a warning sign, but no one picked up on it until it was too late.

That was the thing about Kane—he never made waves, never said anything outright that could get him flagged, but his influence ran deep. He appealed to those who felt like they were being left behind. He talked about the good old days when humans held all the cards, before the Equal Species Act, before the Boston Peace Accords that established the peace between Shifters and humans.

Back then, Shifters were barred from government positions, military leadership roles, even certain private sector jobs. Kane painted it as a golden age when humans were in their rightful place. He'd talk about how Shifters were taking over with our strength, speed, and enhanced senses, that in reality, we were one step above dogs, that we couldn't be trusted with power or put into decision-making positions. He talked about the future if humans failed to act, a world where humans were reduced to supporting roles. But there was still time to stop it.

He promised his followers he'd restore the natural order—code for putting humans back on top and making sure Shifters were cut out of the job market. That it was essential because Shifters were a threat to the *proper* way of life.

Kane built a tight-knit, loyal network around him, and little by little, we saw the changes in morale. The humans in the different units started keeping more to themselves. Conversations stopped when Shifters entered the room. By the time they realized Kane was recruiting his own army, it was already too late. One day, he was a decorated officer with an impeccable record. The next, he and over one hundred other soldiers went dark. Off the grid.

Before Kane, we didn't think about who was human and who was Shifter—we just got the job done. We trained together, deployed together, covered each other's six. We lived by the same code: complete the mission, protect the unit, serve something bigger than ourselves. We had our differences, sure, but out there, it didn't matter. The team. The objective. The mission. That was the foundation of everything.

Kane shattered that. Bringing him down became our top priority for those of us left, but he'd disappear every time we got close.

It was only after the airstrike that I thought took Kane out that we'd uncovered Project Dusk. Project Dusk had been designed to shift the balance of power once and for all. Kane had been trying to turn Shifters human. The initial test subjects—captured werewolves—showed promising results in the beginning. Their ability to Shift slowed, their regenerative properties dulled. But Kane hadn't been able to perfect the formula.

I took another sip as an email notification popped up on my laptop. It was the daily email from Ava, one of our enforcers who I'd tasked with compiling all mentions of ripple incidents in the media and sending them round to everyone.

Ripple.

The parallels were there. Could ripple be a refined version of what Kane and his people were developing in Project Dusk? A way to get rid of the Shifter threat?

I opened my laptop and started mapping the connections. Kane's scent at the cabin had pointed to his involvement with Tristan's Pack, but it had always seemed bizarre—a human working with Shifters who wanted to enslave humans made no sense. But what if Kane wasn't trafficking the humans? What if he was pretending to, but then set them free and recruited them? Who better to enlist against us than humans who had been abused and sold as slaves by Shifters?

My phone was in my hand before I finished the thought. AJ picked up on the third ring.

"Shaw?"

"Hey. I need to know if you've found any new leads on Mina."

AJ was a bear Shifter whose fated mate was human. It was rare, but occasionally, the Moon Goddess paired us up with someone from a different species. Tristan had found out and held Mina hostage, forcing AJ to work for him. When Tristan kidnapped Shya, Mason and I had recruited AJ and persuaded him to turn on Tristan. We'd never have been able to find Shya if it hadn't been for him. We'd promised to help AJ free Mina, but when we got to Tristan's camp, she'd already been sold by the same military guys whose cabin had held Sofia's photos. AJ had been searching for her ever since.

"Nothing new." The pain in his voice was raw. "Trail's cold."

"What if we've been looking in the wrong places?" I stood, pacing as thoughts crystallized. "What if the humans the military guys picked up weren't being trafficked? What if they were recruiting them?"

Silence stretched over the line. "What are you talking about?"

I brought him up to speed about Kane and my theory.

"It could explain why we can't find any trace of them in trafficking circles. Fuck, Shaw! I don't know whether to be happy I have a new lead to chase down or freaked that she might be part of some anti-Shifter conspiracy. She's my fated mate, for fuck's sake! If she is signed up to this, how the hell do I persuade her that Shifters aren't evil?"

"We'll cross that bridge if we come to it. You know I'll help in any way I can. In the meantime, can you look for any new anti-Shifter groups, especially ones with military precision in their operations?"

"Yeah. I'll be in touch."

I ended the call as my eyes went back to the tracker on Sofia's car. She'd set off from Mrs. Patterson's but had pulled over three streets away. I knew she was supposed to see Mai this morning, and Sofia wouldn't want to be late for that.

What the hell is she doing?

CHAPTER SIX

SOFIA

My little ten-year-old red Honda Fit made an ominous grinding noise before shuddering to a complete stop on the side of Maple Drive. I turned the key again, pressing harder—like that would make a difference. Nothing happened except a weak clicking sound.

"No, no, no," I muttered. "Not today. Please, not today."

The universe clearly wasn't taking requests because no matter how many times I tried, the engine stayed dead.

Fantastic.

This was just the latest entry in the growing list of things that had gone spectacularly wrong today. Shannon calling in "sick" again? Check. Missed spa day? Double check. Missing out on seeing my best friend? Oh yeah, let's throw that on the list, too.

And now my car—the one that had seen me through every major life event—had finally given up on me.

I slumped back against the seat, feeling the hot sting of tears behind my eyes. My wolf huffed in frustration, pacing beneath my skin. She hated it when things spun out of control.

My phone rang, making me jump. Derek's name flashed on the

screen.

Oh, hell no.

I ignored it.

Pups?

Damn it, what if something was wrong—with Mai, with Jase, with the Pack? I'd never forgive myself for not answering.

I wiped at the tears escaping from my eyes as I swiped *accept.*

"Is everyone okay?"

"They're all fine, Sofia." His voice was low, steady, wrapping around me like warm honey.

"Thank the Goddess." I blew out a breath, thankful my bad luck hadn't infected anyone else. "Look, I don't have time for whatever this is—"

"You're crying." It wasn't a question. Something in his tone made my heart skip.

"No, I'm not." I wiped my eyes again with the back of my hand. How did he always know?

"Where are you?"

"It's just my car. It broke down, but—"

"Never mind. I got you. I'll be there in ten minutes."

"Derek, wait—"

But he had already hung up.

I growled under my breath and tossed my phone onto the passenger seat.

The nerve of that man. Just declaring he was coming to help like I was some fragile little thing in need of rescuing. The worst part? Some irrational, traitorous part of me actually felt relieved.

A black SUV pulled up exactly ten minutes later—because of

course he was nothing if not precise—and Derek unfolded himself from the driver's seat with his usual ease. He always moved with that quiet, controlled strength that made people step aside when he walked into a room. His dark jeans hugged his thighs in a way that should be illegal, and the black T-shirt stretched across his broad chest left little to the imagination. My wolf immediately perked up under my skin, her restless agitation settling the moment we saw him.

"No," I muttered. "Down. Bad wolf."

"Talking to yourself now?" Derek drawled, coming to a stop beside my window.

"Are you seriously tracking my movements now?" I snapped, irritation flooding through me as I shoved the door open and got out.

"I'm the Pack Beta. It's my job to know where my wolves are."

"Right. And I suppose you also know Mrs. Henderson's schedule?" I crossed my arms. "Or is it just me you're stalking?"

"Only you, gorgeous," he murmured, voice like velvet. "Only you. Besides, you always do Ivy Patterson's shopping on Saturday mornings, and I know you had plans with Wally to see Mai after."

I inhaled sharply, my wolf practically preening under his attention. Nope. Not happening. I rolled my shoulders, forcing my focus back.

"I don't need you to swoop in like some kind of knight in sexy jeans, Derek," I said tightly. Why, oh why, did I have to say *sexy* jeans? "I could have handled this."

"I know. Doesn't mean you should have to." He gestured toward his SUV. "Why don't you yell at me while I drive you to see Mai? You do still want to see Mai today, right?"

I narrowed my eyes at him. "I'm perfectly capable of calling a tow truck."

There was an unmistakable twitch at the corner of his lips. "You could. But they might not be here for another hour. Whereas I'm here now, and I can drop you off at Mai's so you don't miss seeing her. The fact that I get to enjoy your company while I drive you is just a bonus for me."

Damn it, he was right. Now that Shannon was sick, I had to get to work later. My only window to see Mai was closing fast. I let out a slow breath.

"Fine." I shot him a glare—which had absolutely no effect on him—and stomped to his SUV. As I yanked the passenger door open, I could practically feel his amusement rolling off him in waves.

"This is a one-off. Don't think this means I'm suddenly letting you play hero," I said, sliding into the seat.

"Wouldn't dream of it."

The car ride was quiet at first, the low hum of the air conditioning filling the space between us.

"How's the bar holding up?" he asked casually.

"Fantastic. We thrive on chaos."

"So, the same as usual, then?"

"Pretty much." I glanced sideways at him, instantly regretting it when I saw the way his T-shirt clung to the ridges of his abdomen as he leaned slightly forward.

"You need a new car."

No shit, but not only was it an expense I couldn't afford right now, I also loved my Fit.

I scowled. "I like my car. He's seen me through good times and bad. He's never deserted me, and only occasionally lets me down, because he is old and tired. I can't get rid of him just because he is old and tired,

Derek. What sort of person would that make me?"

"He?"

I felt a small blush creep up my neck. "Yes, he."

"Does he have a name?"

I could practically smell the amusement on him.

"Erik."

His grin vanished.

Ha!

"Erik? You named your car Erik?" His voice came out slow, deliberate, like he was trying to decide if I was messing with him.

I smiled sweetly at him. "Yes. *Erik* has always been there for me. He never leaves without warning. Never ghosts me. Sure, he has a few breakdowns, but at least he tries his best to stick around."

Derek's jaw clenched. "Sofia—"

"And when he fails? He doesn't act like nothing happened afterward."

"Is your damn car also your fated mate?"

I grinned mockingly. "Well, given that Erik's more reliable than mine? Maybe."

Derek let out a slow breath, like he was trying very, very hard not to react. "You realize how ridiculous that sounds, right?"

I shrugged. "Not as ridiculous as a man who ran at the first sign of something real, barely even acknowledged me for months, and then started acting like—" I gestured wildly between us, "this—whatever this is—is normal."

A muscle ticked in his jaw. Ho ho, so he did get annoyed. Interesting.

He turned his head, his gray eyes locking onto mine, his gaze piercing and heated. "You really think I don't regret it?"

Something sharp twisted in my chest. Because that was the problem. I knew he regretted it. I knew Derek wasn't cruel, wasn't the kind of man who ghosted someone just for the hell of it. He had his reasons—but I wasn't ready to hear them. I liked this anger too much. It got me through the nights when I couldn't think about anything but him. When I'd wake up with my skin still aching from the ghost of his touch, or when I caught his scent in the bar and felt the overwhelming pull of the mate bond—like stepping into a hot room after a lifetime in the cold. If I let that go—if I let him in—what would be left of me? I didn't know, and I wasn't ready to find out.

"It doesn't matter; I'm more than happy with Erik."

His jaw tightened, but he didn't argue.

"One of these days, we're gonna have to talk about this properly, like adults. No more running away from it."

He did *not* just say that. "No, we won't talk about it. Not today. Not tomorrow. Not any day. There is nothing to talk about."

Derek stopped the car in front of the Alpha House and turned to face me. "Sofia—"

"No. Derek. Nothing, you hear me? Absolutely nothing. Now, thank you for the ride."

"Your car—"

"I'll figure it out."

"Damn it, Sofia, just let me—"

"Stop trying to fix everything!" I spun to face him. "Stop acting like you can just waltz in and make everything better when you're the one who—" I broke off, furious at the tears threatening to fall again.

Something flickered in his eyes, like he'd just worked out

something. Then his hand came up to brush a tear from my cheek, so gentle it made my chest ache.

"I'm not going anywhere," he said softly. "Whether you want me here or not."

I jerked away. "I don't need you, Derek Shaw."

He didn't argue. But when I stepped out, his eyes were locked onto me like I was the only thing that mattered in the world.

I hated that it made something inside me flutter.

So, I did the only thing I could; I slammed the door shut and stalked toward the Alpha House, refusing to look back.

CHAPTER SEVEN

SOFIA

The familiar scents of the Pack washed over me as I stepped into the Alpha House. Mai's pregnancy had changed the underlying aroma of the house—there was something sweeter now, mixed in with Ryan's sandalwood scent. Something that spoke of family, of future, of belonging. Unfortunately, the six enforcers hanging around spoiled it somewhat.

The enforcers barely acknowledged me as I walked in, though I knew they tracked my every movement. Ryan had tripled security since Mai's fainting spell, though I had no idea what he thought all these enforcers would do if she fainted again—catch her mid-air? It made the usually welcoming Alpha House now feel more like a fortress. My wolf bristled at their scrutiny; we used to belong here, used to slip in and out like it was our second home. Now, even this felt different.

A sharp whistle made me glance toward the staircase, where Evelyn, Derek's number two in the enforcers, leaned casually against the banister, arms crossed. Her long, dark braid rested over one shoulder, those sharp green eyes of hers missing nothing as she examined me.

"You made it. I was about to send out a search party," she teased, arching an eyebrow. "Mai will be pleased you're here."

I smiled. Seeing Mai was worth the pain of driving here with Derek. "How's security detail going?"

"You mean, how's babysitting going?" Her lips quirked up slightly. "Ryan's gone full doomsday prepper. Yesterday, he had us practicing 'Operation Stork'—evacuating Mai through three different escape routes while timing how fast we could get her to Thomas's."

"You're joking."

"Nope. We had to wear earpieces and use code names. Mai only agreed to it if she got to name us all. I'm 'Captain Cuddles.'"

I snorted. Evelyn was so not the cuddly type. "That's ridiculous."

"Tell that to Ryan. He's installed panic buttons in every room, and there's a go-bag with Mai's favorite snacks at every exit." Her expression darkened momentarily. "After what happened with Brock and Hayley, though..."

"Fair point," I conceded. "Still, Mai must be climbing the walls."

"Oh, she threatened to Shift and make a run for it yesterday when Ryan suggested bubble-wrapping the staircase." Evelyn's eyes crinkled with amusement. "But the big guy's just terrified. You should've seen him when she fainted—I thought he was going to tear the house apart with his bare hands."

I shook my head. "Yeah, but even so, this is full-blown a military occupation."

"Well... that's love, Sofia. Drives people to do dumb things, especially when they're scared of losing that person." Her gaze flicked over me with quiet assessment. "Not that I'd expect you to understand that... being as stubborn as you are."

I narrowed my eyes. "You trying to say something, Evelyn?"

She grinned, slow and knowing. "Just making an observation."

Before I could respond, Wally's voice carried down from upstairs. "Sofia! Finally!" he called. "We're in the bedroom!"

I shot Evelyn a look that said this conversation wasn't over, but she just smirked and waved me on.

Following Wally's voice, I found Mai propped up against a mountain of pillows in her bed, looking thoroughly fed up. Her small frame was dwarfed by a shirt of Ryan's as it stretched over her growing belly, and her dark hair was pulled into a messy bun. Wally lounged beside her, flicking through what looked like a baby-naming book.

"Sofia, you're a lifesaver!" Mai exclaimed as I handed over the latest book by Rina Meyors and a jar of pickled jalapeños topped with peanut butter—her latest pregnancy craving that had Ryan gagging every time she ate it. "You even remembered the extra crunchy kind!"

"Well, the smooth kind is *obviously* not right with jalapeños," I teased, watching as she eagerly unscrewed the jar lid.

"Don't judge me," Mai mumbled around a mouthful of her spicy-sweet concoction. "The pups want what they want. Last week, it was sardines dipped in chocolate sauce. Tomorrow, it might be something else." She shrugged, licking peanut butter off her fingers. "If I have to be stuck in this bed, I'm at least going to enjoy my crazy cravings."

"And how goes your enforced relaxation?"

Mai groaned, stabbing another jalapeño with perhaps more force than necessary. "If I have to read one more article about proper breathing techniques, I'm going to scream."

"Ryan's been making her practice Lamaze," Wally stage-whispered.

"He's driving me insane! Did you know he actually tried to carry me to the bathroom yesterday? The bathroom! It's ten feet away!"

"Well, you did faint," I pointed out, perching on the window seat.

"While having sex!" Mai threw up her hands. "It happens! Pregnancy hormones are weird! But try telling that to Mr. Alpha-Must-Protect-Mate-At-All-Costs. Now, I'm not allowed to do anything except lie here and think about breathing. He won't even... you know. Says he doesn't want to risk it in case I faint again!"

I clutched my chest in mock horror. "No sex? OMG, Mai, you have to leave him!"

She threw her pillow at me. "It's alright for you; you have a vibrator. Me? I have a Ryan, and now he's gone on strike! Even Thomas said it would be okay if we did it."

"Mai, honey, you're thinking of this all wrong," Wally said. "You just need to tempt him. Make it impossible for him to resist his inner urges."

I fluffed up the pillow and put it back next to her. "You have all this free time now, right? I have faith in my bestie that you'll come up with something that will make Ryan—"

"Make Ryan what?"

I turned to see Ryan standing in the doorway.

"Choose Wally Junior as a name for one of the twins," Wally answered without batting an eye.

Ryan had to have heard our entire conversation, but he went with it as he strode into the room. "We are not naming either of our children Wally Junior," Ryan said firmly. "And we don't know if either of them is a boy."

Mai had insisted she didn't want to know the sex of the babies until they were born. Thomas was the only one who knew, and it was driving Wally crazy that his mate wouldn't spill the beans to him.

"Wallina, then? It has such a pretty ring to it."

"No!" all of us said at the same time.

"How are you doing?" Ryan said, his eyes on Mai. "Not getting too tired?"

"I'm fine. More than fine. Stop fretting."

"Never," he whispered, leaning down to place a kiss on her forehead.

I stayed a little longer, listening to them talk about baby names and nursery colors. Watched them plan futures that seemed so certain, so secure. Mai had Ryan, would never be alone again. Wally had Thomas and now Amara and Ben, a family he'd built from choice and love. Even Jase was finding his place at Shaw Investigations, growing into someone who didn't need his big sister anymore.

⁂

When I left, Evelyn was waiting for me at the bottom of the stairs, a set of car keys in her hand.

"Derek had Ava drop off a loaner for you. Said to tell you your car's going to take a couple of days to fix."

Of course he did. Derek fucking Shaw fixing everything.

Evelyn studied me. "You okay?"

I rubbed a hand over my face. It wasn't Evelyn's fault that Derek always knew how to piss me off.

"Yeah. I'm fine. Just tired. Thanks for these." I took the keys and headed out.

By the time I got to the Bottley, I knew I didn't like the loaner. It was a dark gray Range Rover and it felt too big, too stiff, and it didn't smell right. I parked outside the Bottley, the car's humongous frame making it take three attempts before I got it in the right place, and looked at the bar.

My sanctuary, with its sturdy brick façade and windows reflecting shards of golden sunlight. I loved this place. Like Erik, it had been here when everything else fell apart—when my parents left, when I couldn't find work to feed Jase, when Mai disappeared for four years and I spent every freaking day scared mindless that she might be dead somewhere, when Derek... It was the one place I could always count on. The one constant in a life full of people walking away.

My wolf paced uneasily. She didn't like the direction of my thoughts—she never did when they turned inward like this. But she didn't offer any answers, either.

A sharp knock on my window snapped me out of my thoughts. Jase, his boyish grin lopsided, peered in at me.

"Nice car," he teased, opening my door. "Derek's got good taste."

Did everyone in Three Rivers know about Erik?

"Does the entire town have a group chat about my car troubles that I'm not invited to?"

"Yeah, it's called 'Sofia's Drama Alert,' and yes, we all get notifications." He opened my door with a flourish. "I'm the admin, obviously."

"Obviously," I muttered, climbing out.

He squinted at my face. "Whoa, that's not your 'I just got pampered' glow. Weren't you supposed to be getting hot rocks placed on your chakras or whatever today?"

"Shannon called in sick again."

"You need to fire her ass. She's been pulling this crap for months."

"I know. But we're already short-staffed. I'd rather deal with her flakiness than start from scratch with someone new."

We walked into the warmth of the Bottley, and the smell of mahogany wood, ground coffee, and faintly lingering whiskey greeted me like an old friend. Something inside me unwound slightly just by being here. The lunchtime crowd had mostly thinned, leaving only a few tables occupied. I paused and listened to the quiet conversations mixed with the faint clinking of ceramic mugs against wooden tables, while jazz hummed from the speakers.

Okay, maybe this wasn't the worst way to spend my afternoon if I couldn't make it to the spa.

Jase jumped up onto the countertop. I had thought I'd have to replace the whole thing after it got broken during an attack on the Pack a few months ago, but it had been repaired seamlessly to blend with the older wood so that you couldn't tell anymore which sections were new. The shelves behind it, which had also been shattered, now stood sturdier than ever, bolted into the wall with the extra support beams Derek had added. The alcohol bottles were arranged neatly in rows—whiskeys, rums, and gins nestled between jars of homemade syrup and coffee bean canisters.

After the attack, Derek had fixed this place up piece by piece, night after night. I only knew it was him because his scent was all over this place each morning when I came in. I'd never thanked him, never mentioned it, and he hadn't, either.

Julie, the one staff member I could always rely on, offered me a quick smile as she wiped down the espresso machine. "Rough morning or just rough life?"

I sighed. "Both."

Brian, our teenage goth barista, didn't even look up as he meticulously frosted a scone. "Shannon bailed again?"

"As the sky is blue."

Julie slid a latte toward me. The scent of rich espresso and hazelnut drifted up. "Medium foam, one sugar, extra shot. You look like you need it."

I wrapped my hands around the mug, letting the warmth seep into my fingers. "I think I love you."

"A tragic romance," she sighed dramatically, flipping her dark curls over one shoulder. "If only I liked women."

Brian snorted, tossing a kitchen towel over his shoulder. "I don't know. If anyone could turn Julie, it'd be Sofia's cinnamon roll energy."

I flipped him off halfheartedly but smiled as I took a sip, letting myself just exist for a moment in my space.

Jase leaned against the bar. "Brian may be on to something, you know? Maybe life would be easier if you liked women?"

"You're not wrong, Jase," I muttered as I took another sip. "What are you doing here, anyway? Aren't you supposed to be at work?"

"Just picking up some spare clothes and food. I won't be back for dinner; Carlito's making me catalog old case files."

I suppressed another sigh. I'd been hoping Jase would make it home tonight. Even if Dad wasn't here to celebrate, even if I didn't know where to send the freaking card, last night after work, I'd made Jase and me a cake to share.

"Maybe I can help? Two pairs of eyes would make it go faster."

Jase's expression softened in that particular way that always made me feel simultaneously loved and diminished. "Thanks, Sof, but we have it handled. You know what would help though? Some of your delicious coffee. You know no-one makes it like you do. You mind making me one to go?"

Right. Coffee.

I forced a smile onto my face. "Sure. Don't work too hard, okay?"

At least Jase was here. He might be out all hours, might eat all my food, and leave his dirty laundry everywhere, but I was pretty sure that as long as I kept the fridge stocked, he wasn't going to leave me. Not anytime soon, anyway.

Chapter Eight

DEREK

By the time I'd made it back home, there was a BMW X1 parked outside.

It was the car all Wolf Council members drove.

What was he doing here?

Sam opened the front door before I got to it, stepping aside to let me in. My twin's hair had grown longer since I'd last seen him, brushing his shoulders now. He smiled, but it didn't reach his eyes. Not that it had for months now. Whatever he was doing for the Wolf Council was changing him. My teasing, easy-going brother was almost gone. Now he was a secretive, serious Council man. I hated it, but anytime I tried to talk to him about it, he said what he was doing was worth a few sacrifices. He believed in his job, believed he was protecting all werewolves. I just wished he could do it as the old Sam and that it didn't need this new Sam to make it happen.

"Didn't text. Didn't call. Just showed up," I said, crossing my arms. "Some things never change."

"Miss me that much?" Sam's eyes scanned me with that new clinical gaze he'd developed. "You look like hell warmed over."

"It's my natural glow." I moved past him and headed into the old dining room. I pulled up the feed covering the Bottley.

Sam's eyes lingered on the screen showing Sofia. "Still playing spy?"

My wolf bristled at his tone, but I kept my voice neutral. "I never *played* spy, Sam. Besides, someone has to keep the Pack safe."

"The Pack has Ryan for that," Sam said, settling into my chair without invitation. "And Mai, when she's back on her feet. And a whole team of enforcers." He paused, studying the intelligence reports on the other two screens. "This seems more... personal."

"Everything's personal when it comes to Pack." I leaned against the wall, arms crossed.

Sam picked up one of the photos I'd taken from the cabin in the woods, his lips quirking. "Especially when it involves a certain redheaded barista?"

"Don't start."

"What? Can't a guy be interested in his brother's love life?" Sam's words carried an edge that hadn't been there before.

"If you came here just to bust my balls about Sofia—"

"Relax." Sam held up his hands in mock surrender. "Though, I hear talking to women works better than glaring at them through security footage. Just a pro tip from your more socially adept twin. Why don't you try it sometime? Ask her out for coffee. Though I guess that'd be redundant since she owns the coffee shop."

"She manages it," I corrected automatically. "Lucian Black owns it."

Sam's eyebrows rose. "Ah... yes, the elusive human, Lucian Black. He ever come back?"

I shook my head. Black had left with his wife, Darla Ash, a couple of years ago. According to the staff at the Bottley, they'd gone back to the city to try for a family and left the Bar under Sofia's management. Neither of them had been seen in the Three Rivers since then.

"Not that I know of."

If I wasn't his twin, I would never have caught it, but I knew my brother too well. There was something in the way he breathed out, the way his eyes flickered to the left; he was interested in Lucian Black.

"You're tracking Black. Why?"

Sam frowned, annoyance flashing across his face. "Council business. Forget I said anything."

Right. Council business. Nothing he could talk about.

Again.

I realized just how pissed off he had to have been when I came home on leave from the army and couldn't talk about anything I was doing either.

"How are things at the Council?"

He sighed. "Bad. We stopped the production of ripple in the north, but it's being imported through at least twenty different lines that we know of. And down south, it's becoming a shitstorm. The drug... it's fucking evil, Derek. Driving Shifters to break their Pack bonds."

Pack bonds were everything to us—they provided security and safety, kept us grounded, connected us to each other and our territory. They could only be broken by a werewolf or one of their Alphas.

"And now it turns out that about fifteen percent of those addicted get bloodlust. The media got hold of some footage of bloodlust werewolves attacking humans. It's a fucking mess, bro. We got no cure. No treatment. All those in bloodlust have to be killed, along with most of those addicted to ripple. And look at this shit..." He pulled out a combat knife—wickedly sharp, silver-edged, designed to end a fight in one stroke. "Standard issue now to all Council members and those who work for us."

Werewolves didn't tend to use weapons. Some fucked up point of pride about a werewolf being enough of a weapon. Personally, I was all for using anything and everything that won the fight. But it was a hell of a message for the Wolf Council to be carrying around knives these days.

"They for defense?"

"No." Sam got that grim look in his eyes, the one that had been appearing more and more every time I saw him. "They're to put down any Shifter we find too far gone in their ripple addiction."

Ripple didn't discriminate. Men, women, teenagers, elders—anyone could get addicted to this stuff if they took it. I wondered just how many of us Sam had had to kill.

"Why? I thought the Council was working on a cure for it. I know Mason and Shya are over in Bridgetown."

"Because it's getting worse, and so far, there is no treatment. I've sat with them in the wards we've set up. They're in pain, yet still begging us to give them more ripple. Out on the streets? There are gangs of drug-addicted Shifters with no Pack bonds to hold them back, to keep them under control. They're attacking humans, trying to get money for their next fix, and seeing humans as easy prey." His face darkened. "Some have even turned humans."

Although folklore said we could turn humans into werewolves with one bite, it was only possible if we bit them during a full moon, when the breach pathogen responsible for our transformation was at its strongest in our bodies. It was absolutely forbidden. One of the key tenets of the Boston Peace Accord we had with the humans was that we did not turn humans. It was one of the reasons the Wolf Council existed in the first place—to police this rule and put down any wolf who broke it.

"The human governments are furious; they're blaming the Council for not keeping control. Humans are starting to panic. There are fights breaking out all over the conclave cities." Sam rubbed a hand over his face. "I've heard of at least twenty-three towns that have kicked all Shifters out of their borders, shackled them with silver cuffs on their wrists and ankles. Families, kids, grandparents, everyone, Derek, even though they've been living there, side-by-side with humans for generations. They're saying all Shifters are dangerous. And now," his laugh was bitter, "now, if you can believe it, some cities have banded together. They've raised money to develop a vaccine. Not treatment for ripple but something that will 'cure' lycanthropy."

Anger burned my throat. "They can't *cure* lycanthropy. We aren't a fucking disease. Being me isn't something broken that needs to be repaired. This is who I am. It's every breath, every heartbeat, every part of what makes me alive."

Sam nodded. "Too fucking right. But I've seen the medical reports. The vaccine they're working on is a blocker from the same strain they use in ripple. It permanently inhabits our ability to access our wolves."

They were using ripple against us. Studying it, not to help us with a treatment for its effects, but to see what made it work so well on us.

Motherfuckers.

"What the hell is the Council going to do about it?"

"We've been so busy chasing our tails trying to put out every little fire that ripple causes, trying to stop every addicted Shifter from causing a major incident that we're stretched thin. But we're meeting with a delegation from the human governments. I have to be in Philadelphia in three days. We'll demand they stop their research into their so-called vaccine and try to assure them that we're doing everything we can to stop the situation from escalating."

This whole fucking thing was spiraling out of control. My eyes flickered to the screens again. On one, Sofia was leaning on the counter listening to Ray Tidson. Ray was a roofer who lived across town, but I'd noticed he'd been making a twenty-minute detour every day to get a coffee at the Bottley. He passed three other coffee shops to get there. I knew because I'd checked. Ray was not normally a talker, but he came within five meters of Sofia, and he couldn't shut up. How did she do it? Put everyone around her at ease, make them want to spill their secrets, and share all their news with her?

When I worked in military intelligence, I would have snapped up someone with those skills in a heartbeat. Ray said something that made her reach out and squeeze his shoulder for a moment. My wolf glared out through my eyes and growled. He was as unhappy as I was about her touching someone else. She was ours, not Ray's, not anyone else's. I wanted to run down there and put my fist repeatedly through Ray's face. I'd get an earful from Sofia, but it would be worth it.

On the next screen, there were still the Project Dusk reports. If Kane was alive, ripple sounded like something he'd be knee-deep in. Ripple was spelled with magic, though. Could Kane be working with witches? I knew I should tell Sam my theory, but he had enough to deal with at the moment; I needed to be sure before I dropped this on his plate, too.

"When's the last time you slept?" Sam's change of subject caught me off guard.

"I sleep fine."

"No, you don't. You think I don't know? You can fool Ryan, Mason, the whole damn Pack, but I'm your twin."

My wolf stirred restlessly under my skin. "Back off, Sam."

"How are the nightmares? Still bad?"

"I have them under control."

"Bullshit."

That was it. I'd had enough of him waltzing in here and having an opinion on my life. "You don't know shit. You're never fucking here, so just back the fuck off."

"Not a chance." He stood, moving toward me. "You're my brother. Whatever you're chasing, it's killing you. You can't keep doing this."

"Like you're one to talk." I stood to face him. "What the hell has the Wolf Council got you doing, huh? It's not just the ripple. You're so twisted up these days that my joking, *Star Wars*-quoting brother has turned into… whatever the hell you are now! And you can't talk to me about it. Me. Your fucking twin. You know exactly what I went through in the army. I've seen it all, Sam; fuck, I've done it all. So, what the hell is it you're doing that you can't even talk to me about?"

Sam flinched but held his ground. "This isn't about me."

"Right. Still not talking, huh? So, don't stand there and lecture me about keeping secrets."

He ran a hand through his hair, a gesture so much like my own. He was my twin, the one person I thought I could always rely on, and somehow, we'd ended up on opposite sides of a wall neither of us knew how to break down.

"I came here to check on you, Derek. Not to fight."

"I don't need checking on. I'm fine."

Sam's laugh was hollow. "Yeah, sure you are." He hesitated, then added softly, "Just don't push everyone away, okay? Some of us actually give a shit about what happens to you."

Sam's phone buzzed, and his face changed as he read the message, that new hardness settling over his features.

"Council business?" I asked, not bothering to hide the bitterness in my voice.

He nodded, already heading to the door. "I need to deal with this. But we need to talk, Derek. Really talk."

"Yeah, whenever you're ready to tell me what's going on at the Council, I'll be here."

Sam looked for a moment like he was going to say something. Then he shook his head and walked out.

I turned back to my monitors, my wolf restless and agitated. Sofia was laughing at something else Ray was saying. I picked up my coffee mug and threw it at the wall.

Chapter Nine

SOFIA

I dragged myself into the back office, my feet aching despite the baby-blue sneakers I was wearing. Shya, the Shoe Queen, had bought these for me, and I loved them more than I had any right to love a pair of shoes. A poster was pinned to the door.

WANTED: Dead or Alive (preferably incinerated)SUSPECT: Any rat daring to trespassCRIME: Existing with those tiny demon hands and plotting world dominationREWARD: Sofia's eternal gratitude + lifetime VIP access to all experimental coffee flavors before they hit the menuNOTE: If you hear a scream that could shatter the sound barrier, DO NOT APPROACH. Simply evacuate the premises and wait for Sofia to regain her dignity.

I glanced back down the hall to catch Brian ducking behind the counter, his shoulders shaking with barely contained laughter. Yes, I was a werewolf afraid of rats. They could all judge me after they'd seen one wash its face like a tiny serial killer.

"Very funny!" I called out. "Just remember who approves your time-off requests, Picasso!"

I took the poster inside and pinned it next to the whiteboard that was covered in my scrawled notes—half-formed ideas for seasonal drinks, a reminder to call the supplier about the delayed whiskey shipment.

My office was modest but organized—exactly the way I liked it. A single desk, sturdy and well-loved, was near the far wall, its surface mostly clear except for the neatly stacked pile of invoices I still had to pay. In the corner, a punching bag hung from a reinforced ceiling hook. A fresh pair of hand wraps sat on the shelf beside it. Next to the bag, a small rack of free weights leaned against the wall. Despite the exhaustion I felt, the familiar space soothed me. This was mine. My little corner of order and creativity, the one place where I felt I had some measure of control.

I sighed, rolling my shoulders as I glanced at the time. The afternoon rush was over, Julie and Brian could handle things before I was due back to set up for the evening, and I had twenty minutes before my video call with Lucian. Just enough time to warm up and shake off the tension clinging to me. I tried not to think that I should have been coming in from an afternoon relaxing at the spa. I just hoped Shannon had toe-curlingly delicious sex all afternoon; someone deserved to be having some fun around here.

The thought of texting Lucian, calling today off, passed my mind, but I couldn't stop. Not now. Not when I was finally making progress. It didn't come easily to me, this fighting thing. Not every werewolf was born to be powerhouse fighters like the Shaw brothers. Take Mr. Davaar, who ran the local hardware store—he would only Shift on full moons, and spent that time refusing to leave the safety of his front yard. Or Joyce Rimmer, whose wolf was scared of everything. Every. Thing. I'd once seen her wolf jump fifteen feet in the air when a leaf blew past in front of her.

Being a Shifter didn't automatically make you a warrior. Most of us were ordinary, just trying to live our lives. That was how my mom and dad had brought me and Jase up. My parents had survived Oliver's reign by keeping their heads down, blending in, never drawing attention. They taught us to stay hidden, stay human as much as possible. Shifting meant risk. Playing in our wolf forms? Forbidden. We weren't the kind of Shifters who wrestled in the woods, honing our instincts through play-fights and mock battles. We Shifted only when absolutely necessary.

Early morning, before the enforcers started their rounds, when Oliver's lackeys were still sleeping off the previous night's excesses, we'd sneak out, nosing around the neighborhood, feeling the air on our fur for a few precious minutes before scurrying back inside. We never hunted. Never fought. If another wolf approached, we lowered our heads, tucked our tails, and slipped away.

Jase had turned that around. He'd worked his ass off these last few years, and I was so freaking proud of him for following his dream of being a tough-guy enforcer for Mai and Ryan. Me? I'd been so busy working and looking after Jase that it was only recently that I decided it was past time for me to learn how to defend myself.

I started my warm-up, throwing careful jabs at the punching bag. Each hit sent a satisfying thud through the small room. Left, right, left again. The memory of last night's bar fight flashed through my mind—Derek stepping in, making it look so easy while I seemed to just stand there.

Useless.

That's what he thought of me. What everyone thought of me.

Good for making coffee and pulling drinks. But that was it. I wasn't someone worth sticking around for. I was just another burden, someone who needed protecting, someone you moved on from as soon as you realized that this was all there was.

I hit harder, my muscles protesting. Another punch, this one sloppy with anger. I reset my stance, focused on my form like Lucian had taught me. I would show them they all messed up by leaving me. I would be someone I was proud to be. I wasn't going to let the doubts win. Not today.

The punching bag swayed with each strike, my breathing growing heavier as I found my rhythm. Time got away from me, and I jumped when the laptop binged with an incoming call.

I wiped sweat from my face and accepted Lucian's call. The screen flickered to life, revealing him in his study—all polished mahogany and leather. His jet-black hair was perfectly styled as usual, not a strand out of place despite the late hour wherever he was. Those amber eyes locked onto mine with laser focus, seeming to glow in the dim lighting behind him.

Even through a laptop screen, Lucian Black commanded attention. The crisp white shirt with rolled-up sleeves showcased forearms corded with muscle, and his sharp-featured face remained a careful mask of control. After months of training, I'd learned to read those micro-expressions—the slight tightening around his eyes that meant he was assessing my condition, the barely perceptible downward turn of his mouth that showed displeasure with what he saw.

"You look like hell," he said flatly. "We should reschedule."

"I'm fine." I squared my shoulders, ignoring the protest from my muscles.

His eyes narrowed to amber slits. "Miller, I can count the hours of sleep you've had from here. What happened to rule number one?"

"Self-care is for people without staff shortages," I muttered. "What are we working on today?"

He studied me silently, that penetrating gaze making me feel like a specimen under glass. "Power," he finally declared. "Since you're determined to punish yourself today, let's make it count."

My wolf's ears pricked forward. Power. Exactly what I needed after watching Derek handle Brad last night like he was swatting a fly. Never again.

"Show me your stance."

I settled into position, feeling the pleasant burn in my muscles from the warm-up.

"Lower," he commanded. "You're still too high. A child could sweep you right now. Center of gravity, Miller. We've been over this."

I adjusted, sinking deeper. "Better?"

"Show me the Caldera sequence. Full power." His eyes locked on mine. "Your whole body generates the force, not just your limbs."

I launched into the combination, each movement flowing into the next. Left jab, right cross, left hook, uppercut, knee strike, roundhouse kick. My muscles burned as I tried to maintain perfect form while channeling maximum power through each strike.

"Again," he commanded when I finished. "But this time, someone you love is standing behind you. If your strike fails, they pay. Make each one count."

The faces flashed through my mind—Jase with his crooked smile, Mai and her quiet strength, even my staff who depended on me. Something shifted inside, and my next combination exploded with purpose. Each strike carried intention, each movement had meaning.

"There it is." Lucian's voice held rare approval. "That's the difference between fighting and surviving. Remember this feeling, Miller. Real power isn't anger—it's knowing exactly what you'd burn the world down to protect."

I nodded, chest heaving but standing straighter than I had all day.

The next hour blurred into a punishing rhythm of strike, correct, repeat. Lucian pushed me relentlessly, demanding perfection with every movement until sweat plastered my shirt to my back.

"Time for your favorite part," Lucian said, a rare smile touching his lips. "Blades."

My exhaustion evaporated instantly. I moved to the false wall panel, revealing my private arsenal. With knives, I wasn't just a coffee shop manager trying to be something else. With knives, I became something dangerous.

I selected my practice set—three perfectly balanced throwing blades Lucian had sent to me when we started training. The weight settled in my palm like old friends, and everything else fell away.

My body moved on instinct through the forms—slash, parry, pivot, strike. The blades became liquid silver extensions of my arms, catching light as they cut through air. This dance required no supernatural strength, no wolf reflexes—just precision, practice, and patience. Things I could control. Things I could master.

"Targets," Lucian commanded.

I shifted grip without breaking rhythm and released. The first knife struck center target with a satisfying thunk. The second and third followed in rapid succession, forming a tight cluster that would have dropped any attacker.

"Again," he ordered as I retrieved them. "Add the Viper defense. Your enemies won't politely wait their turn."

I nodded, then launched into the sequence again. This time, I wove defensive counters between each throw—duck an imaginary attacker, slash across their abdomen, weave past their retaliation, release. The rhythm sang through my blood, making me feel more alive than I had in days.

"Better," Lucian nodded. "Your form is improving. You're actually starting to look like a fighter instead of a coffee shop manager playing at one." His eyes tracked the last knife as it hit its mark. "The blades suit you, Miller. They're becoming an extension of you, not just weapons."

From Lucian, that was practically a standing ovation. I bit back a smile despite my burning muscles.

"Rear attack scenario," he commanded. "Keep the blades live this time. Use their momentum."

I pivoted, visualizing an attacker—six-foot-three, broad shoulders, hands reaching for my throat. My body responded instantly, feet planted as I executed the counter he'd drilled into me for weeks. The knife left my hand in a perfect arc of lethal intent, striking exactly where an attacker's shoulder joint would be—not to kill, but to disable.

"Good, but we need someone you can practice against. All the shadow-boxing in the world won't prepare you for an actual body."

"No!" The word burst out forcefully. There was no way I wanted anyone to know about this. "I'm not ready to let anyone else in on what we're doing."

He sighed, pinching the bridge of his nose. "Fine. I'll figure something out. But you won't progress any more without an actual person to practice on."

I tilted my head, unable to suppress a grin. "But you did say I'm progressing, right?"

He scowled. "Don't get cocky. Your progress stops the moment you collapse from exhaustion. When did you last sleep—actually sleep—for a full night?"

I opened my mouth to lie, then closed it at his knowing look. "Define 'full night'?"

"That's what I thought." He crossed his arms. "You can't keep burning the candle at both ends, Miller. All this training won't mean anything if you're too exhausted to use it when it counts."

I wiped sweat from my face with a towel. Lucian was being dramatic. I knew my limits and knew I was okay.

"I'm managing fine."

"Are you?" Lucian's voice took on that stern edge I'd come to know well. "Because I see someone running on fumes and caffeine. What's the first principle I taught you?"

"Balance is the foundation of everything," I recited automatically, slumping against the desk. "But the bar—"

"Will still be standing if you take one damn night off."

"Who's going to cover? Shannon called in sick again, Julie and Brian are already maxed out—"

"And that's exactly why I'm going to send Darla down there to sort things out if you show up to our next session looking like roadkill."

I froze. "You wouldn't."

His smile was sharp. "Try me. And good luck getting her to let you slide, Miller. You think I'm tough? Knowing her, she'll tie you to that punching bag until you sleep for a week."

The threat wasn't empty—I'd seen enough of Darla's protective streak to know she'd do exactly that. Despite what everyone else in the Three Rivers thought, I knew that Lucian and Darla were not human, and Darla was definitely not Lucian's wife. She preferred her partners with skirts and heels.

Being married had been their cover when they lived here, when Lucian wanted to get away from his family, their multiple businesses, and the squabbling between his four brothers, who, by all accounts, kept getting themselves into trouble. Darla was Lucian's bodyguard and had sworn to protect him whether he was the hot-shot billionaire of the family business or a coffee shop owner in Three Rivers. Darla was good at her job, scary as hell, and would remove limbs from anyone who looked at Lucian sideways.

"I appreciate the concern," I said carefully, "but I can handle my schedule."

"Then start acting like it." His voice softened slightly. "Save some of that fire for when it counts, Miller. You won't be any good to anyone if you burn yourself out."

The truth was, slowing down terrified me. Everyone needed something—the bar, my brother, my staff. They kept me busy, kept my mind on them. If I paused, even briefly, I'd have to face thoughts of Derek. His hands, rough and gentle all at once. That smile that lit up something inside me when he turned it on me. The maddening way he made me want to either slap him or climb him like a tree. No. Better to stay busy.

"Get some rest, Miller. I mean it."

I nodded, not trusting myself to speak, and hung up. Slumping down in my chair, the quiet of the office pressed in around me. All I wanted to do was curl up and have a quick nap before the evening shift started. The pile of invoices looked at me accusingly. Damn it, I had to make sure they were paid today.

I grabbed the first one, squinting at numbers that refused to stay still on the page.

My phone buzzed with a text from Julie:

Coffee machine possessed again. Line to the door. Can't handle alone. HELP!

I closed my eyes, swallowing the flash of frustration. Not Julie's fault our ancient espresso machine had a death wish.

A second text lit up: *SOS! People getting angry!!!*

I was already standing, shoving the invoices aside. The accounts would have to wait. Maybe I could do them after closing time?

Chaos crescendoed as I yanked open my office door—raised voices, angry hissing, the distinctive metal-grinding-on-metal sound of impending mechanical rebellion. I rushed into the bar to find exactly what I'd expected: a line stretching to the door, Julie's panicked face, and our espresso machine belching steam like a caffeinated volcano.

I squared my shoulders and marched toward the counter. I was Sofia Miller, and caffeine-deprived customers were nothing compared to what I could handle.

They wanted coffee? Fine. I'd give them the best damn coffee in Three Rivers, broken machine or not.

Chapter Ten

DEREK

The nightmare hit me like it always did—swift, merciless, and too damn real. Harris's blood spattered across my hands as he struggled to breathe, the acrid stench of cordite sharp in my nose. His eyes locked onto mine as his lips twisted into a grotesque smile.

"You'll fail her too. You know you will."

This time, though, the dream shifted to the night before he died. I was in my office at Echo Command, 0200 hours. Intelligence reports scattered across my desk under buzzing fluorescents that hummed like angry wasps. Cold coffee, printer ink, and gun oil—night shift's permanent perfume—surrounded me, while outside, the base's massive generators thrummed.

The rest of the unit had cleared out hours ago, but something kept me here, had kept nagging at me, pulling me deeper into the web of data. This was the moment when I realized Harris was working with Victor Kane, feeding him information, keeping Kane one step ahead of us all this time. Good men in our unit had died tracking him—brothers-in-arms, friends.

I stared at the laptop, my mind refusing to believe the evidence in front of me.

Boot leather whispered against concrete—footsteps I'd recognize anywhere. Even before Harris's familiar scent of gunpowder, mint, and something sharply medicinal reached me, my wolf was alert. The air pressure changed as his broad frame filled the doorway, bringing with it a draft from the corridor that stirred the papers on my desk.

"Still burning the midnight oil, Shaw?" Harris's deep voice carried its usual warmth, but something felt off. Did he know that I'd worked it out? My wolf stirred as Harris crossed to my desk with that fluid grace that had always made him stand out among the humans in Echo Command. Perching on the edge like he'd done countless times before, he pulled two protein bars from his pocket, tossing me the peanut butter one he knew I preferred.

Such a small gesture. How many nights had we shared these awful bars, trading complaints about their cardboard taste while poring over mission reports?

I kept my eyes on the screen, afraid my expression would give me away. "Just reviewing some reports."

"Must be fascinating stuff to keep you here at..." He made a show of checking his watch. "Zero-two-hundred."

I looked up at him. Same pressed uniform, same easy smile, same scar above his left eyebrow from the time he'd taken a hit meant for me in Kandahar. Nothing about him suggested a traitor.

"Found some interesting patterns," I said carefully, watching his reaction as I turned the computer to face him.

His smile held, but something flickered behind his eyes as he read the screen. "Where did you get this, brother?"

"I dug it out of the files we found at Kane's base in Tripoli."

Harris's facade cracked then, his shoulders sagging as he sank into the chair across from me. "I didn't have a choice, Derek, you gotta believe me."

"There's always a choice," I growled. "Those men trusted you. I trusted you."

"They sent me photos of my sister." His voice broke. "They're following her every move, Derek. They threatened to do things… I can't let anything happen to my baby sister."

He leaned forward, desperation etched on his face. "I know I fucked up, but I can make this right, Derek. I can. I just need you to help me one more time."

Was he for real?

"Why didn't you come to me before?" I said, my anger warring with the instinct to help my friend. "We can get your sister somewhere safe, bring in—"

"No!" Harris's response was sharp, panicked. "Kane has people everywhere. The moment we use official channels, she's dead."

I studied him carefully. Everything in my training screamed that this was wrong, that I should report it immediately. But this was Harris. The closest thing I had to a brother here.

I leaned back in my chair. "Okay, nothing official. You have a plan?"

Relief flooded his face. "Kane's meeting some suppliers tomorrow night. I know where. If we move fast, we can take him down before he knows I've flipped. I have a friend back home. I'll get him to pick up my sister, make it look casual. He'll keep her safe until this is over."

I considered it, but we couldn't go AWOL on this, it'd be a suicide mission. Our best chance of getting Kane was with a team.

"If you're right about him having people everywhere, I can hold the

information until the last minute, then tell Command the tip came through our usual agent. That way, it'll still be a legit operation and we'll have backup."

Harris hesitated. "I don't know, Derek. Even last minute..."

"I'll choose the team myself. It'll work."

Harris stood. "Alright, then. Thank you, brother. I'll make this right, I promise."

As he turned to leave, I caught his arm. "Harris. If this goes sideways..."

He gripped my shoulder, his eyes meeting mine. He never did respect Shifter etiquette, meeting our eyes no matter what. "It won't. We're Echo Command's finest, remember? Kane won't know what hit him."

The dream shifted again, back to the moment everything went wrong: the explosion ripping through air, Harris shoving me clear, taking the blast meant for me. Kane knew we were coming. If I had listened to Harris, if I hadn't gone through official channels, maybe he would still be alive. Maybe Harris's blood wouldn't be on my hands.

I looked down at his body in horror as his face morphed into Sofia's. Her green eyes wide with terror, her copper hair sprawled out as blood pooled beneath her, soaking into the dark earth. My hands pressed against her wounds like they had Harris's, but no matter how hard I applied pressure, the blood wouldn't stop. It kept pumping out of her, great gushes of it, in time with her slowing heartbeat.

Her mouth moved, forming words I couldn't hear over the deafening roar in my ears. And then her head lolled to the side, lifeless.

I shot upright, gasping. Sweat drenched my back. The tangled sheets felt too constricting, and I ripped them away, planting my feet on the floor, gripping the edge of the mattress to anchor myself.

Fuck. That was a bad one. They were always worse when I was too busy working to make it to the Bar in the evening, didn't get to see her, smell her, watch her put her hands on her hips and trade barbs with me.

I staggered to the bathroom, not bothering to flip on the light. The moment my feet hit the cold tiles, my stomach revolted. I lunged for the toilet just in time, retching up acid.

When there was nothing left, I slumped back against the wall, the sweat cooling on my forehead and neck. Guilt and shame swirled inside of me—a cocktail I'd grown intimately familiar with since Harris died. But this wasn't about him anymore. This time it was Sofia. Seeing her like that—losing her—night after night; it was killing me.

I needed to move. Needed to do something. My chest still felt too tight, my skin too hot.

Mate. Safe.

Yes, I thought back, we would make her safe. My wolf hated the dreams as much as I did. It was prey we couldn't hunt, couldn't defeat.

I glanced at my watch: 5:03 a.m. I wouldn't be going back to sleep. Instead, I splashed cold water over my face, trying to wash away the memories of the dream. Next, I grabbed my toothbrush and worked mechanically, bristles scrubbing away the bile and the bitter taste of panic from my tongue. Every movement was deliberate, grounding me back in the present, back in control.

My wolf didn't settle, though. His agitation crawled under my skin, demanding action, demanding I check on her.

I pulled on a pair of gray joggers and headed downstairs, my bare feet silent on the hardwood floors. I crossed to the dining room and switched on the wall of monitors. My eyes immediately landed on the feed from outside her apartment, and the footage from her arriving home at 2:35 a.m. I'd already seen it before I went to bed; knowing I wouldn't be able to sleep until I knew she was safe in the apartment. I checked my phone, saw Jase's message from 3:15 a.m. saying he was finally home and that Sofia was asleep. I ran the feed forward. No one else had come in or out of her apartment.

My fingers danced across keys, cycling through exterior cameras. Building perimeter, surrounding streets. Clear.

She was safe.

My wolf settled, appeased for now. But this watching from afar wasn't enough. Never enough.

The buzz of my phone snapped me out of my thoughts, and I nearly knocked the damn thing off the desk. The name on the screen froze me in place: Torres.

I hadn't talked to Torres in years. He was a human who'd trained with me and Harris, but I'd never liked him. He'd always been too quick to laugh when a new recruit wiped out during an exercise or when someone got injured during a sparring match. He was always watching, assessing, cataloging weaknesses instead of building the team.

I opened the message:

Sofia seems nice. Shame if anything happened to her.

My pulse spiked as I tapped on the attachment icon with jerky fingers. The image that filled the screen sent a cold fist squeezing my insides.

Sofia. She was taking a break at the Bottley, hair pulled back, wearing that green sweater I'd never told her brought out her eyes. The photo had been taken through the window—close enough to see a laptop open in front of her, a half-empty mug at her elbow. She had no idea she was being watched.

Fuck!

My vision tunneled red, the instinct to Shift and hunt this threat to our mate surging through me.

No. Focus. Losing control wouldn't solve anything. Wouldn't protect her.

I hit Jase's number, pacing as it rang. He answered on the second ring.

"Yeah," he replied, his voice thick with sleep. "What the hell? It's barely five thirty."

"Active threat. Your place. Don't wake Sofia, but secure the apartment. Now."

I listened to the sound of rustling sheets on Jase's end. His voice hardened immediately. "On it."

I paced again, waiting, listening as Jase moved through the apartment, checking locks and the windows.

My phone buzzed again. I kept the line open to Jase as I checked the messages. Another photo.

This image was of Sofia sitting in her car, wiping tears from her eyes. She was pulled over on the side of the road. It was taken yesterday, before I got to her.

I slammed my fist into the desk, sending a stack of papers and a scout knife clattering to the floor.

"Derek!" Jase's voice cut through my spiraling rage. "Place is secure. No one is here. All doors locked. Sofia's fine. She's still asleep."

I swallowed hard, forcing the wolf to stand down. "Stay alert. No one gets near her."

"You gonna tell me what the hell's going on?"

"I'll handle it. Stay on her when she wakes up. Text me before you leave the apartment. I'm going to send someone in to sweep for bugs and cameras. Do not leave her side today, Jase. You understand? I'll clear it with Carlito, but you need to be wherever she is today."

"Understood."

I hung up as another text came through.

Your protections aren't worth shit, Derek. We can get to her anywhere. Want to keep her safe? Sam Shaw has something of ours. We want it back. USB stick. You have 6 hours. Text when you have it.

My wolf growled inside me, fury barely contained, but I pushed him back. There was no room for emotion now. No doubts.

I had one objective: keep Sofia safe. Nothing else mattered.

Chapter Eleven

SOFIA

Jase was sitting at the corner table by the door to the Bottley, typing furiously on his phone. Not for the first time this morning, I wondered what the hell was up with my brother. His scent had been edgy ever since I woke up to find him sitting outside my bedroom door like some sort of guard dog.

He'd claimed he'd been searching for a lost earring from his latest girlfriend, which was a blatant lie—he didn't have girlfriends these days, not with how busy he was with work, along with the fact he was still pining over Amara. But even when he used to have girlfriends, he never brought them back to our apartment.

Then he told me he had the day off and wanted to spend it with me. A day off? Jase? I wasn't buying it. But I also wasn't going to pass up the opportunity to spend the day with him. Only now, I was beginning to worry. Had he been fired? Was he having issues with the other enforcers? If any of them were messing with my brother, they'd have me to answer to.

The door swung open, and I instinctively straightened, looking up with a bright smile that was all muscle memory. My stomach dipped when I saw who it was.

Derek.

"Morning, Shaw," I greeted, schooling my face into something neutral.

Something about his energy was different today; he almost looked... agitated. He didn't respond right away. Just stood there for a second, his sharp, gray eyes looking me over before he scanned the room.

"Derek?" I tried again.

He gave me a quick nod, then headed straight for the Booth of Brooding, stopping at Jase's table on the way. He leaned down and whispered something to my brother that even I couldn't pick up.

What the freaking hell was going on? I turned back to the counter, trying to ignore the strange knot forming in my chest. It wasn't like Derek Shaw owed me a conversation, and Goddess knew I didn't want to start my Sunday playing twenty questions with him. But still, something about the way he moved, the tension rolling off him... it didn't sit right.

My wolf paced in the back of my mind, uneasy.

I ground the beans and steamed the milk for Mrs. Tuck's Whispering Willow latte. It was one of my most popular creations, a smooth lavender and honey latte with a touch of vanilla, but I couldn't help throwing glances over my shoulder. Derek didn't pull his laptop out like he normally did. Instead, he sat there, his eyes scanning the room every few seconds, his hands gripping his phone like it might sprout wings and fly away if he didn't hold on to it.

Something was wrong.

The tension wafting off Derek was hard to ignore, and it scraped against my frayed nerves like sandpaper. This wasn't normal. Derek

Shaw was… unflappable. Or at least he had been since the moment he swaggered back into the Three Rivers Pack and started taking up space in my life.

And now? He was *flapped*. Big time.

I wiped my hands on my apron and grabbed his order—black coffee and a plain croissant. The most aggressively boring breakfast in existence, perfectly on-brand for Derek Shaw. No frills, no joy, just fuel.

"Your daily dose of bland," I announced, sliding the plate and mug in front of him. "Rushed in early, like the pain in the ass you are, to ruin my peaceful Sunday, or is there another establishment you're planning to terrorize with your charm after this?"

For a microsecond, his lips almost twitched upward. That rare half-smile I absolutely had not cataloged in my mental Derek Shaw expression archive nearly made an appearance, but it was gone before it could fully settle on his face, leaving something much harder in its place.

"That your professional opinion? Me, a pain in the ass?"

"Absolutely. In fact, I'm nominating you for an award. We'll hang your plaque right there: 'Most Dedicated Brooder, Five Years Running.' You can wear your scowl to the ceremony. It'll be very on-theme. We might even get you into the local news."

Not even a twitch this time. Instead, his eyes kept ping-ponging between the door, the windows and back. His jaw clenched as he ran a hand over his military-short hair, fingers tensing at his nape.

This was starting to freak me out.

"Oh no," I said, narrowing my eyes. "Someone's about to snatch the pastries off the counter, aren't they? Quick! Duck and cover."

His gaze locked on something behind me. I turned to see Sam filling the doorway—broad shoulders wrapped in leather, brown hair framing sharp features similar but not identical to Derek's. Where Derek commanded attention, Sam's presence seeped in gradually, like smoke under a door, pressing against your skin until you couldn't ignore it.

I glanced between the twins, and a memory of them in school rose in my mind. Back when they were different. Back when they still smiled those easy teenage smiles.

The memory surfaced without warning: *me alone in the gym, hunting for my favorite blue hair tie—the one Mai had given me for my thirteenth birthday. I was crouched by the bleachers, running my fingers along the dusty floor, when their scent hit me.*

Brock Madden's thugs. Ben and Roscoe.

I swore under my breath. Nothing good ever followed their arrival.

Their presence always meant the same thing—torment for someone smaller, weaker, or just unlucky enough to cross their path.

"Look what we have here," Ben drawled. "Thought I smelled prey,"

I stood slowly, my heart hammering against my chest.

"Looking for this?" Roscoe said, dangling my hair tie from a finger. "Bet it'd look better down the toilet."

"Give it back," I warned, though my voice shook slightly.

Ben laughed. "Or what?"

"Or we break both your legs."

I spun around to find Derek and Sam moving in sync as they approached, their footsteps and expressions perfectly matching.

"A hair tie, Roscoe? Really?" Sam's voice was deceptively light. "Not sure it's your color."

Ben sneered, "This isn't your business, Shaw. Either of you."

"See, that's where you're wrong," Derek said, stepping slightly in front of me as Sam mirrored him on my other side. "Everything to do with Sofia is our business."

"You might want to run along now," Sam suggested with false pleasantness.

"While you still can," Derek finished.

"Fuck you, Shaw!" Ben lunged forward, swinging at Derek. The twins flowed around each other like water, covering each other's blind spots instinctively. As Derek sidestepped Ben's wild swing, Sam was already pivoting, catching Roscoe's arm and twisting it behind his back. Derek's hand snapped out, driving Ben's face into the bleachers with a satisfying crunch.

"My nose!" Ben howled, blood streaming down his face.

"You know," Sam said conversationally, as if he wasn't bending Roscoe's arm at an unnatural angle, "I'm actually disappointed. I expected better from Brock's lackeys."

Sam plucked my hair tie from Roscoe's clenched fist and tossed it to Derek, who handed it to me with a nod. "I believe this belongs to you."

Derek and Sam had walked me home after, cracking jokes the whole way.

They seemed so... not happy, but hopeful maybe was the right word. So confident that life may be shit, but it was going to get better. Now? That optimism had vanished from both of them.

Sam's eyes swept the bar, assessing it the same way Derek had, before heading to me.

"Sofia, you smell amazing as ever."

I smiled but watched as Sam's gaze drifted past me to Derek. As soon as it did, the warmth disappeared, replaced by a razor-sharp edge I wasn't used to seeing directed at his twin. What the hell was going on?

"Good to see you, Sam. You want your usual? I can bring it over."

Sam gave a small shake of the head. "Can't stay long."

"Sam." Derek's voice held more than a note of impatience.

Sam sighed. "I'll catch you later, Sofia." He moved toward the Booth of Brooding with the enthusiasm of someone headed to a root canal.

A violent banging erupted from the register.

"What the f—?"

"Brian!" Julie's warning cut through the café. "Do not finish that sentence!"

"But it won't open!"

I turned to see Brian attacking the cash drawer, black-dyed hair flopping in his eyes as he yanked like he was trying to free a trapped animal. Sighing, I pulled the nail file from my pocket—my secret weapon against temperamental café equipment.

"Here." I jammed the file into the gap and wriggled it. The drawer popped open with a satisfying click.

"I swear this thing has a personal vendetta against me."

"Only because you approach it like it's a UFC opponent," I laughed. "Trust me, in that matchup, the register remains undefeated."

In my peripheral vision, I caught Sam standing abruptly, his chair screeching across the floor.

"I have to take this," he said to Derek. "Don't go anywhere. We're not done yet."

Derek didn't respond, but I caught the way his jaw tightened.

Sam stepped outside and started pacing along the sidewalk, phone pressed to his ear, his free hand gesturing sharply at whatever argument was escalating on the other end of the line. Whatever that phone call was, it wasn't good.

I glanced back at Derek. His hand slipped into Sam's jacket draped over the chair—a movement so casual I almost missed it. Almost. Then his fingers dipped into another pocket, and I caught a flash of something small and black disappearing into his palm.

What the hell?

I froze, my instincts screaming that I wasn't meant to have seen this. That no one was. Heart racing, I turned away quickly, pretending to adjust something under the counter. The theft had been so smooth, so practiced—like a magic trick minus the showmanship. Derek Shaw had just pickpocketed his own brother.

Sam marched back in, phone tucked away, scowl etched deep.

"I have to go," he said curtly, grabbing his jacket and slinging it over one arm. "I'll call when I'm done. We need to finish this, Derek."

Derek leaned back in his chair and spread his hands wide. "Anytime."

Sam's frown carved deeper lines into his face before he turned and stalked out without another glance at anyone.

I stared blankly at the counter, blinking quickly. This wasn't some stupid prank between siblings. The tension humming between them was too real, too sharp, and both Derek and Sam were too on edge right now. But I was having a hard time reconciling this Sam and Derek with the twins I knew and had grown up with. They had always been there for each other. Sure, they bickered and teased, but they had each other's backs, no matter what. And they never stole from one another.

I thought about telling Sam. He deserved to know, didn't he? But—despite everything Derek had done—didn't he deserve the benefit of the doubt? My head spun with questions, but one thing was painfully clear.

Something was very, very wrong.

And whatever it was, Derek was in the middle of it.

Chapter Twelve

SOFIA

Trying to spy on Derek while serving customers was like trying to pat your head and rub your stomach while riding a unicycle. Thankfully, after years at the Bottley, I could make Mrs. Henderson's half-caf oat milk latte with my eyes literally closed.

Which meant I caught Derek glaring at his phone, the muscle in his jaw jumping like it was trying to escape his face, the lines around his eyes carving deeper as he typed furiously. His knuckles went white around his phone before he shot me a quick glance, stood, and stalked outside, the device already pressed to his ear.

I didn't need to hear the words to know the conversation wasn't good. His free hand raked through his hair like he was trying to pull answers directly from his skull, his posture military-straight.

I couldn't pick out most of the words, but twice, he angled his head toward the window as his eyes scanned the road. I could have sworn the words he said at those times were: "Not yet." Then, a few seconds later: "Leave her the fuck out of this."

My stomach bottomed out.

Her. Who the freaking hell was "her"?

Me? Mai? Another enforcer? I shouldn't care about Derek Shaw's drama. Yet here I was, practically straining to eavesdrop like the world's nosiest barista.

A new wave of customers flooded in, but my head wasn't in it.

When Derek stepped back inside, it wasn't the same Derek who had walked out. He moved differently—less of the calm, deliberate grace that usually clung to him like a second skin. This Derek moved with harder edges, every molecule in his body vibrating with tension.

I watched him scan the room for the bazillionth time today. My wolf recognized it for what it was. Predatory. He was on a hunt. His gaze swept past customers and staff alike until it zeroed in on me, a homing missile finding its target.

Our eyes met, and suddenly, breathing seemed like an advanced skill I'd forgotten. He stalked toward me with such intensity that every instinct screamed RUN.

No way. I wasn't running from Derek Shaw.

He stopped close enough that I could feel the heat radiating off him. "Can we talk?" His voice had dropped an octave, rough and gravelly in a way that sent rebellious shivers across my skin. He cleared his throat, glancing at the crowd still filtering in. "Outside. In private?"

I crossed my arms, holding his gaze even as my wolf nudged at me, sensing something I couldn't quite name.

I sighed. Being alone with Derek was dangerous in more ways than one. He'd hear my betraying heartbeat, catch my shallow breaths, smell the desire I fought so hard to suppress. But this might be my only chance to demand answers about whatever the hell was happening.

I glanced toward Julie, who had just finished ringing up Mrs. Redmore's Alpha's Bite cappuccino.

"Cover for me?" I asked, keeping my voice casual.

Julie's smile bounced from me to Derek and back, her eyes lighting up with enough matchmaking gleam to power a small city. "Sure, hon. No problem."

I sighed. Julie could give Wally a run for his money in the gossip department. Knowing her, by the time I returned, the entire town would not only know about our "private chat" but would probably be planning our mating ceremony.

I untied my apron, hanging it on its usual hook, and followed Derek out the back to the alley. The scents hit me all at once—strong, layered, and impossible to ignore, a complex tapestry of scents no human could detect. The sharp tang of spilled beer clung to the pavement near the dumpsters, mingling with the lingering bitterness of roasted coffee from discarded grounds. The faint metallic scent of city rain still clung to the bricks despite the clear skies, mixing with the ever-present aroma of damp earth from where weeds had stubbornly pushed through cracks in the asphalt. The alleyway stretched wide enough for delivery trucks to pull in and unload, but today, it was empty apart from Derek's black SUV parked near the entrance. A set of rusting fire escapes zigzagged up the brick walls, their bolts slowly surrendering to time.

Derek stopped a few paces ahead, his back to me, one hand gripping his neck as he stared at the ground like it might offer answers.

"Well?" I crossed my arms. "You wanted to talk? Then talk. No more lies, Derek. No more bullshit. I want the truth. I saw you steal something from your brother. Either tell me what's going on, or I'm going straight to Sam."

His shoulders tensed at my words, but it took him a full minute before he turned to face me. When he did, his face was carefully blank, but his eyes, normally so guarded, held a cocktail of regret, pain, and something that looked dangerously like guilt.

He opened his mouth, hesitated, and then finally said the last words I expected to hear:

"I'm sorry, Sofia."

I blinked. "Sorry? Sorry for what? What the hell is going on, Derek?"

Without warning, he closed the distance between us in two strides. I instinctively stepped back, my shoulder blades hitting the cold brick wall of the alleyway. My wolf bristled but didn't attack; something about how Derek loomed over me wasn't just threatening—it was protective. Desperate. Dangerous.

"This isn't how I wanted to do this," he murmured as he slipped a hand around the back of my neck, tilting my face to his.

My eyes widened as he leaned down, his lips hovering just above mine, his breath warm and coffee-scented as it mingled with my own. Time slowed to a crawl. The space between us charged with electricity.

Oh, my Goddess, was Derek Shaw about to kiss me? Here? Now? In this grimy alley behind the Bottley with discarded coffee grounds and rusting fire escapes as witnesses? After five years of nothing but cold shoulders and cutting remarks, this was his move?

My traitorous heart hammered against my ribs. My wolf—the same one who'd been snarling moments ago—went suddenly, suspiciously quiet, like she was holding her breath. A thousand teenage fantasies flashed through my mind, memories of wondering how those perfectly sculpted lips would feel against mine.

"What are you—?" I started but then felt a sharp pinch in my neck.

My hand flew up, fingers brushing against the spot where something had pricked me. A syringe? The realization crashed through me just as the effects began taking hold.

"Derek?" My voice slurred, my limbs suddenly weighing about a thousand pounds each.

"I'm sorry, Sofia." His voice sounded far away now, though I knew he hadn't moved. The brick wall behind me seemed to tilt and sway. My knees buckled, and strong arms caught me before I could hit the ground.

I couldn't believe it. Derek fucking Shaw had drugged me! I wanted to scream, or run, or better yet, to punch the look of regret clean off his face.

But the world was already slipping away, everything fading into darkness, his repeated apology—"I'm sorry, Sofia"—chasing me into oblivion.

Chapter Thirteen

SOFIA

Pain was the first thing that registered—a dull, relentless throb pulsing behind my temples, in perfect sync with the beat of my heart. My mouth felt dry, metallic, like I'd been sucking on pennies, and the faint scent of copper teased the edges of my senses. I shifted, fabric rasping under my fingertips. Soft wool, worn surfaces. A blanket?

Claws scraped faintly against the edges of my mind, enough so I knew my wolf was okay. Mad as hell, but okay.

I tried to sit up, but a wave of dizziness nearly knocked me flat again. Everything felt wrong, like my body and brain had been disconnected and poorly reassembled.

Focus, Sofia. Breathe.

I blinked slowly, forcing my vision to stabilize as I took in my surroundings. Dim light cast uneven shadows across wooden beams above me. The room was small but well-kept, with knotted pine walls and a slanted ceiling that spoke of an A-frame cabin. A large window to my right had its thick curtains partially drawn back, offering a glimpse of towering pines beyond, their branches heavy with fresh snow. We had to be north of Three Rivers; back home, all the snow had melted weeks ago.

A bookshelf hugged the left wall, crammed with an odd mix of well-worn paperbacks and sleek, leather-bound volumes. A thick, woven rug covered most of the hardwood floor, its muted geometric pattern blending seamlessly with the room's earthy tones.

The bed beneath me was larger than mine at home, with a woolen blanket draped over me that smelled faintly of cedar and something that reminded me of Derek. On the nightstand beside me, a single lamp cast warm yellow light across the space, and a glass of water sat nearby, beads of condensation sliding down its sides like tiny tears. A soft creak echoed through the space—the building settling, complaining as wind pressed against its walls.

Where the freaking hell am I?

Memory hit me like shards of ice: Derek's quiet, "I'm sorry," the sharp prick of a syringe. Rage bubbled up through my veins as it all came rushing back.

He'd actually done this. He'd drugged me and dragged me Goddess-knows-where like some twisted kidnapper from a crime show.

Who the hell does that?

The anger burned through the fog in my brain, and I jolted upright, managing to stay vertical this time.

I reached for my Pack bonds, the invisible threads that tied me to Jase, to Mai and Ryan, to the whole of the Three Rivers Pack.

Nothing.

My breath caught, chest tightening as I tried again, harder this time, mentally clawing for that familiar connection.

Nothing.

The soft hum of connection I'd always felt while on Pack territory was gone. Panic crawled up my throat, its cold fingers wrapping around my lungs. For a moment, I couldn't breathe. My wolf howled, the sound deafening inside my skull, her confusion and rage so intense my skin prickled with the effort of containing her.

"It's okay, you're safe, Sofia."

Derek stood in the doorway, one shoulder leaning casually against the frame, ankles crossed like he was posing for *Kidnapper Monthly* magazine. He looked so relaxed it made me itch to slap that composure off his face.

"What. The. Actual. Fuck?" I bit out, each word sharp and deliberate. He just looked at me. Fine. "How about we start with something easy, then? Where the hell are we?"

"We're safe. We're at one of my cabins," he said finally. "No one knows about this one."

For a moment, fury completely replaced the gnawing panic in my chest. "Great. A secret little hideaway. Cozy. Did you decide to bring me here because you didn't want anyone else to know how insane you are?"

His expression didn't shift, and that infuriating calm composure of his only ignited something wilder in me.

"Do you have any idea what you've done, Derek?"

"I know exactly what I've done," he said, his tone matter-of-fact, unshaken by my growing rage. "You were in danger."

"Oh, I'm in danger? No shit. I'm very aware I'm in danger." I threw the blanket off my lap, swinging my legs to the floor with more force than I needed, and my feet hit the wooden planks with a satisfying thud. "*You* drugged me. Me! Do you even realize how fucked up that is?" My voice climbed with every word. "And don't you dare stand there like some brooding statue to the Goddess of 'I-did-this-for-your-own-good.' Start talking. Now."

"You're not in danger from me, Sofia."

"Really? So I should feel safe, should I?" I leaned toward him, glaring. "Let me break it down for you. You—" I held up one finger, "lured me into an alley on false pretenses. You—" a second finger, "drugged me. You—" a third finger, "dragged me to this... cabin-in-the-middle-of-bumfuck-nowhere. What about any of that screams, 'Trust me, Sofia, you're safe with me'? Hmm?"

His teeth clenched for a moment before he replied, "I'm trying to keep you alive."

"Alive?" I let out a laugh that sounded borderline hysterical even to my own ears. "Alive, Derek? What happened to basic communication? You know, maybe something like, 'Hey, Sofia, you're in danger, maybe we should handle that.' Did that revolutionary concept ever cross your mind?"

"You wouldn't have listened." His steely gaze locked onto mine, and for the first time since I woke up, his calm façade cracked just a fraction. "You would've brushed me off, just like you've been doing for months."

"Oh, so this is all *my* fault?"

His eyes darkened, twin storms brewing beneath that carefully blank expression. "Sofia, stop going crazy, I'm trying to explain. You're in danger—"

Stop going crazy?

"Fuck you!" I shot to my feet, keeping one hand on the bed to steady myself.

Derek exhaled sharply, brushing a hand through his dark brown hair, frustration radiating off him in waves. "Look, Sofia, you're my fated mate. I wasn't going to let…"

His words faded to white noise as my arms fell limply to my sides, my chest tightening like someone had landed a direct hit to my sternum. For a moment, my entire mind went blank, the breath stolen clean from my lungs. I'd dreamed of hearing him say those words for years. Years! And now he just casually dropped it into conversation like he was commenting on the weather.

"Excuse me?" I said slowly.

"Sofia—"

"No." I held up my hand. This was the final straw. "I know I'm your fated mate, but thank you for finally acknowledging it. Unlike you, I've known it for years, even though I've tried hard to forget it. But I've clung to the thought that the Moon Goddess made a mistake. She makes mistakes all the time. Look at Jem and Hayley—that was a total fucking disaster. And you and me?" I jabbed a finger between us. "This has got cosmic clerical error written all over it."

I knew I was ranting, but right now, I didn't care. My eyes flickered to the ceiling as I dramatically lifted both hands skyward, tilting my chin up like I was waiting for divine intervention.

"Any moment now, she's going to course correct," I declared loudly. "Right, Moon Goddess? You're gonna pull the plug on whatever cosmic prank this is and hit reset, right?"

The floor beneath us didn't rumble. No divine light flooded the room. The absurdly cozy fire behind Derek crackled in its stone hearth, stubbornly refusing to offer any signs of divine intervention.

Just perfect.

When I glanced back down, Derek was glaring at me, arms crossed. "Guess you're stuck with me."

"Oh, hell no." I jabbed a finger in his direction. "Just because the Goddess put us together doesn't mean shit. I'm saying no, thanks. I'm fine on my own. I'm happy on my own. I don't want anything to do with you. You hear me, Derek Shaw? Nothing, abso-fucking-lutely nothing to do with you! You're taking me back. Right now."

"No."

"That's it? Just 'no'? No discussion. No reasons?" I glared at him, hands planted firmly on my hips, mentally scanning for ways he could possibly piss me off more. Nope, I was pretty sure this was Sofia DEFCON 1—full nuclear meltdown imminent. "Fine. I'll call Jase, and he'll come pick me up. Where—?"

My voice broke off as my hand instinctively patted my back pocket. Empty. I froze for a heartbeat, then frantically checked my jeans, the side table, even the blanket I'd thrown aside. Nothing. No phone.

"Where is it?" I snapped.

"Gone."

He really had a thing with one-word answers these days.

"What the hell do you mean, 'gone?'" My voice rose, panic inching closer to the surface, clawing at my composure. "It doesn't just vanish, Derek. Where is it?"

"I got rid of it," he said, his tone maddeningly calm. "I didn't have time to install a signal jammer. Yours was wide open—they could've tracked it."

My brain short-circuited for a moment, grappling with the implications of his words.

"You *what*?" The words came out loud, echoing off the cabin walls. "You really have gone crazy! That was my phone, Derek! My only way to call for help, to check in with Jase—"

"They'd find you through it," he repeated slowly, like he was talking to a three-year-old. "It wasn't safe."

Oh, that did it.

I shoved my feet into my sneakers, spun on my heel, and stormed toward the door. I was ready to run until my legs gave out or we found civilization, whichever came first.

"Where are you going?"

"As far away from you as possible!" I wrenched the door open. Cold air bit at my cheeks with sharp little teeth, but I didn't care. I had to get the fuck out of there.

CHAPTER FOURTEEN

SOFIA

My pulse pounded as I crunched through snow, breath clouding in the frigid air. I turned in a slow circle, taking in my surroundings. The cabin stood in the center of a clearing, a wide expanse of snow-covered ground stretching about twenty meters in every direction before the tree line swallowed the landscape.

The trees themselves were ancient, towering pines and skeletal birches, their branches heavy with fresh snow, forming an impenetrable wall around us. The wind whispered softly through the forest, carrying the faint scent of pine and wet earth. There were no voices. No hum of cars in the distance. No telltale warmth of Pack on the edges of my senses. My wolf whined as she stretched—searching, yearning—for anything familiar.

The only break in the unrelenting stretch of trees was the narrow, winding track leading away from the cabin, the single path carved through the snow. My gaze followed it, noting the tire tracks still visible in the frozen ground. They led straight to Derek's black SUV, parked a few feet from the cabin's covered porch.

The snow around the cabin was largely undisturbed, save for my footprints and Derek's. An axe leaned against the cabin wall, its handle worn smooth, blade crusted with a fine dusting of ice. Nearby, a tree stump sat half-buried, surrounded by scattered wood chips.

I turned again, slower this time.

Apart from being north of Three Rivers, I had no idea where I was or how to get home.

Fuck!

Derek stood on the porch of the cabin, arms crossed, watching me.

"You going to tell me which way is home?"

"Nope."

Fucking Derek Shaw.

"Well, I guess I'll just have to work it out, then." I strode toward the track. It had to lead somewhere with people.

"That there is an old logging track," Derek said, his tone just as maddeningly composed as ever. "Splits more times than I can count. Junction after junction. You don't know where you're going; you'll just go deeper into the forest. Take you days, weeks even to get to the other side."

I spun back to him, narrowing my eyes. "Newsflash, Derek: I'm not some helpless child you can scare into staying put."

His mouth curved slightly, though there was no humor in it. "No. You're not. But if you get lost in these woods, you'll need to hunt to survive. Plus, there's a good chance the cold will kill you first."

I looked away quickly, letting my gaze skate over the forest again. Derek knew I wasn't a good hunter. Knew I had never really been taught how to catch prey in my wolf form.

I turned in another slow, deliberate circle. Maybe he was bluffing. Then again, maybe he wasn't.

The towering trees stretched in every direction I could see. The wind, whispering through the branches, carried no scents of human life, just pine and ice. The only movement came from the occasional swirl of frost kicked up by the breeze, tiny whirlwinds of glittering ice that danced across the clearing before settling again in perfect stillness.

My wolf whined, deeply unsettled.

No Pack. No bonds. No way home.

If I Shifted into my wolf form, I could probably follow the SUV tracks back to a road, as long as I could find the road before there was another snowfall. I glanced up at the sky, at the heavy clouds gathering above me.

Damn it.

The last thing I wanted was to be caught out in a snowstorm; it would be a death sentence.

I clenched my fists so tightly my nails dug into my palms, sharp little crescents biting into my skin. My breath came too fast, too shallow, misting in front of me in frantic, uneven puffs.

No. I couldn't accept this.

I wouldn't accept this.

I dug my heels into the icy ground, forcing my breaths to slow, making sure the out-breath was longer than the in-breath. In for four, hold for seven, out for eight. The tightness in my chest didn't ease, but it made my lungs work properly, made my wolf settle, made me feel grounded and in control again.

I was not going to panic.

Derek hadn't moved from his spot on the porch. He obviously wasn't worried I'd get far out here. There was no triumph in his expression, though, no smugness that I was stuck. Just that same unbearable calm, like he knew this was hard for me, but he was waiting for me to come to terms with it.

"This is kidnapping, you know," I said flatly.

His jaw ticked. "I know."

"You don't even care, do you?"

"I care," he said, his voice steady. "But I care more about keeping you alive. If I hadn't moved when I did, they would have—" He stopped himself, jaw clenching. "Just trust me on this."

Something in his tone made me pause. It wasn't just determination—there was an edge of urgency I'd never heard from him before. His eyes scanned the tree line with the kind of focused intensity I recognized from when he was working.

I narrowed my eyes at him, but he didn't waver, didn't flinch. He really believed this was the right move.

And that pissed me off even more.

I exhaled slowly, forcing my shoulders to relax, shoving my anger down deep where it wouldn't get in the way of what I needed to do next. If Derek wasn't lying, then escaping through the forest wasn't the answer. But he had given me an idea of what might be.

His SUV.

I just needed to get my hands on the keys; then I could leave his sorry ass stranded while I drove myself home.

And in the meantime, he was going to tell me what the freaking hell was going on.

Chapter Fifteen

DEREK

I knew she would be mad, knew it was possible she was never going to forgive me for this. But I hadn't seen any other option. Telling Sam would have been too risky. He worked for the Council; his job was to see the big picture these days and I couldn't gamble that he would refuse to give me the USB if it came down to that or Sofia.

So, I'd stolen what Torres had wanted, a Darth Vader USB, of all fucking things, but I hadn't handed it over. Not yet. I needed to know what was on it first. Needed to know what was so damn important that Torres would threaten Sofia to get it. And I had no illusions that this would end there. No, he knew my weakness now. He'd threaten her every time he wanted something, just like Kane held Harris's sister over him.

Instead of delivering, I'd texted Torres, asking for more time. He'd called, that Southern drawl unchanged.

"I gave you six hours. It's been over five. You always were an overachiever. The great Captain Shaw must have it by now."

"Not yet. Like I said, I need more time."

"But Sofia doesn't have more time, Derek. I have men there now, on standby, just waiting for my order to swoop in. And if you fail… well, to be honest, I haven't decided yet whether my order will be to kill her or to take her prisoner so we can all have some fun with her. That depends on how much you piss me off with your bullshit."

"I ain't stall—"

"I know you're at the Bottley, Derek. I know you met Sam."

I did a scan of the area, cataloging everyone who had eyes on me right then, everyone who wasn't Pack, but there was no one. How the fuck did Torres know so much? Maybe I could use it against him.

"Then you also know he got called away. I'm meeting him again later. I can get what you want then."

"No. You now have thirty minutes left. Go find your brother and get me what I need."

The dial tone was loud in my ear. I analyzed possible scenarios in my head. Telling Sam, telling Ryan. All options took too much time. I could hunt Torres's men, the ones he had stationed there, but I had no idea how many of them there were, and if I missed just one, then Sofia would pay the price. I couldn't let that happen. The only way to turn this around was to find out what was on the USB, try to use that against Torres. But I couldn't do that and keep Sofia safe. Not there. Not when I didn't know how many men or how many cameras they had.

That left only one option: buy time by taking Sofia and the USB somewhere secure. I had less than thirty minutes to get us both out of Three Rivers. I had safe houses set up; I just had to get us to one. I glanced through the window at Sofia. Her copper hair caught the sunlight streaming through the window, turning it into liquid fire as she moved behind the counter. She was smiling, that bright professional one she used for customers, but I could see the tension in her shoulders, the slight strain around her eyes. I should be taking care of her, not making her a target. But after all I'd done to her, she didn't trust me at all.

Yeah, I might be an overachiever, but even I couldn't get Sofia Miller to willingly agree to leave with me without an extremely detailed explanation.

I sent Evelyn a quick text.

Active threat. Lock down 3 Rivers. Anyone not Pack must be evacuated. I'm going AWOL. Protect the Pack.

My car was already parked in the alley. I had vials of ketamine and benzodiazepines in the truck; all enforcers did as part of our kit. It was the only way to put down an out-of-control werewolf without injuring them or us. I really wished there was another way.

Sofia stomped past me back into the cabin. Dark clouds rolled in from the west—a big storm coming, judging from the scent on the air and the dropping temperature.

I turned and followed the trail of faint, wet patches on the wooden floor left by her sneakers. She stood in the main living area in front of the stone fireplace, hands on her hips again. Never a good sign.

"Well?" she asked.

"Well, what?"

"Explain. All of this. Actually, no," she held up one hand in a stop gesture, "hold that thought. I need coffee. You better fucking have coffee, Derek."

I nodded to the modern kitchen to her left. Even I wasn't stupid enough to kidnap Sofia without bringing coffee.

She yanked open the first cupboard, then froze. Her hand hovered over the bags of the Ethiopian coffee beans—the ones she stocked at the Bottley and the ones she always put in her own coffee. She moved to the next cupboard, with the honey-roasted cashews and those weird kale chips she always claimed were "basically like eating air, but addictive air."

"How did you...?" She opened another door, revealing the granola I'd overheard her raving about to Julie a few months ago and some dark chocolate-covered almonds. "Just how long have you been planning this whole kidnapping adventure of yours?"

"I didn't plan this, Sofia. It was an on-the-spot decision, but that's not to say I don't have a few places like this fully stocked just in case."

She opened the fridge and paused as she took in the stacked shelves. "Uh-huh. And how long, exactly, do you think we're going to be here?"

"As long as it takes to figure out the next step."

"Mmmm." She didn't say any more while she made herself some coffee.

I watched, entranced. I loved watching her do this. She somehow made this small act into a ritual, each movement precise and practiced. First, she pulled out the grinder, her fingers trailing over the settings until she found the exact coarseness she wanted. The rich scent of freshly ground Ethiopian beans filled the kitchen as she worked, her expression softening.

She measured the grounds by eye, no scoop needed. The water had to be exactly the right temperature; she told her customers regularly that too hot would burn the beans, too cool wouldn't extract properly. While she waited for it to heat, she warmed the French press with hot water, swirling it gently before discarding it. The grounds went in first, then she poured the water in a slow, steady spiral, making sure it was all saturated. She tapped her foot, maybe to a tune in her head, maybe counting the seconds while she waited for it to steep.

I knew better than to say anything right now. She needed this. Needed to feel something was the same as always. That not everything had changed. Then, she pressed down with a practiced motion, smooth and steady, separating the grounds from the liquid. The sound of coffee pouring into her mug was almost musical. Two sugars, a splash of cream, and then that first sip—her eyes closed briefly, savoring it like it was the most precious thing in the world.

I could watch her do this all fucking day.

She seemed calmer when her eyes met mine.

"Right. Let's get this over with. You're going to tell me what is going on and why I am here, and I promise to drink my coffee and not try to rip your head off. Deal?"

I nodded and gestured to the soft leather chairs in front of the fire. She grabbed a blanket from the back of one of the chairs, wrapping it around herself like armor as she curled into the seat.

I crossed to the fireplace, crouching to add another log. Before she'd woken up, I'd chopped enough wood to see us through at least a couple of weeks. Not that I thought we'd need to be here that long.

I wanted to explain, to make her understand but I wasn't sure how much I could tell her without putting her in more danger. How much did she need to know?

"You're in danger."

"Yeah, you said that already."

"I mean it, Sofia. There are serious guys from my past. I don't know what they are into now, but they threatened your life unless I got something for them."

Her mug paused on the way to her mouth. "It was the thing you stole from Sam?"

"Yes. A USB."

"What's on it?"

I shrugged. "I don't know yet. I tried to hack into it while you were... sleeping. I'm going to need more time."

She put her mug down on the table in front of her and leaned forward. "Well, what are you waiting for?"

A low rumble of thunder rolled in the distance. We both looked at the windows as they trembled slightly in their frames. I stood up, and the power cut off.

Fuck!

Chapter Sixteen

DEREK

The nightmare seized me, vivid and unrelenting as always. Harris lay dying in my arms, his blood soaking into my hands, my uniform, the ground beneath us. I looked down, and it wasn't Harris anymore—it was Sofia. Her hair spread across the dirt, her green eyes locked on mine, filled with pain and betrayal as the light dimmed from them. I tried to move, to stop the bleeding, but my body wouldn't respond. All I could do was watch as crimson bloomed across the earth.

"Your fault, Shaw," Torres whispered, familiar and mocking. "Just like Harris. You couldn't save him. You wouldn't be able to save her, either."

My wolf thrashed violently inside me, howling in rage as Sofia's form began to fade, slipping through my grasp like smoke. I tried to hold on, to anchor her to me, but she disappeared.

"Derek! Wake up!" A voice cut through the fog of my nightmare. Hands were shaking my shoulders. "Derek! It's just a dream!"

My body reacted on pure instinct, military training taking over before conscious thought could catch up. The world tilted and spun as I surged up, twisted on the sofa as my hands found wrists to immobilize, and I used my weight to pin down the threat.

"Derek! It's me—Sofia. You're okay. Everything is okay. It was just a nightmare!"

Reality crashed back in waves as her lavender scent cut through the lingering terror. My vision cleared, and I found myself staring down at Sofia, her eyes wide but steady as they met mine. She was alive. Breathing. Whole.

And I had her pinned beneath me, my hands locked around her wrists in an iron grip above her head.

Oh shit!

"Fuck," I choked out, releasing her wrists like they'd burned me. I rolled away, putting distance between us as shame and guilt collided in my chest. My back hit the wall, and I stayed there, trying to ground myself in the solid wood against my spine while my heart hammered against my ribs.

"Damn it, Sofia. I'm sorry." My hands were shaking; I clenched them tight.

She sat up slowly, rubbing her wrists in a way that made my wolf whine with distress. But when she spoke, her voice was gentle. "I'm fine. Are you okay?"

A harsh laugh escaped me before I could stop it. Was I okay? I'd just attacked her—the one person I was supposed to protect above all others.

I dragged a hand down my face, trying to wipe away the last remnants of the dream, but Sofia's blood seeping across the dirt stayed burned into my mind.

"I—shit. I didn't mean to—"

"You didn't hurt me, Derek." She scooted to the end of the sofa, watching me. The power was still out, but I'd left the fire on in the lounge, and the light bounced off the doors and walls and flickered on her face. I hadn't been able to hack into the USB before the battery on my laptop died. So, I'd made Sofia a cold dinner—which she'd eaten in silence—and we'd both gone to bed, me here in the lounge. Her in the bedroom.

"What the hell was that?"

I didn't answer. She deserved better than this. Better than a broken soldier who couldn't tell the difference between nightmares and reality. Better than someone who could hurt her without even being conscious of it.

"Does this happen a lot?"

"It's nothing," I said, forcing my voice to stay steady. "Just... an old ghost that's not worth dragging up."

A soft, disbelieving snort escaped her. "Oh, sure. Nothing screams 'nothing' like waking up ready to kill someone." Her tone softened, though the sarcasm remained. "Stop dodging, Derek. For once in your life, just... talk to me."

I glanced at her wrists; could already see the bruises forming there, even in this dim light.

"It's not really a dream. More of a memory. About Harris. He was my brother in the army. My best friend."

"And?"

"And, what?"

"And what happened? That wasn't a happy memory you were just reliving."

I sighed, dragging a hand through my hair. How much to tell her? "We were out in enemy territory. We were hunting a rogue operative called Kane, but he was always one step ahead. He knew we were coming. It was an ambush. Harris saved my life. Took the hit instead of me." The words came out mechanical, divorced from the emotion churning in my gut. "He died right in front of me. Bled out in the dirt. Because of me. If I'd been faster, smarter, or just... better, he'd still be here."

"That's not your fault, Derek," Sofia said softly. "You know that, right?"

"I know that I made some bad decisions, and Harris died in my place." I clenched my jaw, then forced it to relax. "And now? If I make the wrong move, you'll be next. I can't—" I cut myself off sharply, looking away before I could reveal too much.

But Sofia never was one to let me retreat.

"You're not going to lose me, Derek. But locking everything away doesn't stop it from leaking into your life. The boxes you've put these memories in, they will crack open."

She stood and took a hesitant step forward, like a wolf approaching a wounded deer. I stilled as she crept closer, not sure if I was more scared of her touching me or that she wouldn't. Her fingers brushed my forearm, then she took my hand in hers. The touch sent electricity through my veins, and my wolf surged forward, desperate to have more contact.

"You shouldn't have to see this," I said quietly. "Any of it."

"Mmmm." Sofia's thumb traced small circles on my palm. "Maybe you should have thought of that before you kidnapped me to a one-bedroom cabin."

A ghost of a smile tugged at my lips.

She pulled me over to the sofa, curling up next to me. No part of us touched except for her hand in mine. She pulled the blanket tighter around her and me with her free hand and closed her eyes.

"Try to sleep," she murmured. "I'll make sure you don't start brawling with the furniture again."

"Sofia…" I started, not sure what I was going to say.

"Shh." She squeezed my hand gently. "Just rest. We can go back to me hating you in the morning."

Her breath brushed against my neck, and I fought back a desperate growl. Her warmth seeped through the blanket, through our joined hands, through every inch of space between us until it felt like she had wrapped around me completely. My muscles ached with the effort of staying still, of not pulling her closer, of not burying my face in the crook of her neck, and losing myself in her.

I let my eyes drift over her as she settled in, her lips slightly parted as sleep pulled her under. I wanted to kiss her so fucking much it hurt. I wanted to trace my fingers over the delicate dip of her collarbone, to slide my hand into her wild curls and tilt her face up so I could claim her properly.

Instead, I stared up at the cabin's dark ceiling, listening to the storm rage outside and Sofia's steady breathing beside me. For the first time in years, the aftermath of the nightmares felt lighter. Not gone—never gone—but… manageable.

My wolf settled, content. Sofia's scent surrounded me like a shield against the darkness, and I found myself matching my breathing to hers.

I didn't know how she did it. How she could always quieten the demons in my mind and make me feel at peace. Maybe she did deserve better, maybe she would go back to hating me in the morning, but if

I knew one thing, it was that I was never letting her go. Not again.

CHAPTER SEVENTEEN

SOFIA

The first thing I registered was the sound of something clattering—not in a threatening, someone's-breaking-in way, but the distinctly less menacing someone's-fighting-with-pots-and-pans way. For a split second, I forgot where I was, my brain tangled in the usual fog of sleep. Then it hit me: the cabin, Derek, his nightmare, us falling asleep together on the sofa.

Derek had slept peacefully the rest of the night. I'd woken a few times, watching him sleep through bleary eyes. He looked... softer asleep. His features were more relaxed than I could ever remember seeing them, the hard lines of his jaw and brow smoothed out. I'd let myself melt into his warmth, let myself forget all the reasons why this wasn't okay. Why Derek wasn't safe for my heart.

I groaned, dragging the blanket over my head. I'd called a temporary truce with Derek and wasn't sure I had the energy yet to go back to hating him. Maybe after food.

There it was again—the scrape of metal on metal, followed by a muttered curse I couldn't quite make out. Derek Shaw, Mr. Brooding, was apparently trying to cook.

The smell of something... charred wafted to my nose.

What the hell was he doing?

Whatever the answer, it wasn't good.

The wild howling of the storm still rattled through the cabin walls, but at least the power seemed to be back on. I stayed bundled on the couch for a moment longer, then with a resigned sigh, I tossed the blanket off and padded toward the kitchen, still in the vest and panties I'd slept in.

The smell hit me harder when I got closer—something between burned toast and eggs that had suffered too long in a pan. The back of my throat tightened.

Derek was topless, because why not cook topless, and held a spatula in one hand, his other braced on his hip in that stubborn stance that screamed "I know what I'm doing"—and probably meant the opposite. He was peering into the frying pan in front of him as if it was a ticking time bomb that he wasn't entirely sure how to defuse.

I leaned against the doorframe, crossing my arms as I watched. He shifted a pan just slightly, tilting it at an angle. Smoke rose faintly. My wolf wrinkled her nose.

"You know, you should just admit defeat and let the stove win."

My words were meant to be teasing, and they came out steady, but my brain? My brain had gone completely off-script. Because—sweet Goddess—Derek was built.

I knew that already, obviously. It wasn't exactly a secret. But there was knowing, and then there was *seeing*.

His back was a marvel of sculpted muscle, each ripple shifting under his skin as he moved. His arms—Goddess help me—were thick with power, veins subtly raised along his forearms as he gripped the spatula like he was preparing for battle. And his abs? Yeah, I'd like to say I wasn't staring, but that would be a total lie. Rock-hard, perfectly defined, with just the right amount of that deep V leading down into his low-slung sweatpants.

Focus, Sofia. You are mad at him. You are mad at him. You are—

"Are you just gonna stand there gawking, or are you gonna help?"

I snapped my gaze up so fast I nearly gave myself whiplash. Derek had turned to face me now, his stupidly handsome face smug as hell, like he knew exactly what I'd been thinking.

"I was not gawking," I shot back, lifting my chin.

His smirk deepened, the bastard, as his eyes trailed over my body. Something passed over his face, some emotion I couldn't place, there and then gone in a blink. The spatula in his hand lifted slightly, and he gestured gracefully at whatever sad mess was sizzling in the cast iron pan on the stove. "You hungry?"

I arched an eyebrow, stepping closer until I could see the damage. Charred edges lined three what-could-maybe-pass-as-pancake blobs.

"Oh, I don't think I'm that hungry."

"I *can* cook, you know," he said defensively, lifting the spatula higher like it was a badge of honor he'd earned along with his military stripes.

"Boiling water doesn't count."

"I can do more than just boil water," he grumbled, clearly offended.

I leaned in deliberately, peeling one of the ruined pancakes off the edge of the pan. The thing had the consistency of cardboard. Scraping it off made a sound no food should ever make.

"I *can* cook," he repeated stubbornly.

I stepped closer to the stove again, inspecting the damage for any sign that something might be salvageable. My wolf grumbled, unimpressed.

"Move," I said with a sigh, waving him aside.

Derek's brows lifted, but he didn't budge. "What are you doing?"

"Saving breakfast." I pushed past him to grab the mixing bowl on the counter.

"I had it under control."

I snorted as I cracked more eggs into the bowl, deciding omelets were the safer bet.

He stared at me for a moment, then grabbed a knife from the counter and stepped to the other side of the kitchen, where he started chopping vegetables more efficiently than I expected.

"You've gotten better at that," I said lightly, the remark slipping out without thinking. I remembered the mangled chunks of carrots he used to chop for the meals his brothers used to make back when the Shaw brothers, Jem, and Mai would all eat together after their parents died. I'd go over sometimes to see Mai, when I was sure my parents wouldn't catch me.

Derek didn't look up, but something shifted in his shoulders, his movements slowing slightly. "Military training," he replied simply.

I tilted my head, genuinely curious for the first time since waking up. "They teach soldiers how to cook?"

He paused just long enough to shoot me a faint, mock-serious grin. "They taught knife skills, not pancake flipping. Big difference."

I laughed softly, despite myself—the sound surprising me as much as it seemed to surprise him.

"Put the veg over there. I'll cook it in a minute."

"You're surprisingly bossy in a kitchen. I like it."

I snorted at that, flipping the pancake with an intentionally theatrical gesture. "Somebody has to take charge, or we'd be eating your burned excuses for food."

He shrugged, leaning against the counter with the knife still in hand. "I delegated. That's teamwork."

I turned slightly, leveling him with a look. "Oh, is that what we're calling it? Letting me clean up your messes is 'delegating' now?"

A faint glint of amusement sparked in his eyes, but he didn't answer, just popped a piece of bell pepper into his mouth.

I pointed toward the bowl of grated cheese he must have prepared earlier. "Make yourself useful and sprinkle that in the eggs."

"Yes, ma'am."

"You've also gotten better at taking orders." I glanced sideways at him. "Teenage Derek never would've listened to me in a kitchen."

"Teenage Derek had other priorities."

"Like causing chaos with Sam?"

He smiled. It was a soft, almost sad smile, and for some reason, it made my heart ache.

"I missed this, you know? Missed you," he said.

I froze. For a moment, the only sound was the crackle of the fire and the muffled howling of the storm outside.

Then I forced myself to meet his gaze. "Then why did you leave me?"

He blinked. "Leave you?"

"You know what I mean," I said, my tone sharp. "You left me to join the military. And when you came back, we had that stupid, perfect date; then you acted like it never even happened."

"Sofia, the military... I didn't leave *you*. I went. I went to do something important—for the Pack. For you. I went to learn the skills I need, so I could protect you."

"Bullshit. You left, just like everyone leaves."

He frowned at me. "Everyone who?"

"My parents. My best friend!" The words tumbled out before I could stop them. "And you? You even managed to do it twice. Twice! What the hell is so wrong with me? Am I really that unlovable?"

CHAPTER EIGHTEEN

SOFIA

Derek's eyes ignited, storm clouds brewing there, darker than anything I'd seen before. He stalked toward me, his presence a force of nature all its own, and I had to force myself to stand my ground, my legs screaming at me to back away. His hands came up and cupped my face, his firm fingers brushing against my skin. My breath hitched from the warmth of his touch, the closeness erasing any oxygen left in the room.

"Don't ever think that," he growled.

His hands were warm against my skin, grounding me, but I couldn't let his words erase years of doubts, years of watching people walk away without looking back.

"You don't get to say that, Derek. Not after everything." My voice was hoarse, but I forced myself to look him in the eyes, to let him see every ounce of hurt and anger that had built up inside me for so long. "You don't get to tell me I'm wrong when I've spent my whole life watching people I love leave me behind."

His grip on my face tightened just slightly, like he was afraid I'd slip away from him if he didn't hold on. "Sofia—"

"No. Let me finish." I took a shaky breath and pushed forward, because if I didn't say this now, I might never say it at all. "Do you know what it's like to always be the one left behind? To watch everyone else move on while you're stuck in the same place, pretending you're fine when you're not? My parents left, Derek. They walked out of my life like I was a houseplant they could put in the window, and hope would survive on its own. Mai left. She had her reasons, and I forgave her, but for four years, I had to wake up every day not knowing if my best friend was dead or alive. And you?" I let out a bitter laugh, shaking my head. "You didn't just leave me once—you did it twice. The first time, I told myself I understood. You had your dreams, your duty. But the second time? After our date? After you made me believe, just for one night, that I was worth staying for? That was the worst of all."

His breath hitched, his fingers flexing against my skin. "You think you're unlovable? Sofia, you are the most lovable person I have ever met. You walk into a room, and you change the whole damn atmosphere. You make people feel seen, safe, like they matter. You make strangers feel like they belong. You made me feel like I belonged." His thumb brushed against my cheek. "Do you have any idea how rare that is?"

His voice grew rougher, like the words were clawing their way out of him. "Do you know how many nights I lay awake in the barracks, thinking about you? How many times I wanted to call you just to hear your voice, just to remind myself there was still something good in the world?" He stepped closer, his body heat radiating between us. "You are warmth, and light, and fire, Sofia. You are all I thought about, all I can think about. The thought of you was the only thing that got me through the training, the missions."

"If that were true," I managed, "then why, Derek? Why did you ghost me when you came back?"

His eyes searched mine, then his face went carefully blank as he took a step back. "Now is not the time to get into this," he said, his voice a low snarl, his wolf creeping closer to the surface.

I raised an eyebrow and took a deliberate step toward him, my body nearly pressing against his. The thin fabric of my vest did nothing to shield me from the heat of his bare chest.

"No?" I jabbed a finger into his chest, feeling the solid wall of muscle beneath my hand. "When is the time, Derek? Because I texted you. I called you. Hell, I even drove over when I finally got desperate enough to think you might've been hurt. And what did I see?"

I paused, just long enough for the memory to burn brightly in my chest. "You. Stumbling out of some bar halfway across town, hugging Shya like she was the answer to every question you'd ever asked."

His eyes widened at the mention of Shya, but I pressed closer, feeling the quickening of his breath. "Yes, I know now she was working undercover for you. I know she only has eyes for Mason. But I had to work that out for myself because you never gave me any explanation! Well, guess what? I'm done waiting. You've got nowhere to run now, Derek. So stop with the bullshit and tell me the truth."

The air between us turned electric, the charge crackling as my wolf and his wolf clashed with unspoken tension. It wasn't just anger swirling here—not anymore. It was pain, betrayal, longing, and something deeper, something primal that made my skin flush hot.

Derek's lips curled, his teeth bared in frustration. "You think I wanted this? You think it was easy for me to walk away from you? To hurt you?"

"You certainly made it look easy! You didn't just walk away, Derek. You fucking ghosted me! For months! Why? You owe me that, at least."

He sucked in a sharp breath. "Because they knew where to find me!"

I blinked. "What? Who knew?"

He raked a hand through his dark hair. "The hunters. At the fairground. On our date. They were tracking me. They knew you were my weakness, that I'd do anything to protect you. That made you a target."

The memory surged forward unbidden—laughter, bright lights, warm skin against mine on that stupid Ferris wheel. And then the shadows, the men watching from a distance, the sound of footsteps trailing after us, the way Derek had gone quiet and tense. Him telling me to get somewhere safe, to call Ryan. Hunters grabbing me, dragging me into darkness. Them ordering Derek to surrender or they would hurt me. Derek hadn't hesitated. He'd given himself up without thought.

"After, I realized the hunters had come specifically for me. I didn't know who they were or how they'd tracked me. I didn't know how much they knew about me, about you."

"So you ghosted me... why?" I swallowed hard, painfully aware of his proximity, of how his scent curled around me.

"I was trying to protect you." His voice dropped lower, the rumble of it sending heat pooling low in my belly. "I had to make them think you didn't matter to me, Sofia. I couldn't let them see you as someone they could exploit to get to me. I put you in that position. I had to fix it. Had to make sure you were safe while I went after them, so I could shut their whole operation down. If they even suspected..." His voice broke for a heartbeat, his chest visibly heaving before he forced it back under control. "If they knew how important you were, they would have come after you."

"Well, you did a great job, Derek," I said, my voice soft. "You had everyone convinced, especially me, that I didn't matter to you at all. That I was nothing to you."

His flinch was so small, so quick, I almost missed it.

"You hurt me more than anyone ever has," I continued, the floodgates finally breaking. "My parents leaving hurt. Mai leaving hurt. But you, Derek?" Tears pricked at my eyes, but I refused to let them fall. "You're my fated mate. You were the one who was supposed to stay."

For a moment, he looked torn between reaching for me and holding himself back.

"The fated mate bond doesn't mean shit, Sofia," he said finally.

And there I was, thinking he couldn't hurt me any worse than he already had, but he continually surprised me.

"This isn't some mystical, Goddess-divined feeling. I have always loved you. Me, not the bond telling me to. Me," he slammed a hand against his chest as if to emphasize the point, "loving you because you are the most fucking amazing person I have ever known."

I blinked.

"I've loved you all my life," he said, his voice dropping to a whisper that caressed my skin. "Every choice I've made, it's always been for you. Joining the military? Learning how to fight? Leaving after... after that date? Even this," he said, gesturing to the small cabin around us. "All of it. For you. Everything I do, everything I have done, it has always been for you. I'd do anything for you. Protect you from anyone or anything. Even if it meant walking away. Even if it killed me every single fucking day to do it. My past, my job now, it makes you a target. I thought staying away would protect you, but they found you anyway."

His hand reached out toward my face, but he didn't touch me.

"I'm sorry. I'm so fucking sorry for hurting you. For walking away. For pretending I didn't care. For all of it. I know I can never take it back." His voice was raw, his eyes never leaving mine as his warm breath mingled with my own. "But I swear to you, I'll spend every moment of the rest of my life—every fucking second of it—trying to make it right. If you'll let me."

CHAPTER NINETEEN

SOFIA

His gaze was locked onto me. It was full of longing. Raw and unfiltered and terrifying in its honesty.

My breath caught, stuck somewhere between my lungs and the tight knot in my chest. He didn't look away. Didn't break the connection. And for the life of me, I couldn't either.

I watched, unable to look away, as his hand came up slowly, the movement careful, hesitant even, as though he wasn't sure how I'd react. Hell, I didn't know how I would react, either. He brushed a strand of hair behind my ear, his knuckles grazing my skin in a way that sent a shiver racing through my entire body.

Then he leaned in, his breath ghosting over my lips. My heart was pounding so hard it must have been the only thing he could hear. He paused, something in his expression almost asking for permission. I stayed still, too terrified to move in case he didn't kiss me. But then he closed the gap between us, and his hot lips crashed into mine.

It wasn't soft. It wasn't hesitant. It was ferocious—years of tension, frustration, and something deeper colliding in an explosion of sensation. He kissed me like a man who had been drowning and I was his first breath of air, his lips hot and urgent against mine.

Every nerve in my body lit up, the anger and hurt I'd been holding onto morphing into something else entirely, something molten, something dangerous. I wanted this. It felt right, like a piece of me that I'd been missing finally clicked into its proper place.

Derek's hands moved from my face, one sliding down to cup the back of my neck, anchoring me to him, while the other pressed firmly against my lower back, pulling me closer until there was no space left between us. My hands slid around his neck, desperate for something to hold on to as he kissed me deeper, harder.

He tilted his head, and I gasped as his teeth grazed my lower lip just enough to send a new jolt of need through me. My stomach flipped, a white-hot heat pooling low as his touch became more insistent, more consuming.

"Derek," I whispered against his lips, though it came out more like a plea.

He groaned, the sound vibrating against my skin as he broke the kiss, instead trailing his lips down the side of my jaw. Goosebumps erupted across my skin when he found that sensitive spot just below my ear.

"Say it again," he muttered, his voice rough.

"Derek," I breathed, arching into him as his lips continued their exploration down my neck.

His hands slipped down my back, over my ass, and then he effortlessly picked me up. I wrapped my legs around him, and my eyes widened as I felt the hard length of him against me.

Everything was heat—his body pressed against mine, the fire crackling in the hearth, the storm of emotions rolling through me.

He carried me back to the sofa, then lay us down, him on top, my legs still wrapped around his waist. His cock rubbed against my core, and I almost purred in pleasure.

It felt so freaking good.

He arched his hips back, then slowly drove them forward, the building pressure on my clit delicious. His eyes were fixed on my face, watching my reaction.

"You like that."

I bit my bottom lip and nodded.

He grinned and did it again.

My panties felt soaked, and I squirmed underneath him, wanting more.

In answer, Derek tilted me back, resting me against the arm of the sofa as he hovered over me, his dark eyes locked onto mine. There was a flicker of something softer, something reverent, in his look, and suddenly, I didn't care about all the reasons I should stop this. Everything about Derek—his touch, his scent, the feel of him against me—overrode any semblance of rational thought. Whatever this was between us, I wasn't ready for it to end. Not yet.

He lifted my arms above my head, slowly peeling off my vest, then my panties, until I was naked. He looked down at me, his eyes roaming everywhere, like he was drinking me in, storing it all in his memory.

"Fucking gorgeous, you know that?"

"I—"

"Fucking gorgeous," he repeated, his eyes coming to mine.

I didn't say anything, didn't know what to say.

"Tell me to stop, Sofia," he murmured, his voice full of something raw, something dangerous. "Tell me to stop, and I will. But if you don't..."

He left the sentence unfinished, letting the promise of whatever came next hang between us.

"Don't... don't stop," I whispered.

He let out a breath. "Thank fuck for that." His lips hovered an inch from mine, his eyes open, watching me. I lifted up, wanting to feel his mouth on mine, but he pulled back.

"Derek!" I warned.

"I want to taste you."

"So kiss me!"

"Not that taste of you."

Oh!

He grinned at the look on my face.

"Any objections?"

Any objections? Was he crazy? I shook my head, feeling a little breathless.

His grin widened, and he slid down my body, trailing kisses as he went. He settled between my legs, and I saw his nostrils flair. He smiled up at me, and the look on his face was one of such contentment, of someone exactly where they had always wanted to be.

Holy fucking Goddess, it was hot.

Then he dipped his head, and his tongue flicked my clit, once, twice, three times. Each one leaving me gasping, panting for more.

"Derek!"

He chuckled, then his lips encircled my clit and gently sucked.

Oh. My. Goddess.

I was going to come apart.

The heat of his lips on me was driving me wild; I never wanted him to stop. I needed him, needed more. His tongue twirled around my clit, then slid lower, again and again, licking, sucking, consuming me.

My hips bucked, and I gasped as he slipped one finger inside of me. "Oh!"

Derek paused and looked up at me. "Oh good or oh bad?"

"Oh good. Very, very good."

"You want more?"

"Yes."

"Yes?"

"Yes. More. Please, more!" I begged.

He slid another finger inside, stretching me as they moved in a slow, steady rhythm. The sensation was incredible, unlike anything I had ever felt before. I moaned, my hips bucking against his hand as he worked me closer to the edge.

His tongue continued to dance around my clit, teasing and tormenting me. I could feel my body tightening, the muscles in my stomach and thighs clenching as I fought to hold on to my control. But Derek was relentless, his fingers pressing deeper, his tongue flicking faster.

I gasped, my body trembling with anticipation. And then Derek Shaw, the fucking bastard, stopped.

I looked down at him, outraged. "What. The. Hell?"

"Not yet, Sofia. I say when you can come, and I want to savor every moment of this."

His fingers lazily started moving again, slowly building up the pace until their rhythm synced with the beat of my heart. My body was on fire, every nerve ending alight with pleasure. I could feel the orgasm building inside me, a fierce, overwhelming force that threatened to consume me.

"Please," I begged, my voice hoarse. "Please, Derek."

He stopped again, his mouth releasing my clit, his fingers slowing their relentless strokes.

"You... Derek!"

"It'll be worth it, I promise."

He kept me riding on the edge, his fingers pumping in and out of me, his tongue licking and sucking at my clit. I was writhing beneath him, my body desperate for release. But he always slowed down or backed off whenever I was close. It was torture, sweet, delicious, infuriating torture.

"Derek, please," I begged again, my voice strained. "I can't take much more."

He didn't reply, his focus entirely on the task at hand. He hummed against me, encouragement and approval all in one. The vibration sent another ripple through me, and I felt myself spiraling higher, the coil inside me tightening with every flick of his tongue and firm grip of his hands. His fingers moved in a swift, decisive motion, striking my G-spot with perfect precision again and again as he took my clit in his mouth and sucked, his tongue swirling against it. It was too much; I couldn't take anymore.

"Please, Derek, please, let me come!"

He released my clit. Then blew on it softly, the cool air brushing against me only sending me higher.

"Come for me, gorgeous," he ordered, then took my clit in his mouth again.

I cried out, my body convulsing, my thighs trembling with the intensity of it as the orgasm finally broke through.

Wave after wave of pleasure washed over me. Derek didn't stop, his fingers and tongue continuing to work their magic, drawing out every last shudder of pleasure.

Even then, he didn't end it, his mouth and hands slowing but not leaving me as I came down from the high. By the time he finally moved back, pressing a soft kiss to the skin just above my hip, my whole body was trembling.

His dark eyes locked onto mine as he braced himself above me. My cheeks burned, my body still humming from what he'd just done, but there was something in his gaze that rooted me to the spot.

I reached for him, my hand sliding down the broad, hard expanse of his chest. He sucked in a quick breath, his muscles tensing beneath my touch.

"Sofia." His voice was soft but firm as his hand wrapped gently around my wrist, stilling my movement.

"Let me," I whispered, not caring how raw or desperate I sounded. "Let me touch you. I want to touch you. I *need* to touch you."

He brought my hand to his lips instead, pressing a lingering kiss to my palm. The tenderness of the gesture sent a fresh wave of heat through my chest.

"Not yet," he murmured, his eyes soft and full of something I couldn't quite name. "I want to take things slow."

Slow? Was he freaking serious? After what he'd just done, after dismantling me so entirely that I doubted I'd ever be the same?

"Okay," I bargained. "No sex, but I still want to touch you."

He rested his forehead against mine. "Not yet. When you touch me, I won't be able to hold back. I need you to be sure, really sure, coz there'll be no going back afterward, Sofia. You touch me, and all our past is left behind. We start anew." He leaned down, his chest brushing against my breasts, and whispered, "You touch me, Sofia, and I won't be able to stop, so I need to know you want it, really want it."

I honestly did not know what to do with that information right now. Did I want him? Hell, yes. Did I trust him? Hell, no.

I pulled my hand back, my pulse still racing with frustration as much as anything else. "You're impossible, you know that?"

His lips twitched into a small, knowing smile. "You have told me on a number of occasions."

I groaned in frustration, tugged the blanket back over my tangled body. "I'm going for a shower."

He smirked at me. "Good decision."

He rolled off me, and I stood up on shaky legs.

"Need some help getting there?" His voice was teasing and fully satisfied.

Smug bastard.

I turned my head and stuck my tongue out at him.

The sound of his laughter followed me into the bathroom.

When the cold water hit my skin, I gasped, but not from discomfort. The chill was welcome, a sharpened blade cutting through the haze of heat Derek fucking Shaw had left in his wake.

Chapter Twenty

DEREK

I listened to Sofia's footsteps fade down the hall, followed by the creak of the bathroom door and the rush of running water. My wolf whined softly, already missing her presence, her warmth, her scent. But I knew she needed space right now—space to process, to think, to possibly rebuild her walls brick by careful brick.

That was okay; I'd knock them down again.

Besides, I'd just found the perfect way to get her to stop arguing with me. Hearing her moan underneath me, hearing her beg me for more... if I lived to be three thousand, I would never forget it. And I fully intended to do it a million more times. When she was moaning, she wasn't arguing.

I stood from the couch, stretching my muscles and trying to calm my own desires down. It had taken all my military training not to sink my cock inside of her. She'd been so wet, so fucking ready for me. But I'd meant it; she needed to be sure before I fucked her. Because even my training wouldn't be enough to hold me back when I was finally, after all this time, deep inside of her.

Shaking off the feeling, I headed for the kitchen. I wanted to cook for her, wanted to show her I could make something edible. I was going to learn how to do it properly; she deserved a home-cooked meal every night, and I was going to make damn sure I could give it to her.

My hands moved automatically, gathering the ingredients we'd prepared earlier and heating the pan. Eggs I could handle. Probably. The sizzle of butter hitting hot metal filled the quiet space as I beat eggs in a bowl, trying not to think about the way Sofia had felt pressed against me, or how she had tasted, or—

My phone buzzed. The storm must have passed enough for the signal to return. I wiped my hands on a dish towel and pulled it out of my back pocket.

A message from Torres.

Fuck.

Everything in me tensed as I unlocked the phone, knowing whatever waited wouldn't be good. I still hadn't cracked the USB, still had no plan to turn this around.

The message loaded with a photo first—Sam walking past the Bottley, timestamp from twenty minutes ago. My brother looked distracted, completely unaware he was being watched. Being hunted.

The text followed:

We know you have it. Nice job taking the girl. But you can't hide everyone. Bring the USB to the Bottley or your brother has an accident. Warn him, and he has an accident. Tell anyone, and he has an accident. Are you clueing in to the theme here, Shaw?

I was out of time. Something inside me snapped. The world narrowed to a pinpoint of rage and fear as my wolf surged forward, howling for blood. How were they still in Three Rivers? I'd ordered Evelyn to evacuate anyone she didn't recognize. I felt useless, hiding out here while my twin was walking around with a target on his back.

The sound of the running water turning off in the bathroom made my chest squeeze tighter. How the hell was I supposed to protect both Sam and Sofia?

I knew Sofia. If I told Sofia about the text, she'd insist on coming with me. And then all this would be for nothing. I'd taken her to keep her safe, and instead, I'd be delivering her back to the place where she was in most danger. The thought made bile rise in my throat. No, Sofia had to stay here.

Her footsteps padded across the bedroom floor. She'd be out soon. The only option would destroy whatever progress Sofia and I had made.

Fuck.

I couldn't lose either of them.

My gaze caught on my backpack in the corner.

Fuck, fuck, fuck.

She'd hate me for it. Maybe forever this time.

The bedroom door handle turned. Time was up.

I crossed the room and dug in my pack, pulling out a piece of rope. It was cold in my hands as Sofia stepped out. My eyes traced over her—damp hair curling around her shoulders, one of my shirts falling to mid-thigh, a pair of tight blue jeans showing the curve of her calves. The sight of her, covered in my scent, hit me like a lightning bolt—she was everything I had ever wanted, ever needed. She looked soft, vulnerable, and utterly perfect. And I was about to shatter whatever trust she'd just given me.

The eggs sizzled in the pan behind me, forgotten. The domestic scene I'd tried to create—breakfast, normalcy, maybe even a bit of happiness—crumbled as Torres's threat echoed in my head.

She frowned at me, maybe picking something up in my scent. "Derek? What's wrong?"

I had to do this. I couldn't back out now. It was the only option.

Fuck!

She froze when she saw my expression, her earlier softness hardening instantly into wariness.

"You're probably going to hate me for this."

Her eyes dropped to the rope in my hand, and I watched the exact moment understanding dawned. Her breath caught, and her eyes widened as they shot back up to meet mine.

"You wouldn't dare!"

I took a step toward her. "I don't have a choice."

She took two steps back. "There is always a choice, Derek."

She must have seen the resolve on my face because she suddenly lunged forward and tried to wrench the rope from my hands. I had to admit, it caught me by surprise, and she almost had it. Then I moved, using her momentum against her as I grabbed her wrists. She didn't give in easily—not that I expected her to—kicking, twisting, trying to throw her weight against me.

"Don't you fucking dare do this, Derek!" she snarled, struggling against my grip. "Let me go!"

"If you'd just listen—" I started, then cursed as she nearly slipped free. "Damn it, Sofia, stop fighting me!"

She did not stop fighting me. In fact, her struggles got even more intense. I pivoted, slipping the coil of rope around both her wrists as she thrashed against me. The rope tightened with a sharp tug, binding her hands together, and before she could react, I picked her up and carried her to the bed.

She kicked, she screamed, she howled like a fucking banshee, but I dropped her on the bed and looped the other end of the rope around the heavy iron frame in a double constrictor knot before she could yank it out of reach.

She stared in shock at the rope, then pulled hard against it, the binding digging into her skin. When it didn't budge, her head snapped around to face me.

"Are you out of your damn mind?" She jerked against the restraint again.

I kneeled on the bed with one knee, inspecting the rope. My fingers brushed lightly over her wrist, where red marks were already blooming. She just glared at me, then yanked harder against the rope.

"Stop that. You're going to hurt yourself."

I went back to the lounge and grabbed a rectangular piece of black cloth from my bag pocket.

"Don't you dare touch me," she snapped, trying to twist her bound arms out of my reach when I got back. As gently as I could, I took her hands in mine.

"You make it a habit to tie up helpless women?"

"You're hardly helpless, Sofia," I replied. "I've seen you fight, remember? Now hold still. I'm just putting the cloth between the rope and your skin. It'll stop the fibers from cutting into your wrists."

"You're fucking unbelievable, you know that? After what we just did? Are you seriously going to leave me tied to the bed?"

"I have to go out for a bit. Sam's in trouble," I said. "I don't have time to explain right now. But I need to know that you are safe here and are not going to try to escape."

She started pulling against the rope with everything she had.

I glanced at her, then looked away. There was no choice.

"I'll be back before dawn."

"Don't do this, Derek," she snarled, her voice full of anger. "Don't you fucking dare!"

I paused halfway to the door, my back to her.

"You walk out that door, don't bother coming back at all. I can't fucking believe you're leaving me again!"

My whole body went rigid. It physically hurt to do this, to leave her.

"I'd rather have you alive and hating me," I said quietly, "than dead because I failed to protect you."

Then I turned off the stove, threw the eggs in the garbage and walked out, listening to her sobs all the way to my car.

CHAPTER TWENTY-ONE

DEREK

As the car hummed along the empty stretch of road, my thoughts kept flicking between the USB in my pocket and the look on Sofia's face when I'd tied her to that fucking bed.

What the hell was on this thing that Torres wanted it so badly? What had Sam gotten himself messed up in? The tightness gnawing at my chest refused to ease. *She's safe*, I told myself for the hundredth time. She'll hate me for it, sure. But she'll be alive to do it. That thought would have to keep me moving forward.

My wolf paced restlessly against my skin. He hated being separated from her.

It won't be for long, I promised.

I didn't know what I was going to do when I got back. Hand the USB over? Try to warn Sam? Find Waylen and see if he could hack into it? I had no fucking idea right now. For once, I had no plan.

I crossed into Three Rivers territory, and despite everything, my bonds with the Pack and the land hummed with joy. No matter how long I was away, coming back always felt like stepping into a warm embrace.

I'd gone twenty miles past our border, when the flash of headlights ahead yanked me from my thoughts. A BMW X1. Angled across the road, blocking my path.

Sam.

A quick glance in my rearview mirror showed me Ryan's truck rolling up behind me, cutting off any retreat. He must have felt it in the Pack bonds as soon as I crossed into Three Rivers territory.

Fucking perfect.

I rolled to a stop a dozen feet short of Sam's cruiser. My wolf bristled at being trapped between them, but I kept my movements deliberate and controlled as I stepped out of the car.

Sam got out of the cruiser with his usual fluid grace. His jaw was set, anger radiating off him. I guess he'd worked out who took his USB.

Behind me, Ryan jumped out of his truck. Alpha authority rolled off him in waves, heavy and oppressive. His blue eyes locked onto mine, and I didn't need the Pack bond to feel the frustration thrumming beneath his calm exterior.

"You!" Sam pointed his finger at me as he strode forward. "Where the fuck is my USB?"

Ryan came to a stop in front of me. "More importantly, Derek, where is Sofia?"

I looked at my big brother and sighed. "She's safe."

"Safe? Half the Pack's out looking for her. You think hiding a member of my Pack without my knowledge counts as safe? Don't fucking test me. I haven't told Mai yet—she'd be out of bed searching for Sofia no matter what the Doc or I ordered and wouldn't hesitate to torture you to get answers. So you're gonna tell me right the fuck now where Sofia is so I can bring her home, and my mate and my pups aren't put at risk from whatever clusterfuck you're caught up in."

"And once you've done that," Sam growled, stepping closer, "you can hand over my USB. You know, the one you stole."

I looked at Sam and knew I had to know what was on that stick. Whatever Sam was into, it was not good, and it was past time he stopped handling shit like this on his own.

"I'm not giving it back."

I felt a warning tug along my twin bond with Sam, and then he snapped. He slammed me against the SUV, his arm on my neck.

"The fuck you are! You don't trust anyone except yourself these days—that's your problem, Derek. But in case you forgot, I'm your brother. We both are. Or doesn't that mean anything anymore?"

"Trust goes both ways, bro. I don't see you opening up about what the Council has got you doing."

Before I could respond, Ryan grabbed Sam's shoulder and hauled him back.

"Enough. What the hell is going on, Derek? You got two minutes to explain or I'm throwing you in one of the cages until I sort this out."

"Someone's after Sofia. They said I had to get Sam's USB, or they'd take her out. I did what I had to do."

Ryan's lip curled in a snarl. "Why didn't you come to me?"

"There wasn't time. They were tracking Sofia, had photos of her. New photos, taken in the last couple of days. I took Sofia and the USB somewhere safe, but this morning, I got another text and another photo. This time, it was of Sam. I know these guys; they're serious. One of them, Torres, was in my unit. They want that USB and don't give a fuck who they hurt to get it."

"Torres Stappen?"

I frowned. "Yeah."

"You think you're one step ahead?" Sam glared at me. "Well, congratulations, Derek—you just walked right into their trap."

A trap? "What are you talking about?"

"Evelyn got your text. The enforcers have been scouting out any unknowns in our territory and escorting them out. They followed two of them back to a warehouse in Jacksonville. Came back, got a team together. When they hit it, whoever was there cleared out, but they left something behind." Sam's eyes hardened. "A body. Your old army buddy Torres."

The world tilted sharply as pieces clicked into place.

"Someone's still using Torres's phone. Setting me up."

It was Kane. It had to be.

"No shit." Sam's face looked grim. "What was their last message?"

"To bring the USB to the Bottley, or they'd take you out."

Sam looked at me for a beat. "And? Were you gonna give it to them?"

I gave him a flat stare. "I hadn't decided. I was gonna improvise."

"If they'd done any research on you at all, they had to know you don't work well with threats. You'd be looking at ways to get round it. No. They know they need to force you into a corner. They'll need something concrete to make you turn over the USB," Ryan said. "They're baiting you. Either to attack you when you get there..."

"Or to lure you away from wherever you've stashed Sofia," Sam finished.

Sofia.

My heart slammed against my ribs. "I left her alone."

I spun toward my car. Ryan stepped into my path.

"Try to stop me leaving, and I'll—"

"Sam will go with you," Ryan cut me off sharply. "I'll head back to Three Rivers in case there is an attack there."

I moved to go around him, but Ryan blocked me again.

"Move," I growled.

"When you get there, keep your head. I know she's your mate, but you're no good to her dead."

My wolf bristled, but I forced myself to nod. He was right. I had to stay focused.

We peeled out onto the road, Sam and I heading one way, Ryan the other.

Please let her be safe. Please let me not be too late.

CHAPTER TWENTY-TWO

SOFIA

I strained against the knots for the hundredth time, but Derek had tied them tight. Too tight. The damned rope dug into my wrists, rough and unyielding. My skin was raw underneath the rope, but I didn't care. I was still too freaking angry. I could still taste his kiss on my lips, feel the crushing heat of his body. How could he do this to me, after everything? After...

I couldn't think about that now. Shoving the memory aside, I thought about Shifting, my wolf stirring restlessly beneath my skin, responding to my panic. But if I Shifted with my hands tied, there was a good chance I'd break both my wrists. No, I had to get out of this in human form. I looked around the room for anything that I could use. Bedside lamp? Nope. It was a modern design with a chrome-plated spiral stem and an LED light running the length of it. Glass of water, maybe? If I could reach it, I could break it and use the glass to cut through the binding. I strained against the rope as far as I could go, my shoulders screaming at me.

Just a little further.

My fingertips touched it, and the glass moved. Further away.

Damn it!

I wasn't going to cry. I wasn't. I shifted my weight onto my hip, trying to find a better position to reach the glass as a sharp pain stabbed into my hip. What the—? I awkwardly dug into my pocket and found the nail file I kept for the cash register.

"Freaking yes!"

I was going to kiss that bloody cash register when I got back! I angled the nail file awkwardly between my bound hands, struggling to flip it so the rough edge faced downward. My fingers, already tingling from restricted circulation, fumbled and nearly dropped the file.

Fuck!

No. This was going to work. It had to work. I began sawing—short, desperate jerks of my hands, using what little mobility I had in my wrists to work the file against the tight binding. My wrists burned where the rope had rubbed it raw, but the rough hemp fibers started to fray, each tiny snap feeling like a small victory.

The faint vibration of an engine thrummed low in the distance. I froze, my senses perking instantly. Did Derek forget something? If he came back now, he'd take the nail file and retie the rope.

Damn it.

But the engine noise was quieter, smoother than Derek's. This one was different—lower, rougher. And there were more than one.

How likely was it that Jase had noticed I was gone and had brought the cavalry? Compared to, say, the guys who had Derek fucking Shaw spooked enough to kidnap me and high-tail it out of Three Rivers?

Panic clawed its way up my chest as tires crunched against the snow. I scraped the file frantically against the rope.

"Come on, come on!"

Engines turned off. Car doors slammed—one, two, three, four. My wolf's hackles rose.

"Come on, come on, come on!" My breaths were coming short and shallow now. I had to get out of here. They could not find me trussed up like a gift-wrapped present.

Blood welled, then dripped from my wrists. The nail file bit deeper into the fibers as voices, low and controlled, drifted through the window.

"Perimeter clear."

Another fiber split.

"Secure all entrances."

The file was nicking my skin with each stroke, but there was no stopping. Blood mixed with sweat, the metallic tang filling my nostrils.

"Standby for breach."

"Come the fuck on!" I hissed at the nail file, tears of frustration blurring my vision. The fraying strands of rope groaned louder under each stroke.

The steps outside the cabin creaked. One last swipe and the rope snapped.

Freedom.

The sound of the door being kicked open made my head jerk up.

Move, my wolf urged.

No shit.

I scrambled off the bed and ducked low, quieting my breath as I crept into the bathroom and shut the door gently. There was a small window to the right of the shower. The image of the tub of mint choc chip ice cream I'd eaten in one sitting last weekend flashed into my mind, and I glanced down at my hips.

Goddess, if I get out of this, I promise I'll never eat ice cream again... Well, not a whole tub of it in one go, anyway.

Keeping as low as I could, I edged toward the window. I could hear breathing in the lounge. They would be in the bedroom in seconds. I grasped the window handle, testing it. Locked. Of course. My fingers, slick with blood and sweat, trembled as I fumbled with the latch.

"Hurry, hurry, hurry," I muttered, giving the latch a vicious twist. It released with a soft snap.

The floorboards in the bedroom creaked. My head snapped toward the bathroom door. Shadowy shapes danced in the gap under the door.

I was out of time.

I shoved the window up, biting back a groan as it protested. Ice-cold wind drifted in, bringing snowflakes with it.

Fabulous. Now it was snowing.

I kicked off the edge of the sink to boost myself up, forcing myself through the open window. The frame scraped against my arms and thighs, and I bit my lip to stifle a curse. I dropped headfirst to the frozen ground, managing to twist at the last moment to land on all fours. The snow and wind chilled me instantly, cutting through Derek's too-big shirt like it wasn't even there.

My wolf urged me forward.

I flattened myself against the side of the cabin, pressed between the rough grain of the wood and a tall stack of firewood. I took a deep breath as I looked around. No one between me and the woods. Their scent was here, though—cold steel, adrenaline-spiked sweat, the acrid polish of gun oil. They didn't smell of werewolf. Or bear. Only humans. A squad hunting its prey. That's what I was to them: prey.

"East side!" shouted a voice from inside.

Crap, crap, crap. Move, Sofia.

I didn't have time to make a plan. I pushed off the wall and sprinted toward the tree line.

My bare feet sank into the snow with every step, the cold biting at my soles, soaking the bottom of my jeans. Adrenaline drowned out everything but survival. The shadows of the forest loomed ahead, and although every instinct screamed to look behind me, I didn't. They were back there, and they wouldn't hesitate.

Derek's words from earlier slipped through my mind: *"You don't know where you're going; you'll just go deeper into the forest. Take you days, weeks even to get to the other side... Plus, there's a good chance the cold will kill you first."*

Well, guess what, Derek? You and your awesome plans left me no choice.

I heard another shout, then the whizz of a bullet race past me. The tree line was just ahead. I just needed to make it that far. I dug deep, running faster than I had ever run. Another bullet zinged past, this one thudding into a tree trunk to my left. The bark exploded, pieces whipping past my face. Then I was through, weaving between trees, putting as much distance between me and them as possible.

Chapter Twenty-Three

SOFIA

The snow started falling heavier now, muffling sounds in that way only snow can do.

Would they follow me? I could only hope they were looking for Derek, and when they didn't find him, they would leave.

Snow crunched behind me.

"Northwest push!" It wasn't a shout, more of a murmur. They must be using radios.

Well, there went my hopes of getting out this easily.

My wolf clawed inside of me, wanting out, desperate to fight, to run faster, to Shift, but I couldn't. Not yet.

Soon.

I needed time to Shift. If I stopped now, they would catch up.

Instead, I ran. At first, blindly, just trying to put some distance between me and them. But I was a barefoot barista, and they were trained professionals. I could scent them and hear them, but they didn't need werewolf senses to follow my footprints.

I glanced up as I ran. "Come on, Goddess, more snow. I need more snow!"

It had to get heavier for there to be any hope that the snow would start to cover my tracks before the men found them. I changed direction—left, right, backtracking, anything to confuse those on my tail. My legs burned, but I pressed forward, wading through the snow between the trees and hopping over gnarled roots half-hidden under all the white fluff.

"She's heading deeper!" Another murmur, closer than I wanted.

Damn it. I wasn't losing them.

I cursed myself for not grabbing my sneakers—they were my favorite ones from Shya, as well. For not being better prepared. For trusting Derek.

And now? Now I was running through the goddamn woods with no shoes, no phone, no plan, and most definitely no backup.

A new scent cut through the air—water and ice, minerals and stone. A river. I angled west toward it, pushing through a thick patch of undergrowth.

The trees thinned out, revealing a narrow river, its surface completely frozen over. It wound through the forest like a silver ribbon, disappearing around a bend about fifty yards downstream. The surface was rough with frost, creating a pattern of tiny crystals. It looked solid enough to hold my weight, but one wrong step and I would be in freezing water.

"Footprints heading west."

I was out of options. I tested the ice with one foot. Even with my numb feet, it was painfully cold. It held, though. I stepped fully onto the ice, my heart thundering against my ribs as I listened for cracking. Nothing.

A fallen branch caught my eye—pine, with dozens of smaller

branches fanning out from the main stem. Perfect. I snatched it up, backing onto the ice while holding the branch behind me like a broom. The smaller twigs scraped against the frost, blending my footprints into the frost as I moved.

The sound of pursuit grew closer—boots crunching through snow, branches snapping.

Fuck it.

I turned, holding the branch behind me, hoping it would work. Then I started jogging downstream. I had to buy myself some time. If they found my tracks leading onto the ice but not leading off... Well, they weren't stupid. They'd figure out what I'd done quickly, but it might be enough.

My feet felt like blocks of ice by the time I spotted a low-hanging branch stretching over the steep bank and onto the river. I reached up, using it to haul myself onto the bank. Only my feet wouldn't cooperate. They were completely numb, refusing to grip properly as I stumbled forward. I made the bank and got maybe fifteen paces before I crashed to my knees, pain shooting up my legs.

Shaking all over, I hissed through chattering teeth, "Up! Gotta get up, Sofia!"

Shift. Now!

She was right. I turned over, fumbling with my clothes, my fingers not working properly. It felt like it took forever to peel my jeans and shirt off me. Then the Shift gripped me hard and fast, pain ripping through every muscle and bone. I sucked in a sharp breath as my body contorted, bones snapping, fur bursting from my skin, claws replacing fingers, teeth sharpening and lengthening, leaving my jaw aching.

The forest seemed to tilt for a heartbeat as the change finished, leaving me crouched low, my newly sharpened senses catching every sound, every scent in an overwhelming punch to my senses. Even here, even now, being hunted in a forest far from my Pack, my home, the joy of being in my wolf form thrummed through me.

Steam curled up off my fur in the cold air, and my paws pressed against the snow-covered ground instinctively, my body ready to run. I had a chance now.

I darted left, only to change my mind and dash back to snag Derek's shirt between my teeth. Don't ask me why, but I couldn't leave it behind.

Everything felt sharper now—smells, sounds, the pounding rhythm of my heart. The forest stretched endlessly ahead. My ears flicked as the sound of boots crunching on frost reached me. They were on the river.

I surged forward, paws not sinking into the snow as much as my two feet had. I veered left, then right, dodging through the trees in unpredictable patterns. Low-hanging branches scraped at my sides, the rough bark pulling at my fur, but I took no notice. Anything to buy me distance. My breaths came in sharp bursts now, white clouds that puffed and vanished, and still, I pushed harder.

"Team C, focus southwest. She didn't double back." The voices dropped further behind, their sounds crisscrossing through the forest.

Perfect.

My nose twitched. There. The scent of asphalt, something metallic that didn't belong in the forest, and a faint trace of gas.

A road. Derek had lied. There was a way out of here.

It would be easier to hide my tracks on the road, and I could follow it to safety.

Almost there.

And then I saw it—the break in the trees, the stretch of pale, open road beyond.

Yes!

I darted forward, then skidded to a halt as a man stepped into my path, his gun pointed right at me.

I froze, claws digging into the cold earth. The world around me halted, a breathless silence enveloping me for a long second before time snapped back into place. My heart thudded in my chest so hard I swore he could hear it. The man wore black combat fatigues and had sharp angular features and a thin nose leading to pale eyes. Dark hair was pulled back severely from his face into a tight knot at the base of his skull. A thin sheen of sweat glazed his temples despite the freezing temperature, the only sign that he'd been running.

I was more interested in his gun. Longer than a regular handgun, with some kind of scope on top and an extra grip underneath, it looked like something out of a military movie—sleek black metal with extra attachments that probably had specific purposes but just made it more menacing. The scariest part was the thin red beam coming from beneath the barrel, creating a steady red dot that hovered over my chest.

"You're good, little wolf," the man drawled, his voice smooth and calm. There was nothing rushed or uncertain in him. He knew he had me. "But not good enough." The corners of his lips tilted into the faintest smirk, as if the chase had been amusing for him. Like I'd just been a game that he'd now won.

I snarled, my paws inching forward.

"Nuh-huh. Don't even think about it. I'll put you down faster than a blink."

I snarled again but stopped moving.

"Good decision. Now, do you know where the USB is? If you do, you'll save yourself a load of trouble by taking me to it."

I bared my teeth as instincts pulled me in different directions. Part of me wanted to lunge for his throat, to tear into him until he stopped being a threat. But another part—the part that had never learned to fight, never been trained for situations like this—screamed at me to run. To find an opening and bolt into the forest's shadows. I wasn't Derek. When I Shifted, it was usually to run through the forest on full moons or burn off stress after a long day at the bar. I'd been in battles, had fought for my Pack, but always as a Pack, a team. I followed their lead. I had no idea how to get out of this on my own.

The man must have sensed my uncertainty. His laugh grated against me, a soft, mocking sound as he shifted his weight.

"No? Silent treatment, huh? Alright, that makes sense. The quiet ones always think they're the toughest. But I gotta tell ya, sweetheart," he swung the barrel slightly, the laser sight shifting to hover in front of my left paw, "bravery doesn't count for much when you're on your own."

The crack of the gunshot cut through the forest like a thunderclap, the bullet biting into the ice just inches from my paw. Pain flared as shards sprayed against me, and the scent of my own blood hit my nostrils. I danced back, not putting weight on my front left paw, refusing to look at the tiny crater he'd torn into the earth in front of me.

"Still no, huh? Doesn't matter. Pretty sure your friend will be much more talkative when he finds out we have you."

I couldn't let that happen.

Think, Sofia.

I had nothing. I was coming up blank. Okay, had to think faster!

He turned his head an inch to the side and said, "Alpha two, I got her."

"Copy. Moving on your position."

He stepped forward, the barrel of the gun dipping slightly. "Easy now, little wolf. We don't have to do this the hard way, sweetheart." His voice was casual, almost gentle, like he was coaxing a frightened pet.

The world slowed around me. My wolf saw only one choice.

I exploded forward, muscles bunching and releasing in one violent surge. The shirt dropped from my jaws as I became pure predator—teeth bared, claws digging into frozen earth for traction. My instincts screamed for his throat, that vulnerable pulse point where life could be severed in one powerful bite. But survival meant being smarter. I angled low toward his right thigh, aiming to cripple, not kill.

The space between us vanished in a heartbeat. I saw his eyes widen—just a fraction—before his training took over.

He pivoted with military precision, every movement a brutal economy of motion. The gun barrel swept up and away as he stepped left, bringing the weapon's stock down like a club. It connected with my ribs with a sickening crack that reverberated through my entire body.

"Nice try," he snarled, all pretense of gentleness gone.

Before I could recover, he slammed the butt into my flank with crushing force. Pain shot through me like white-hot lightning. The world spun as I was hurled sideways, a sharp yelp tearing from my throat before I could stop it.

I hit the frozen ground hard enough to drive what little breath remained from my lungs, tumbling through snow in a disorienting blur of white and gray. The metallic taste of blood filled my mouth.

Every instinct screamed to stay down, but I forced myself to roll, paws scrabbling desperately against the ice as I struggled upright. My left side burned like fire, each breath a stabbing agony, as I bared my teeth and snarled at him.

"Feisty." His voice had changed, edged with something darker now—respect mingled with cruelty. He tapped his fingers rhythmically against the weapon's stock, an almost hypnotic gesture from a predator toying with wounded prey. "I like that."

The red dot of his laser sight found my chest again, unwavering.

"But you're not getting out of this."

Chapter Twenty-Four

SOFIA

My claws flexed into the frozen dirt under my paws, my body crouching low as I stalked forward.

His smirk turned razor sharp as he adjusted his grip on his gun. "Go on, then," he invited. "Give it your best shot. I'll beat the shit out of you, and then you'll still be leaving with us."

I erupted into motion, anger crackling through me, eyes locked on his neck—on the pulse just under the skin.

His smirk flickered. Briefly. Almost imperceptibly. He waited until I was close, then he moved—faster than I'd expected. He twisted sharply, pivoting on the balls of his feet, and the stock of his gun slammed into my shoulder with bone-cracking force.

Pain flared. I buckled for a second. He could have hit me again, but he didn't. He just chuckled as he stepped back and circled me.

"Not very good at this, are you?" Slinging the gun over one shoulder, he withdrew a blade from a sheath on his hip.

I knew shit about guns but blades... blades I knew. It was a Ka-Bar tactical knife with a seven-inch serrated blade and black coating designed to prevent reflection. This wasn't some hunting knife—this was a weapon specifically designed for close-quarters combat. The kind of blade that could pierce werewolf hide and do serious damage.

Alrighty, then.

I darted in, feigned for his throat, but as he swung the knife, I dropped low and left.

My teeth dug into his calf—a quick, precise bite meant to rip enough muscle to slow him down. He staggered back, swearing as blood seeped through his pant leg.

"You're just pissing me off, you know that?" he spat, his balance already recovering, though there was a new tightness to his voice. "That won't end well for you."

I growled low and deep, our eyes locking. I'd hurt him. I could do it again.

He dropped into a defensive stance now, no longer relaxed or bored. Blood still leaked from the tear in his calf, painting dark drops against the frosted ground, but his grip on his knife remained firm.

I was running out of time. The others would be here any second. I had to end this.

I lowered myself back into a crouch, growling softly. As if bracing for another blind, wild charge. His hand twitched expectantly, and he shifted his weight to counter. I went right first. His knife angled up to block the attack.

Got you.

I dove left, ripping into his other leg.

I heard the sound of crunching snow and knew backup was coming. I could feel it, sense it, smell it: humans approaching fast from multiple directions.

Seconds. That's all I had.

Before I could decide whether to kill him or flee, the air shifted. A faint gust of wind rustled through the trees, colder, heavier, laden with a scent I recognized.

The man froze. His eyes darted upward, past me, a flicker of fear flashing there.

"What the—?"

The sound of trees groaning under massive weight forced my head to whip around. I barely had time to register the black shape swooping down before it reached us. I'd seen this only once before, and it sent shockwaves of fear lacing through me then as well.

Lucian.

Not the man—not the grumpy Bottley owner with the perfect hair and casually terrifying stares I'd spent months trying to impress. No. This was something entirely different.

This was a dragon Shifter.

Lucian was enormous, his wingspan blotting out the sky as he dove straight for us. Scales, obsidian black creating an iridescent effect, rippled in the low light like liquid shadow. His landing shook the ground, a gust of scorching air rolling off him as he folded massive wings close to his body. The air shimmered with heat, snow beneath his talons already melting into steaming rivulets. His claws—black as midnight and long as daggers—sank effortlessly into the earth, carving deep grooves. Amber eyes, still that same striking color as in his human form, glowed like molten gold against the darkness of his scales.

The man rolled sideways just as Lucian's tail came sweeping down, smashing against the ground with enough force to crack the earth. He scrambled to his knees, reaching for something—another weapon, a communicator, something—but Lucian didn't give him the chance.

His head shot forward with terrifying speed, teeth bared, twisted ninety degrees, and clamped onto the man's torso.

He screamed. The sound cut short as Lucian jerked upward, dragging the man into the air with ease, teeth slicing through him like butter. A sickening crunch, then silence swallowed the woods again, broken only by the thud of body parts hitting the ground. Lucian had dropped what was left of the body with the grace of a hunter discarding prey that wasn't worth a meal.

My legs trembled slightly—not in fear, exactly. But the raw magnitude of him, the sheer primal power, left me simultaneously reassured and unnerved.

He swung his head around, his eyes fixed on me before he exhaled loudly. I watched, fascinated, as the long exhale started his Shift back to human form. It was sudden and seamless. One moment, massive claws and tail; the next, Lucian standing over the shredded remains of the man as though he hadn't just incinerated the concept of physical limits. Fully dressed, naturally. Because, of course, dragon Shifters got to retain their perfectly put-together civilian facade while we wolves had to navigate the logistics of Shifting back completely naked.

He studied the corpse. "You got two hits in, both on his calves. You need to hit the vital points, bleed them out quick." He raised an eyebrow at me. "They were good hits, though, so I suppose there is that."

I huffed out a sharp breath, absolutely livid. I'd got myself free after being tied up, escaped from a cabin and covered more than ten miles in the freaking snow, then fought a guy with a gun and knife. And Lucian had the freaking nerve to critique where I bit the guy.

Lucian's gaze shifted behind me, where the sounds of the others were close.

"We need to move," he said bluntly, stepping around the body and gesturing for me to follow. "Car's a mile west of here."

I glanced back, saw Derek's shirt half-buried in the snow where I'd dropped it, and scooped it up without hesitation. I bit into the fabric, holding it firmly in my jaws as I loped after Lucian, silent but intent on the one thought driving itself deep into my mind like a bullet. Derek better still be alive.

Because when I found him, I was going to make him regret leaving me.

CHAPTER TWENTY-FIVE

DEREK

I pushed my SUV to its limits. The engine roared in protest as I drove the accelerator into the floor, tires skidding on the trail to the cabin. It was nearly dark, but Sam's truck stayed close, his headlights bouncing wildly in my rearview mirror.

Mate in danger! Move faster! Don't stop. Don't fail her again.

My wolf was feral, clawing at me, howling to get out. To hunt.

The cabin appeared ahead, a gray smudge against the snow-laden trees. My eyes scanned the area, taking it all in, assessing and cataloging everything. The tire tracks came first—deep-set grooves in the driveway, scattered with fresh patches of snow. There were no cars here now. Whoever was here had already left. The front door was smashed in, hanging at an angle on its hinges.

Fuck!

Hope that they hadn't found Sofia vanished. They must have laughed. I'd tied her up and left her as a present for them.

The SUV screeched to a halt, tires kicking up snow and gravel. I didn't turn it off, just leaped out and tore toward the porch.

Inside, the air smelled wrong—men, intruders, metallic and cold, blood, sweat, and gun oil. My wolf snarled, rage rising. Enemies had invaded our space.

I didn't stop to think. I raced to the bedroom. Her scent was strong here, laced with fear. I knew she was gone, but the sight of the empty bed almost undid me. The rope hung loosely from the bedpost, frayed and empty, the fibers stained with a streak of blood. Her blood. My gaze locked on it, my chest tightening with something I couldn't name but sure as hell could feel.

My wolf yelled at me to do something, to move, to find her, but I was frozen, rooted to that goddamn rope.

She was gone. Really gone.

"Derek!" Sam's voice was sharp, cutting through the fog of panic.

He strode past me, then crouched near the bed, his fingers brushing a small smear of blood on the floor next to the rope.

"If she got hurt when they cut through the rope, there'd be signs of a struggle." He picked up the cord, then looked at me. "No. Sofia did this. They didn't catch her here."

I latched onto the words like a lifeline. "You're saying—?"

"I'm saying if you stop panicking and pay attention, you'll see she got out," Sam said, meeting my gaze evenly.

I took a breath and then another. I was no fucking use to Sofia if I panicked. She needed me clear-headed and focused so I could find her.

A cold breeze brushed against my left cheek. I spun, striding to the bathroom. Empty, no signs of a fight, but the window was open. "Good girl."

I spun and sprinted for the door, Sam on my heels.

Outside, below the window, I could see where she landed in the snow. And the footprints, both hers and the people who'd followed her.

"She's barefoot. She won't last long out here unless she Shifted."

Sam glanced at me. I knew what he was thinking. He knew as well as I did that Sofia's skills and instincts as a werewolf weren't great.

"Trail's there. Heading northeast." Sam pointed toward the tree line.

We set off at a fast pace. We needed to move quickly but not so quickly that we ran straight into a trap. It took me half an hour to find the place where she Shifted. Snow had covered her tracks, but her scent was sharper here, stronger. My wolf rose up again, snapping at his cage. He wanted blood. Wanted violence. Wanted her.

I crouched, running my fingers over the place until I found her jeans. It was a desperate move, Shifting when she was being hunted. But at least in her wolf form she would be able to move faster, more able to withstand the cold.

Sam placed a hand on my shoulder. "She was still alive here, and she increased her odds of surviving by Shifting."

I didn't wait to hear more. I shot forward, following the trail like a beast possessed, the sounds of my brother's soft footfalls behind me.

The trail was broken and chaotic, weaving this way and that. She'd been trying to evade them.

There were signs of her pursuers, though. Broken twigs, disturbed snow, their scents converging and separating as they coordinated their hunt. Too many of them.

I gritted my teeth and kept moving.

The scent hit me before I saw it—coppery and rank. Blood. Fresh. Some of it Sofia's.

I slowed. Sam went left, covering me as I approached two mounds of snow. I brushed the flakes off with my boot.

Huh.

What the hell had happened here?

I turned my head to the side. "Clear."

Sam appeared next to me, his eyes scanning the ground. "This doesn't make sense."

No, it certainly did not fucking make sense.

Sam crouched beside the body parts, his expression unreadable. "It looks like one cut, straight through his torso."

"Why wouldn't they take the body with them?"

Sam looked at me sharply.

"Not whoever or whatever did this." I gestured at the body. "The dead guy wasn't alone. I've scented at least eight men tracking Sofia. Why wouldn't they take the body of their man?"

Sam stood. "Maybe they're coming back for it."

I inhaled deeply, trying to match all the scents. Sofia. She was in pain, angry, full of adrenaline. The dead man, already smelling of decay. Seven of the men who'd been hunting my mate. Something new here. Something almost reptilian. I'd never smelled anything like it before. And one more. One that hadn't been in the forest so far. A scent I recognized from Three Rivers, though not recently.

"Lucian Black," I growled. I spun to Sam, grabbed his jacket with both hands, and slammed him against the nearest tree.

"When you came home, you asked about Black. You were tracking him. Why? Who the fuck is he?"

"Let me go, Derek, before I put you down."

I lifted him higher. "I'd like to see you try. You've been keeping things from me. Things that affect me and my mate."

"I didn't know Black had anything to do with Sofia apart from being her boss. You really think I'd keep it a secret if I thought for one second that he was a danger to her?"

I searched his face, then dropped him. He was right. Sam might work for the Council, but we always came first.

I ran a hand through my hair. "Sorry. I—"

"I know." He straightened out his jacket. "But you're not the only one who cares about Sofia. She's your mate; that makes her my family."

I sighed. "Point taken. But I still need to know why you were looking into Black."

Sam gave his head a small shake. "I had a meeting last week with a guy who feeds me information now and then. He called and asked if I could meet him at his apartment. When I got there, he was gone. Car still there, wallet on his bedside table. I haven't been able to find any trace of him. But in his wallet, he had a handwritten note that just said 'Lucian Black' with a question mark on it. I don't know if it's connected to his disappearance. I don't even know if it's the same Lucian Black who used to live in Three Rivers." Sam's eyes went to the two mounds on the ground. "The Black we knew was human, and a human couldn't have done that. But I'm beginning to think it isn't a coincidence his name was in that wallet."

My gaze locked onto the trail where the scent of Lucian intertwined with Sofia's. "He took her."

We followed the trail onto the road, going slower now, the icy ground crunching beneath our boots as twilight edged closer to night. Anger festered under my skin like a hot coal, but I shoved it down.

Getting distracted by emotions right now would help nobody—not Sofia, not me.

"Trail's thinning out," Sam voiced what I already knew.

I stopped. Sofia and Lucian's scents ended here. They must have gotten into a car.

Sam crouched by a set of tire marks embedded in the semi-frozen ground. He dragged his fingers along the ridges.

"Tracks are fresh. An hour, two at the most," he said, tilting his head slightly. "It's big. Probably an SUV."

I nodded tightly. Lucian had gotten her into the car—had gotten her out of here before I could find her. Had she gone willingly?

"She's gone."

Sam pushed himself upright, brushing gravel and snow from his hands.

"What's Sofia's relationship with Black?"

I had my hand around his neck before he could blink. "There is no relationship with Black. She's my mate. Mine."

Sam held up his hands. "Alright. She's your mate. No one's saying any different. Now back off."

I let go of Sam's neck. "We need to find out who the fuck Lucian Black really is. And why he has my mate."

CHAPTER TWENTY-SIX

SOFIA

I didn't remember falling asleep in the car with Lucian, but the tension in my muscles told me I must have been unconscious. I didn't know for how long, but my body Shifted back while I was asleep. I ached all over, but the sharp stabbing pains in my ribs and shoulder had gone. It was one of the advantages of being a were; accelerated healing when we Shifted meant most damage could be fixed.

Blinking awake, I found a blanket draped over me.

Right. Because of the whole naked thing.

My limbs had locked up from the cold and the fight, every joint stiff and sore as I sat up, careful to keep the blanket around me. Streetlights streamed through the tinted windows of Lucian's truck. Their harsh electrical glow lit up buildings that stretched toward the sky, endless rows of brick and glass boxed together like they were fighting for air. It smelled strange—no, wrong. My senses, always heightened for a time after I Shifted back to human, flinched against the assault of so many unnatural scents: gas fumes, rotting food seeping from distant dumpsters, the iron tang of steel in every direction. My wolf paced inside of me, restless and mistrustful. She wasn't used to this, and neither was I.

"Where are we?" My voice cracked, hoarse like I hadn't used it in hours.

Lucian glanced at me in the rearview mirror, his piercing gaze scanning me as if to assess my state. The look didn't last longer than a moment before his attention went back to the road.

"Someplace safe."

Hmmm. "I see you haven't gotten any more talkative in the last few months."

He didn't answer, just kept his eyes ahead. Derek's shirt was on the seat next to me. It was still damp but it smelled of Derek, of Pack, and I needed that right now. I slipped it on, then climbed into the front passenger seat.

I watched the city go by in silence, knowing there was no point in pushing Lucian.

After twenty minutes, Lucian pulled up to a structure that stood like a relic from another era—a four-story warehouse wedged defiantly between gleaming high-rises. Red brick and black metal composed its industrial façade, weathered yet imposing, with large windows that caught and fractured the streetlight glow. A row of luxury cars lined the block in front, suggesting this was no ordinary warehouse.

Two figures materialized from a discreet side entrance. They moved with the confidence of people who owned their space. The man stood tall, with razor-sharp cheekbones and meticulously combed dark hair, his black suit fitting him like armor. Beside him, a woman with hair the color of polished sterling pulled into a severe bun surveyed the perimeter, her tailored blazer and trousers projecting authority without effort. Both wore earpieces that occasionally caught the light and though their postures appeared casual, their eyes never stopped moving—cataloging, assessing, memorizing every detail of the street around us.

Lucian slid out of the car, and I scrambled after him, tugging Derek's shirt down over my bare thighs. The guards' eyes flicked over me—a half-naked woman with just an oversized shirt covering her girly bits—they obviously decided I wasn't a threat. They smelled human, but I saw their nostrils flaring as they caught my scent. The man's lips twitched in what might have been amusement. What did he smell? Wolf sweat? Fear? Derek's pine-and-moss scent clinging to me like some tragic cologne?

I wondered if they were dragon Shifters like Lucian. He had once told me that due to a witch's spell, he smelled human when he was in human form, but I wasn't sure if it was just him or all dragon Shifters who had that ability.

"Sir." The man straightened. "We weren't expecting you this evening."

Lucian strode toward the doors. "Change of plans, Artie. Are we clear for tonight?"

"Yes, sir. Cleanup is done. Just fight prep for tomorrow evening left."

Lucian nodded once. "We'll be upstairs, then."

Cleanup? Fight prep?

"What is this place?" I whispered, hurrying to keep pace with Lucian.

"This is Virtue and Vice, or the V&V, as we call it." Lucian pushed through the heavy doors. "One of my businesses. Well, two, really. One side is the nightclub. Very exclusive. Caters to all the rich, young punks who like to flash their cash. The other, we use as a fight club."

I nearly tripped, wondering which one was supposed to be Virtue and which one Vice.

"A fight club? Seriously?"

"Keep up, Miller."

Right.

I hurried after him through steel doors and into a nightclub that defied every small-town expectation I had. The space soared through all four stories, cathedral-like in its emptiness without its usual crowds. Multiple mezzanine levels wrapped around the walls, their sleek railings gleaming even in the minimal lighting. Wooden booths with plush leather seating offered views over what I was guessing would normally be a packed dance floor. The whole place screamed money—from the state-of-the-art sound system speakers mounted strategically throughout to the premium finishes on every surface.

What truly captured my attention was the architectural impossibility hanging against the far wall—a two-story glass box suspended from the ceiling like a jewel in a setting. Tinted windows wrapped it, concealing whatever lay inside. Reynolds, the fancy restaurant back in Three Rivers, had impressed me, but this? This existed in another dimension of wealth entirely.

Lucian crossed the cavernous room in purposeful strides, his shoes clacking against the pristine floor as I jogged to keep up. Halfway along the east wall, he pressed something invisible, and a section of wall slid open without a sound.

"This way."

A red-carpeted staircase spiraled upward, plush fibers caressing my bare feet. At the top waited another door, and beyond it—the suspended box.

It was an office, commanding views from three sides through floor-to-ceiling windows. To my left sprawled the empty dance floor we'd just crossed. To my right opened what had to be the fight club—a sunken arena reminiscent of ancient Rome, with tiered seating circling a central pit and private viewing boxes perched above like opera boxes. In the sand-covered floor gleamed an intricate design—two Vs intertwined that, from this height, resembled a dragon's tail coiling upon itself.

The north-facing window stole what little breath I had left. The city unfurled before me—a tapestry of light against darkness, steel and glass towers piercing the night sky like man-made constellations. Beautiful, yet utterly foreign to my wolf senses. Where Three Rivers offered pine-scent and birdsong, this landscape presented only the mechanical pulse of traffic lights, rumbling trains, and the constant drone of air conditioning. My wolf pressed against my skin, unsettled by this concrete maze where everything natural had been conquered and contained.

The office itself matched the opulence below. Dark hardwood floors disappeared beneath oriental rugs in deep crimsons and blacks. The furniture was all clean lines and rich materials. A massive mahogany desk dominated one end of the room, its surface gleaming and spotless except for a pile of papers placed exactly parallel to one edge, a sleek laptop, and a single crystal tumbler. Behind it, a high-backed leather chair looked more like a throne than office furniture.

Shelves held a collection of books and artifacts—ancient-looking weapons mounted on stands, delicate pottery pieces that looked centuries old, and leather-bound volumes whose spines gave titles in languages I didn't recognize. A discrete bar to my left was stocked with bottles whose labels, at first glance, cost more than my yearly rent. A seating area took up the nearby corner, with deep leather armchairs and a low table made of what looked like a single slice of dark wood.

Sitting in one of the armchairs was Darla Ash. Lucian's pretend wife when he was away from his family business and bodyguard when he was not. Tonight, though, she looked like neither—more like an exasperated older sister about to deliver a lecture. At 5'10", she uncoiled from the chair with effortless grace, platinum blonde hair cropped short and spiky. Her pale blue eyes performed a clinical assessment as she approached in simple black jeans and a pink shirt.

"Well," she said flatly, "you look like shit."

Chapter Twenty-Seven

SOFIA

"Two days off the grid? Wasn't your smartest move," Darla said bluntly.

I cocked an eyebrow. "You weren't worried, were you? Darla Ash, worried about little old me?"

"Don't push your luck," she warned, but the faint twitch of a smile tugged at the corner of her mouth.

"Come, sit down. Collapsing on Lucian's floor isn't a good look."

Lucian snorted. "And Darla should know; she's done it more than once."

I forced myself to move toward the nearest chair, my legs shaky, though I wasn't sure if it was from exhaustion or sheer emotional overload.

"I was bleeding out from a bullet wound I got defending you. And you started that fight, so it was entirely your fault."

As much as I wanted to hear this story, I wanted answers to the questions that had been swirling around in my mind since I woke up. "How did you find me?"

Lucian settled opposite me. "You missed training."

"He panicked," Darla interjected, moving to his side. "So we pulled Bottley's security footage."

"You—" I began.

"Saw you slip out back with Derek," she continued, cutting me off. "His car left minutes later. So we figured you were with him. After that, it was just a matter of checking hotels, motels, anywhere you might be holed up, and tracking down all his holdings."

"The cabin wasn't easy to find," Lucian added, voice tight. "He's good at covering his tracks. Better than I expected."

"You want to tell us what happened out there? Lucian said he found you being hunted through the forest by armed men. Where was Derek?"

I frowned at Lucian, wondering if dragon Shifters could communicate telepathically.

"I called from the car while you were unconscious," he explained, reading my expression.

Or he really was telepathic and had just read my mind.

My parched throat tightened as I swallowed. I'd kill for a glass of water, but pride kept me from asking. I trusted Lucian and Darla, but I didn't know much about dragon Shifters and what they could do. Before I'd met them, I'd thought dragon Shifters were a myth, made up by wolves to scare their cubs—stories of fire-breathing monsters who could level mountains with a single roar. Now I was sitting in one's office, wearing nothing but a T-shirt, completely at their mercy. It was surreal how quickly impossible things became an everyday reality.

I pulled Derek's shirt tighter, hating that I still wore it, hating him, hating that I couldn't make myself take it off.

"I don't know exactly. I don't even know who those men were.

Derek tied me to the bed—"

"Tied you to the bed?" Darla's lips curved into a wicked smirk. "Didn't realize you were into that."

"It wasn't the fun kind of tying up! He left me there like bait!"

Lucian's forearm muscles tensed as he methodically rolled up his sleeves. "He restrained you and didn't even leave you a weapon?" His voice had dropped dangerously low. "Exactly what has he dragged you into?" Something flickered in Lucian's eyes—a flash of gold that disappeared as quickly as it came.

I shook my head. "I wish I knew."

"None of this tracks," Darla said, frowning. "You sure this isn't some werewolf courtship ritual gone sideways?"

My jaw dropped. "Courtship ritual? Injections, kidnapping, being tied up and hunted through the woods by armed men? What exactly do you think werewolves do for foreplay?"

"Darling, I dated a she-wolf once. Trust me, some of her kinks made me blush."

I opened my mouth, then shut it firmly. I decided I didn't want to know.

Darla smirked at me. "Good choice."

Lucian leaned forward, elbows on his knees. "Think back. Has Derek been acting strange lately? Anything unusual at all?"

Exhaustion hit me like a wave, dragging my shoulders down as I sank deeper into the chair. I caught a whiff of something in the air—the lingering scent of expensive cologne and gunmetal. Someone else had been in this office recently, someone who carried weapons.

"He did steal a USB from his brother, Sam."

"Wait," Darla said, her voice sharpening. "You mean Sam Shaw? As in the Wolf Council member?"

"Yeah. Why? Does that make it better or worse?"

A look passed between Darla and Lucian, one I couldn't decipher.

"I don't know yet," Lucian said, his eyes returning to me. "In the meantime, you can stay here. As long as you need."

"Here?" I was going to stay in his office? I glanced around, not seeing a bed.

He gestured upward. "There's another floor above this one. It's yours if you want it," he said, his tone softer now. "You'll be safe here. Or I can arrange for a driver to take you back to Three Rivers. It's your call. Just let us know what you want to do."

I pushed myself awkwardly to my feet, my bare toes curling slightly against the smooth floor as I took a hesitant step toward the far window, the one looking out over the city. The throb in my ankle reminded me of my sprint through the forest, branches tearing at my skin, rocks digging into my feet. A bruise was blooming along my calf where I'd crashed into a fallen log.

A distant siren sounded from outside. Three Rivers was out there somewhere, along with everyone who'd be worried about me—Mai, Wally, Jase. I should want to go back, shouldn't I? To my apartment, my job, my life.

But something twisted in my gut at the thought. Going back meant facing Derek. Meant answering endless questions, enduring concerned looks. Meant becoming Sofia-the-reliable again. The one who held everything together. The one who put everyone else first.

I didn't want that yet. Didn't want to return to pulling espresso shots and solving other people's problems. Didn't want to face Derek knowing he'd abandoned me again. Not yet, anyway. For once, just once, I wanted to put myself first.

I turned back to face them, my spine straighter. "I think I'll sleep for a week. After that..." I shrugged. "I don't know. But whatever happens next will be my decision. Mine. No one else's."

Darla searched my face for a moment before giving me one of her rare smiles. "That's our girl."

Behind me, Lucian's phone vibrated on his desk. He glanced at it, his expression hardening for a fraction of a second before he schooled his features back to neutral. Darla caught his eye, a silent conversation passing between them. Whatever was happening, it wasn't over. Not by a long shot.

But Darla's words had stirred something faint but steady within me. My anger hadn't cooled; my frustration hadn't eased. Derek's name still burned in my chest like a brand. But for the first time in days, I felt a flicker of control—a tiny ember of hope igniting somewhere deep where bitterness hadn't yet reached.

It wasn't much. But tonight, it was enough.

Chapter Twenty-Eight

DEREK

We made it back to Three Rivers by early morning, the sky just beginning to bleed from black to gray at the edges. My mind kept running through every possible scenario of what might be happening to Sofia, each worse than the last.

My wolf paced restlessly beneath my skin, growling for action, for violence.

Find her.

We will, I promise.

But we both knew I couldn't make that promise.

We headed straight to Shaw Investigations, the PI agency my brothers had built from nothing. The sign above the door was simple, understated—just like Sam and Mason themselves. With Mason now Alpha of the Bridgetown Pack and Sam spending most of his time with the Wolf Council, Carlito Mendez was running the day-to-day operations. He'd turned out to be exactly what the business needed—methodical, ruthless when necessary, and completely unbothered by Pack politics.

I gripped the handle of the glass front door, the metal cool against my palm, and pushed it open with more force than necessary. I'd called ahead from the car, first to Ryan, then to Carlito—letting them know we would need Waylen's tech expertise on this.

Ryan had been waiting for us in the parking garage, leaning against his truck, arms crossed over his broad chest. His face was carved from stone, jaw tight enough to crack walnuts. Seriously fucked off didn't begin to cover it. I knew the feeling—it was churning in my own gut, threatening to spill over into something dangerous.

He'd taken one look at Sam and me as we climbed out of our cars, then just growled, "Inside."

Right.

The office was already humming with early morning activity. Dean, the receptionist with the keen eyes that missed nothing, gave us a tight nod as he pressed the button under his desk that unlocked access to the main office. I returned the nod briefly, already moving past the desk, not breaking stride. The lock disengaged with a barely audible click as we pushed through.

Inside, the space opened up, desks arranged in neat rows around the perimeter. Some staff were already glued to their screens, others examining photographs and documents pinned to walls in organized grids. The scent of coffee and paper mingled with the distinct odors of the people themselves—some freshly showered, trailing clouds of citrus shampoo and sandalwood shower gel, while others clearly hadn't made it home last night, their clothes carrying the stale sweat of overtime and the lingering garlic from someone's pasta dinner.

You could tell which corner belonged to Waylen from a mile off—a disaster zone of organized chaos that he somehow made function like a well-oiled machine. Energy drink cans formed precarious towers beside his multiple monitors, some with post-it notes stuck to them, his writing a crazy scribble only he could decipher. Tangled charging cables snaked across his desk like electronic spaghetti, connecting at least three phones, two tablets, and what looked like several external hard drives. The wall behind his station had transformed into a maze of sticky notes, printed code snippets, and newspaper clippings connected by red string like something out of a conspiracy theorist's basement. A half-eaten bag of Cheetos lay open next to a mechanical keyboard that glowed with rainbow backlighting, but there was no Waylen in sight.

The door to the briefing room swung open, and Carlito stepped into the frame, filling it with his presence despite his average height. He was lean and muscular, the kind of build that came from years of constant, hands-on work rather than flashy gym training. His skin was sun-worn and tanned, etched with a few scars that peeked out from beneath his rolled-up shirtsleeves. The inked lines of a tribal tattoo curled around his right forearm—the old Pack symbol from a Los Angeles territory, where he'd grown up. Behind him, I could see Jase pacing back and forth like a caged animal, his agitation a mirror of my own.

"In here," said Carlito, his voice carrying the subtle accent of his hometown.

We followed him into the room, and I felt Carlito's eyes tracking us, lingering a moment longer on Sam before cutting to me. His gaze was assessing, missing nothing.

"You look like shit," he said bluntly.

Carlito had been brought into Shaw Investigations by Mason and Sam. He'd been in the army before that. His superiors had blamed him for an op that went wrong, and he'd been dishonorably discharged from his unit. He'd gone lone wolf after that, taking mercenary jobs that grew increasingly dangerous until Mason and Sam tracked him down. He'd been here a couple of years now, and the Pack and the job seemed to suit him. Waylen liked to joke that Carlito's supernatural ability wasn't just his skills in tracking and combat; it was the way he could make anyone in the room feel three inches shorter just by existing.

"Noticed that too, huh?" Sam said as he walked past Carlito and into the room. "I thought maybe his mirror broke."

"When was the last time you looked in one, Sam? You and your brother both look like you've been marching through fields of shit for weeks."

I'd had enough. Every minute spent on banter was a minute Sofia might be in danger. My patience, already stretched to breaking point, snapped.

"We don't have time for this. We need to find Sofia, not exchange beauty tips."

"Where the fuck have you been?" The words exploded from Jase, his voice raw with worry and rage.

"Calm—"

"Calm down?" Jase's hands fisted in the front of my jacket as he slammed me into the wall hard enough that the edge of a monitor rattled on the adjacent table. His face was inches from mine, but I could feel the tremor in his hands, smell the fear beneath his anger.

"Where the hell is my sister?"

I kept my gaze steady, accepting his rage. My wolf wanted to fight back, to assert dominance, but I locked it down tight. There was no point in reacting—Jase needed to get this out of his system, and the Goddess herself knew I deserved it.

"I don't know."

"That's enough," Sam said, yanking Jase back.

"It is not enough!" Jase's body twisted in place like he was on the verge of taking a swing at me. "She's out there with who knows who—doing who knows what—because of him." He jabbed a finger in my direction.

"I fucked up." There was no use sugarcoating it. Jase deserved the truth, and I wasn't about to hide behind excuses. "But we're going to find her. That's why we're here."

Sam nodded, squeezing Jase's shoulder briefly. "We'll find her. You know we will."

"You'd better. You got any ideas why the fuck Lucian Black would take her?"

I shook my head, the name igniting fresh rage in my veins. I'd spent the drive here trying to come up with a reason, but I had no fucking clue, and it was eating away at me. Who the hell was Lucian Black? He was supposed to be a human owner of a coffee shop. How had he managed to slip under every radar? What gave him the right to take her?

My hands curled into fists at my sides. I was going to hunt him down, and if he had touched her, I would kill him. Slowly. The parade of possibilities of what he was doing to her stormed through my mind again. Was she scared? Hurt? In pain and wondering where the fuck I was? That last thought hit me like a sucker punch to the gut, driving the air from my lungs and making me want to double over. It was the worst kind of pain—the kind you know you deserve.

Sam must've felt the rage radiating off me. He always could, with our twin bond strung taut between us, no matter how far apart we drifted or how pissed I was at him. His scent shifted subtly—deliberately smoothing out the sharp edges of his own anxiety, releasing calming pheromones that would affect both Jase and me. It was an old trick we'd learned when we were kids—control your own chemosignals first, and the wolves around you will follow suit. Sam had always been good at it, like some damn wolf whisperer.

"Derek." Sam stepped close, folding his arms but keeping his movements slow, deliberate. Everything about him was now measured, he was a grounding force, dragging me back from the cliff edge. His eyes locked on mine.

"We'll find her," he repeated.

I took a deep breath, inhaling the scents of the room, using them to anchor myself in the present. The clean, familiar, steadying scent of my twin. The lingering coffee in the air. Getting my anger under control took effort, but I managed it. I needed a clear head right now. I couldn't help Sofia if I was blinded by rage and guilt.

The door swung open next to me, and Waylen burst into the room, an open laptop in one hand, a sheaf of papers in the other. He was like a caffeine-fueled hurricane, with his lime-green glasses hung crookedly on his nose and his body jittering as it always did when he was riding the high of discovery.

"Got something," he said, not bothering with hello. "On Lucian Black."

"Finally," Sam said as Waylen dumped his laptop and papers on the table, shoving aside two of the work tablets that Carlito kept in here for meetings.

Waylen hit a key and spun the laptop toward us. A shit-eating grin spread across his face. "Lucian Black isn't Lucian Black."

I wasn't in the mood for games. "Translate, wizard boy," I said, nodding at the screen name he always used—*Waylen the Wizard.*

Waylen snorted. "Relax, Shaw. I'll get there." He jabbed a finger at the screen. "His real name is Lucian Stone."

The name tickled something in my brain. "Stone? Why does that name sound familiar?"

"Because it should." Waylen hammered a few more keys, pulling up documents on his screen. "Lucian Stone is the eldest son of the Stone family. East Coast heavyweights who have their fingers dipped in everything: real estate, politics, clubs, and restaurants. You name it, they own it—or crush it."

He pushed his glasses up his nose. "The Bottley Bar was bought five years ago through so many shell companies it'd give the IRS a migraine. This guy created fake businesses to hide other fake businesses that hide his real business. Pro-level coverup."

Ryan moved closer, arms crossed. "Someone like Stone doesn't just show up in Three Rivers to sell muffins and coffee."

"Exactly," Waylen said, snapping his fingers like someone had finally caught on. "This guy stepped out of some *Game of Thrones*-style dynasty and decided to..." He waved his hand with mock flair. "Make lattes with little hearts on top. Makes no sense, right?"

"Why, then?" Carlito asked. "What the hell was a guy like that doing here?"

Sam's eyes narrowed. "He smelled human. He and his wife. But no way a human could cut a guy in half. Any records suggest supernatural involvement?"

"Nothing concrete. But if they're pure human, you can dip me in mayonnaise and serve me for lunch." He tapped on his laptop again, then pointed at the huge screen on the far wall. "Lucian's name is on most of the Stone's major holdings. He's the CEO, the shot-caller. Which makes it even weirder that he was playing barista in Three Rivers."

"And why take Sofia? A guy like that doesn't do anything without a reason for it."

Ryan narrowed his eyes. "The USB—you think Lucian knows about it? Took Sofia as leverage, maybe?"

I spun round to face my twin. "Sam, just what the fuck is on that drive?"

Chapter Twenty-Nine

SOFIA

I woke to golden sunlight streaming through the windows, the gauzy white curtains doing little to filter the morning glare. For a moment, I just lay there, letting my senses adjust to the space. The bed beneath me was too soft, too luxurious—nothing like my worn mattress at home or the threadbare sheets I'd had for years.

City sounds drifted up: car horns, the distant wail of sirens—were the sirens never-ending in this place?—a steady hum of traffic. No bird calls. No rustling leaves. No familiar sounds of the Three Rivers forest that usually met me each morning.

I'd slept in Derek's shirt. His scent still clung to it but it was fading fast. For some reason, that made me sad, and a tear trickled down my cheek, which was ridiculous. It shouldn't affect me. I didn't care about Derek or whether his clothes still smelled of him or not.

What had I expected? An explanation? A promise that this time would be different? That he wouldn't leave me again?

A bitter laugh escaped my lips before I could stop it, echoing in the too-large room.

Dream the freaking hell on, Sofia.

I felt like such an idiot. I couldn't believe I'd let my guard down. Again. Every time I trusted him, he found new ways to stomp all over my heart.

My fingers clenched on the expensive sheets.

"Fool me once," I muttered to the empty room, "shame on you. Fool me twice, shame on me. What the hell is fool me thrice? Give up now and become a lesbian?"

I swung my legs over the side of the bed, my bare feet meeting a cold marble floor. The chill shot through me, but I welcomed it. Anything to shake off the self-pity.

My wolf huffed; she didn't like being in this strange place any more than I did.

Going home?

Not yet, I thought back as I studied the room. I hadn't really taken it in last night; just had a quick shower to wash off the smell of my blood and panic, then collapsed on the bed and fell asleep.

Sunlight bounced off the muted grays and whites that dominated the room's décor, creating an almost clinical atmosphere. No photos on the walls, no personal touches. Just pristine surfaces and sharp angles. Through the window, I could see skyscrapers stretching toward the clouds, their glass faces reflecting morning light like mirrors. The view should have been breathtaking, but it just made me feel smaller. More adrift. In Three Rivers, I could always orient myself with the forest I'd known my whole life. Here, everything was straight lines and right angles, man-made patterns that felt alien to my wolf.

I needed a plan. Needed to work out what I wanted. Should I go back to Three Rivers or just... disappear for a while? Mai did it. She vanished for four years. Maybe I could do the same—work for Lucian here, live in the city, try to be someone else. No one would really miss me. Mai had Wally to gossip with, and they had more in common with each other than me these days with all the baby stuff. Jase didn't need me anymore—sure, he'd have to learn to cook, but if it was that or starve, I was confident he'd work it out. Julie could run the Bottley. Even Mrs. Patterson would manage; Jase would help her out if she needed anything.

I could do this. I really could stay here. Take the time to work out who I was and what I wanted. There was something freeing about that thought but also something achingly lonely. Werewolves are Pack creatures—we're not meant to be alone. But maybe that was the problem. I'd been trying so hard to make sure everyone else was okay that I'd forgotten how to take care of myself.

I stood up, then froze when I caught sight of myself in the ornate mirror hanging on the wall by the door to the en-suite.

Holy freaking crap!

I almost didn't recognize the person looking back at me. The woman in the mirror looked so tired and worn out. Dark circles shadowed my eyes, my skin paler than I remembered. Stress and constant work had hollowed my features, carving away at the softness I used to see there.

And my hair... I ran my fingers through the tangled red mess, grimacing as they caught on knots. What had once been vibrant waves now hung limp and dull, desperately in need of some TLC. Between the forest chase and sleeping on it wet, my hair looked like a family of squirrels had staged a territorial war in it, complete with fortifications and battle trenches.

A knock at the door interrupted my thoughts, quick and sharp.

Before I could respond, it swung open, and Darla strode in with that deliberate grace that made her look both dangerous and completely at ease. Her eyes swept the room in that quick, assessing way she had, taking in everything from my disheveled state to the crumpled shirt of Derek's I still wore. Her trademark smirk played at her lips as she crossed to the bed, moving with the casual confidence of someone who knew exactly how deadly they were.

"Got you some clothes," she said, dropping a pile on the bed. "Figure you'd want out of that shirt."

I hadn't even thought about clothes.

Damn it, I had to get my life together.

"Thank you."

"Breakfast in five. Then training."

I frowned. "Training?"

A slight smirk tugged at her lips as she paused in the doorway on her way out. "Yup. Training. Your choice—wallow up here or get stronger."

She turned without waiting for a response, the door clicking shut behind her with quiet finality. I stood there for a moment, staring at the space where she'd been, then slowly, deliberately, I pulled Derek's shirt over my head, the soft fabric whispering against my skin one last time before I let it fall to the floor.

The clothes Darla had brought were the perfect fit—black leggings, fitted sky-blue tank top, white sneakers in my size, everything designed for movement.

I could do this. I could be a new person. Be the person I'd always meant to be.

And next time I saw Derek fucking Shaw, I would show him who

I really was.

Chapter Thirty

DEREK

"I have no fucking idea what's on the USB." Sam met my stare across the table, his expression hard.

"Run that by me again?" He had to know what was on it. It was his fucking USB, for fuck's sake.

"I downloaded the encrypted files from the laptop of a Council member named Jessica Chu. I've been investigating her for the last few weeks. She always seems to turn up where there is a ripple outbreak. There's been too many coincidences, and she has too many connections to people of interest."

"You stole files?"

"Yes." Sam's jaw tightened. "I stole files from Chu; you stole the USB from me. See a theme here, bro?"

"What kind of connections?" Ryan asked, leaning forward.

"She's been meeting with people off the books. Three weeks ago, I tracked her to a warehouse in Detroit. She met with Danila Norris, a witch who the Council believes is involved in the ripple trade. Jessica should've arrested her. Instead, they had tea and cookies, chatted for two hours, and then Elara left and flew home. Chu made no mention of this meeting to the Council."

"Did you take your concerns to the Council?"

Sam opened his hands wide. "The Council's compromised. I don't know who I can trust. Chu's been meeting with people she shouldn't, voting in erratic ways. I saw an opportunity during a break in Council meetings to gain access to her laptop. I didn't have long, but I was able to download a bunch of files before I had to go. When I looked at it, I couldn't crack the encryption, and I couldn't risk taking it to anyone at the Council."

"So, that's why you're in back in Three Rivers," I said, the pieces clicking into place. "You needed Waylen to crack the encryption."

A small smile tugged at the corner of Sam's mouth. "Best hacker I know."

"Did someone say encrypted drive?" Waylen practically vibrated in his chair. "Give it. Give it now."

I pulled the USB from my pocket.

"If you fuck it u—" Sam started.

"Please," Waylen scoffed, snatching the drive from my hand. "Who do you think you're talking to? I don't fuck things up. I make them sing."

He plugged it in, and the screens around us immediately lit up with scrolling code. His fingers flew across the keyboard with that focused intensity I'd seen on him during crucial operations. The wizard was in his element now, his glasses reflecting cascading lines of text as multiple windows popped open across his screens.

"Oh," he breathed, eyes widening behind his glasses. "Oh, this is interesting. They're using AES-256 with some kind of custom key derivation function." Waylen's fingers never stopped moving as he spoke. "We've got what looks like standard file encryption, but there's some weird header data that doesn't match any protocol I've seen." He pulled up a hex editor on another screen, displaying blocks of alphanumeric characters.

"Weird how?" Sam pressed.

"The metadata structure is all wrong. See this block?" Waylen pointed to a section of the screen. "That's not following any standard format. Someone's built a custom encryption solution with multiple authentication checks. Probably a dead man's switch, too." His grin widened. "Clever."

I stood up, pacing around the table and back. Sam shot me a wary look.

"How long is this gonna take?" I asked Waylen.

"You can't rush a masterpiece, Derek."

Fuck. I hated this. Hated waiting around when I needed to be out there. Hunting. I picked up one of the tablets from the table, needed to do something, anything, and started scanning the documents Waylen had pulled on Lucian Stone.

My phone buzzed in my pocket, breaking through Waylen's muttered commentary about encryption patterns. I looked at the name flashing on the screen.

Huh.

"It's Torres."

"This should be interesting," Ryan said. "Put it on speaker."

The room went quiet, everyone's attention shifting to the phone as I placed it on the table and hit the answer button.

"Hey, Torres—oh, no, wait. You can't be Torres, can you?" I said, anger creeping into my voice. "Unless your corpse has discovered a way to talk."

A laugh came through the speaker, with a slight tinny echo that told me whoever it was was using a voice modulator. Interesting. Because they thought I would recognize their voice? Or that I would record it and run it through voice recognition software? Was it Kane?

"You always were a smart one, weren't you, Derek? But not smart enough to keep your mate protected, were you?" The voice had an edge of amusement that made my wolf snarl. "Such a pretty thing with all that red hair. Shame she escaped. I had plans for her. Still do, if I'm honest. I want a taste of her. See if she lives up to the promise of her photos."

Red bloomed across my vision. My wolf clawed to get out, desperate to rip out the throat of anyone threatening our mate. The tablet shattered in my hand, the screen fracturing into a spiderweb of cracks. The scent of my rage must have filled the room—Ryan shifted his weight, and I knew he was ready to intervene if I lost control.

Across the table, Jase's hands curled into fists. Sam placed a warning hand on his arm, but his own expression was dark, dangerous.

"You'll try, and you'll end up just like your guy," I managed through gritted teeth. "It wasn't a pretty sight; his body got ripped clean in half trying to get to her. Messy stuff." I took a calculated guess that they didn't know who had killed his guy either.

"Casualties happen," the voice replied smoothly, but I'd caught the slight pause before he'd spoken. He was rattled by the body, just like we were. "It's all part of the mission. And I've got guys lining up around the block to be part of this one. Just imagine how many more will be happy to risk their lives for a taste of your mate?" the voice continued.

Sam scribbled a note on a piece of paper and held it up.

He's trying to bait you.

No shit.

Carlito stood up, walked around the table, picked up the other tablets, and moved them out of my reach.

I forced myself to sigh loudly. "That all you got? Coz I've got things to do, and you're boring the fuck out of me."

The voice laughed. "I like you, Derek. You've got balls. If things had worked out differently, I could have had a place for you. But let's cut the shit. The USB, Derek. Hand it over, and this all goes away. I'll even think about leaving your mate alone."

"No." The word came out flat, final.

"No? Just like that?"

"Just like that."

A sigh crackled through the speaker. "I thought you might say that. Never could make things easy on yourself, could you? Well, never mind. You won't hand it over, we'll just have to come get it."

The line went dead.

I stared at the phone, my mind racing. Kane was coming for Three Rivers. Sofia was out there somewhere in Stone's hands. And I couldn't be in two places at once.

CHAPTER THIRTY-ONE

SOFIA

The training room smelled clean, sharp, and clinical, like everything inside had been scrubbed within an inch of its existence. Smooth, gray mats covered the floor under the fluorescent lights, their muted color sucking in the glow and reflecting none of it back. Mirrors lined two of the walls, though, ready to catch everything.

In the corner, a weapons rack gleamed like a prize case. Daggers, throwing knives, staffs, training blades—all polished, all waiting.

Holy mother of the sharp and shiny!

My fingers itched as my eyes skimmed over the knives. The collection was like something out of my dreams—if my dreams involved drooling over deadly weapons, which, okay, fine, when they weren't filled with Derek fucking Shaw, they totally did.

Each blade was a work of art, from slim throwing daggers that looked like they could slice through air itself to curved hunting knives that practically begged to be held. There were even a few pieces I didn't recognize, their exotic shapes making my inner knife nerd do a happy dance. They weren't just weapons; they were possibilities, representing a different way to fight back, to protect myself. These weren't the practice blades I was used to—these were serious weapons for serious fighters.

I wondered if Darla would let me play with— I mean, train with them. My fingers twitched again, already thinking about the balanced weight of those throwing knives, the satisfying thunk they'd make hitting their target.

"You're imagining naming them, aren't you?" Darla stood dead center in the room, arms crossed, waiting with a predator's stillness that made my wolf bristle. Even in workout clothes, she radiated that effortless lethality that reminded me she wasn't just a skilled fighter—she was something else entirely, something ancient and dangerous. Darla didn't flinch; Darla didn't second-guess herself. She was power wrapped in silk and she owned it for all to see.

"No." I shook my head vigorously. "Not at all. Though that silver one with the curved blade is definitely giving me strong Stabby McStabberson vibes."

Darla's lips quirked into a faint smile as our eyes met. "Really? I've been calling it Slice and Dice for years." She uncrossed her arms. "But we'll get to the fun toys later. First, I need to see what Lucian's been teaching you. Lose the shoes."

I complied without argument, kicking off my sneakers and leaving them near the doorway. Barefoot now, the cold mats felt fresh against my skin as I stepped forward.

She began circling me with quiet deliberation, her movements precise and fluid. Her pale blue eyes dragged over every inch of me—not out of scrutiny, but something more detached, clinical. It wasn't disapproval, exactly, but neither was it approval. It was observation, the way a mountain lion considers the balance of weight and weakness before deciding if it's worth the effort to strike.

"You trained with Lucian," she said finally, her voice clipped and direct. It wasn't a question.

I nodded.

"But fighting isn't all about what someone else teaches you. It's also about what you're willing to let out. How much you're willing to unleash. So..." She stopped in front of me. "Show me. Show me what you've learned."

I hesitated for half a second, but she caught it.

Her smirk grew wider. "Come on. Show me those teeth."

I bounced up and down on my feet, loosening my muscles. "Don't worry, I'm not here to hold back."

"Good." Her tone was almost... pleased. Her sharp eyes swept over me one last time as she took a half-step back. "Because if you do, I'll make you regret it."

Before she could plant her feet, I struck with a quick jab aimed at her center. She batted it away like swatting a fly.

Okay, then.

I snapped a low front kick. Her leg glided back, avoiding impact, one eyebrow rising. "Not bad."

I threw myself into the next set, striking harder, thinking less. Combinations Lucian had drilled into me until they lived in my muscles. Each movement flowed into the next, my fists cutting through the space between us. Darla deflected everything, her motions compact, effortless.

"You're still playing." Her voice cut with disappointment.

Narrowing my eyes, I didn't respond. Words were distractions.

Instead, I pushed forward again, refusing to slow down. Darla caught my wrist mid-strike, twisting just enough to make me stagger. I used the momentum, breaking free and spinning into a back-kick that grazed her ribs. She let out a sharp exhale.

"Better. Channel that rage. Make it work for you. But don't let it control you."

I clenched my teeth, frustration bubbling beneath the surface.

Don't play, but don't get too angry?

Right. Like I had enough experience to know where that line was.

I rolled my shoulders, resetting, and adjusted my stance. More focus, more control; I could do this. I launched forward again, my movements sharper, like my body and mind were finally in sync. Every punch, every kick, every dodge came from a place of strategy, not chaos.

Darla's eyes narrowed as I landed a solid palm strike to her shoulder that sent her skidding back a step. For the first time, Darla looked... engaged. The smirk melted into something more serious, something closer to satisfaction.

Sweat trickled down my back, my breath coming in short, sharp bursts. My legs burned, my arms ached, but I didn't stop. Couldn't stop. The more Darla pushed, the more I found something inside myself to keep going. I could feel something breaking free, a weight lifting as I fully sank into the rhythm of the fight.

"They underestimate you," Darla said, her voice cutting through the haze in my mind. She blocked a strike aimed at her ribs and countered with a hook that barely missed my jaw. "Use that. Make them regret it."

Her words hit something deep within me, igniting a spark I didn't even know I carried. Images flashed in my mind—of Joey and Brad's fight, of Derek tying me to that freaking bedpost, of every person who ever looked at me and saw nothing more than a cheerful barista or a girl too polite to fight back.

They were wrong. All of them.

I roared, my wolf rising to meet me in a seamless merge of strength and precision. My body was fire, and I was its master. I was faster now, sharper. Every punch, every kick, every move felt like a revelation, an unraveling of the girl I used to be.

I feinted left, drawing Darla forward, before spinning into a high kick that connected with her shoulder. She staggered—just for a heartbeat—but it was enough. Enough for me to see it. I wasn't an opponent she could afford to underestimate anymore.

"Time!" she called. Darla straightened as she eyed the sweat trickling down the side of my face. "Lucian and I, we both saw this in you. The edge. The fire. The strength. We knew what you were capable of, even when you didn't."

I swallowed hard, something catching in the back of my throat.

"The question," she continued, stepping even closer, "is what will you do with it?"

I swiped the sweat away with my hand. "Teach me everything. No more holding back."

She grinned, her smile sharp and wild. "Finally."

CHAPTER THIRTY-TWO

DEREK

"Got it!" Waylen's shout made us turn toward him. He'd been working on the files for the last two hours, and his eyes were wide behind his glasses. "I'm through the encryption. And holy shit, you guys need to see this."

He opened a file browser, revealing dozens of folders with cryptic names. Waylen clicked through them rapidly, pulling up documents and scrolling through data.

"It's a whole intelligence operation," he muttered. "Look at this—personnel files, financial records, operation plans, the works."

A PDF opened on one screen, showing a profile with a photograph.

"Simon Webster," Sam breathed, leaning forward.

Fuck me.

Webster wasn't just any witch—he was why we banned all witches and their magic in the north. Fifteen years ago, he designed a spell to put all werewolves under his control. Mind-control that would've turned us into puppets and slaves. He'd nearly succeeded. In the end, the spell failed. The investigation afterward claimed the spell was impossible to pull off, but it didn't stop the Wolf Council from implementing a no-witches policy. Webster had disappeared, going underground. There had been rumors for years of him down south, organizing witches, trying to regroup and rebuild, but no firm proof that he was even still alive.

"Damn, I thought he was dead," Carlito said.

"Not according to this," Waylen said, typing rapidly. "And look who he's been playing with."

My jaw clenched as Kane's face appeared on screen. Not just Kane—Torres, Mitchell, Brooks, other men who had been in my garrison. All names I thought I'd buried, all threats I thought I had eliminated.

"These are bank transfers," Waylen explained, opening a spreadsheet and highlighting transactions between numbered accounts. "Webster's coven is channeling funds through these shell companies to support... this."

He clicked open another folder containing research documents and chemical diagrams. I couldn't make sense of the molecular structures, but I recognized what they represented. Everyone in this room would.

"Ripple," Ryan said quietly.

"They're working together," Sam muttered, his eyes scanning the data. "Webster's coven and Kane's military group. Combining resources, expertise..."

I'd been worried Kane was involved with ripple but to join up with Webster? That escalated the threat he posed a hundredfold.

"Wait," Carlito said, moving closer to the screens. His eyes narrowed as he studied the transaction logs. "These payment structures—some of them match patterns I've seen before. Back when I was tracking weapons shipments in South America."

Sam's head snapped up. "You're sure?"

"Positive. Same shell company cascade, same routing methods through tax havens. They're not just moving money—they're moving equipment."

"What kind of equipment?" Ryan demanded.

Carlito's expression darkened. "Could be anything. Lab equipment, weapons, chemicals."

"Show me," Sam ordered, and Waylen switched to another spreadsheet with shipping manifests.

While Sam and Carlito dissected the data, I spotted a minimized folder of JPEG files. I reached past Waylen to open it. Inside were dozens of surveillance photos—people in various cities, going about their daily lives, oblivious to being watched. Just like Sofia's photos from the cabin. The systematic nature of it made my blood run cold. Who were these people? Other loved ones of targets they wanted to blackmail? How long had they been planning this? How deep did it go?

"There's something else," Waylen said, his voice uncharacteristically grave. "I've been tracking the magical component of ripple—specifically how it makes users want to break their bonds. Remember when Seth, Mai's douchebag ex, tried breaking her bond with Three Rivers? He couldn't do it alone, but brought in a witch, whose spell nearly worked. That was our first clue."

He pulled up more files, fingers flying. "Then Jase and Mai rescued Esme, our now kick-ass resident witch, from a ripple-making factory where they were forcing her to put the spell on all shipments. That confirmed our theory that ripple is a chemical compound requiring a witch to add a spell to each batch."

Waylen pulled up what looked like a research summary.

"What Esme told us is critical—the spell can only be added at the final step. It's labor intensive. Their supply is bottlenecked by having to station a witch at every factory, limited by how many spells each witch can cast before burnout. That's slowed their production and made them easier to track."

He scrolled down to highlight a section. "According to these records, they're trying to streamline it. They're testing a setup with ten witches in one fortified central location who capture spells in these."

Waylen clicked on a file and opened an image on the main display. It showed a small, round metal box, about the size of a dollar coin and two inches deep, with intricate engravings around its edge.

I leaned closer to get a better look. "Is that even possible?"

"Theoretically. Witches have been working on spell containment for decades. If they've cracked it—if they can store spells in objects for later use by non-witches—it's a game-changer." Waylen's eyes were wide. "Think of the potential. Anyone—human, witch, Shifter—having access to magic, from acne-clearing charms to mass amnesia spells. And witches could charge a fortune for these containers."

His fingers moved over the keyboard. "The power balance between our species would shift permanently. They'd have unlimited resources and legions of humans, Shifters, and witches willing to do anything to protect access."

Carlito twirled a pen, studying the box with intense concentration. "Break it down. How does this apply to ripple specifically?"

"Right, so, according to these production estimates," Waylen said, opening a spreadsheet, "an average witch can cast the spell maybe two hundred times a day. Ten witches, that's two thousand containers. They ship the containers out to the factories where a worker breaks the box over a shipment—which could be ten thousand pills—and the spell is effective on each and every pill."

"They'll up their production exponentially," Sam said grimly.

Waylen nodded. "And it makes their operation much harder to track. No need for witches at each production site anymore."

He opened another folder containing what appeared to be operation plans and media strategies. "They're not just making ripple. They're orchestrating everything—the attacks on humans, the media coverage, even channeling funds to human politicians pushing anti-Shifter legislation."

Sam exhaled sharply. "They're manufacturing a crisis. Creating exactly the kind of chaos that would justify extreme measures against Shifters."

"The vaccination program," Ryan said darkly. "The cities wanting to 'cure' lycanthropy."

"But why?" Jase asked. "What's their endgame?"

"War," Carlito answered quietly. "They're pushing us toward war. Create enough incidents, enough fear, enough division…"

"And humans will demand action against the Shifter 'threat,'" Sam finished, his voice hard with realization. "Hell, they already are. FOX ran three segments last week about 'Shifter containment protocols.' The *Post* had an editorial calling for mandatory registration." He slammed his palm on the table. "All while witches position themselves as the reasonable alternative—the saviors with their magical solutions to the 'werewolf problem.' Perfect timing for Webster to step back into the spotlight, isn't it? Not as the monster who tried to enslave us, but as the visionary who warned everyone about us all along."

"This drive contains proof of everything," Waylen said, ejecting the USB and holding it up. "The entire conspiracy laid bare. Who's behind ripple, the attacks, the political plays—all of it."

"Which is why Kane's so desperate to get it back," I said. "Anyone who's seen this information is a threat to their entire operation."

Ryan straightened. "We fortify Three Rivers immediately. Call in every enforcer within a hundred miles, set up defensive perimeters, double our patrols. They want us? We'll be waiting for them."

"Can we count on Council support?" Carlito asked Sam.

Sam's expression darkened. "I honestly don't know who I can trust right now. Most of the Council are in Philadelphia meeting with human government officials."

Right. I'd forgotten about that. Sam was supposed to be there, too.

Ryan turned to me. "Derek—"

"I'm going after Sofia," I cut him off. "They'll eliminate anyone connected to this USB. That includes her."

"Agreed. Get her and bring her back to us."

"And if Stone doesn't want to give her up?" Carlito asked quietly.

My wolf surged forward, teeth bared. "Then he'll learn what happens when you take a wolf's mate."

I turned and headed for the door. "Waylen, find me Stone's location. Text me when you have it."

"I'm coming with you. She's my sister," Jase said, stepping into my path.

I shook my head. "You're needed here. Protect Mai and the babies. Help Ryan coordinate the defenses."

"But—"

"Listen to me." I gripped his shoulder. "If something happens to me—if I fail—Sofia will need you. You're all she has left, Jase. She would seriously kick my ass if I told her I got her little brother killed."

The fight drained from his face, replaced by something rawer, more vulnerable. His jaw worked for a moment before he spoke. "Just... bring her back, okay? She's all I have, too."

I headed for the door, mind already mapping routes, strategies, contingencies. I'd find her. I'd bring her home. And then I'd make damn sure Kane never got close enough to threaten her again.

Behind me, I heard Sam mutter, "Be careful, brother."

I didn't bother responding. Careful wasn't part of the plan anymore. Not by a long shot.

CHAPTER THIRTY-THREE

SOFIA

I'd been waiting for over an hour to talk to Lucian and Darla. I still didn't know what I wanted to do. Still wasn't sure if I wanted to stay here or go back to Three Rivers. Lucian had waved me into his office, but he'd been stuck on the phone since then, and Darla got called downstairs to deal with some issue with one of the bouncers half an hour ago.

"Segregating Shifters into separate districts from humans in the conclave cities isn't a solution," he said. "It's a guarantee of more violence. Are you seriously considering voting for this nonsense?"

The voice on the other end sounded exasperated. "Of course I am, Lucian. Have you seen the latest statistics? Attacks on humans by Shifters are up forty percent in the last six months. The public is demanding action."

Lucian's voice hardened. "You're talking about forcing people from their homes, splitting up communities that have lived together peacefully for decades. The public might be demanding action, but this is not it. You're a politician; you're supposed to lead based on the evidence, on what is right, on the public good, not follow the baying crowds."

I got the impression that Lucian was losing this argument. There had been a lot of talk about werewolves on ripple attacking humans. Of humans needing to take a stand to protect themselves, of a war coming. I didn't understand it. I'd lived my whole life in Three Rivers; I made great coffee and looked after my neighbors. I couldn't imagine what I'd do if those same neighbors turned on me and ordered me to leave the only place I'd ever known. How had the world come to this?

Needing a distraction from my spiraling thoughts, I crossed to the window overlooking the fight club. Even above the dance music pulsing through the building, I heard the impact of fists on flesh, the crowd's roar rising and falling like ocean waves. Two men circled each other in the ring, sweat gleaming on their skin as they darted in and out, each one hunting for weaknesses.

The larger fighter's face was a mess—a gash above his eye had split open, blood streaming down his cheek, yet he showed no sign of slowing. His opponent's ribs were mottled purple and black where the skin had been pummeled, probably by numerous blows.

Without scenting them, I couldn't be sure, but my guess was they were both Shifters. They were too fast and were taking too much damage to be humans.

The larger of the two fighters was a blur of motion as his fist arced toward his opponent's jaw. The smaller Shifter slipped under the punch. His footwork was smooth, deliberate, as he leaped up and brought his foot down on the other guy's knee. There was a sickening crack as his leg buckled under him. He roared, pain and adrenaline feeding him as he drove up into the smaller one's solar plexus.

Not wanting to watch any more, I turned away. The dance floor on the other side of the building offered a different kind of escape. I crossed to the opposite window, fingers trailing against the glass as I watched bodies move beneath the pulsing lights. They looked so free, so uncomplicated in their joy. Just strangers finding connection in the music, in the movement, in each other.

What would it feel like to go down there and join in? To let loose for once? I ran a bar and still couldn't remember the last time I'd been dancing. How long had it been since I'd gone out and had fun? My wolf whined as the gaping hole in my chest seemed to expand. She didn't want to let loose, didn't want to have fun, didn't want to do anything if it meant doing it without Derek.

The truth of it hit harder than I expected. How long had I been clinging to the idea of Derek, even while telling myself I wanted nothing to do with him? Every time he walked into the Bottley, every time his scent reached me or his voice floated across the room, it was like picking at a wound that never properly healed.

I closed my eyes, but that only made it worse. Memories flooded in—the way he touched me in the cabin, the look in his eyes as he tied the rope around my wrists, the ache of being left. Again. The military, the silence after our date, and now this. Three times, he'd walked away. Three times, I'd had to piece myself back together.

My decision crystallized like frost on glass. I couldn't stay in Three Rivers, not with him haunting every corner of it. His scent would linger in the bar; his presence would shadow every street. Even the forest itself held too many memories of him. I couldn't do it again. Couldn't see him there and not have him. But I couldn't stay here either. The city was not for me. It was too loud, too crowded, too smelly. No, I needed to find somewhere else, somewhere I could fit in, where I could belong without the memories and reminders of what I couldn't have.

Tomorrow. I'd leave tomorrow. Pack light, head south, maybe. Somewhere without coffee shops or Pack politics or gray-eyed Betas who looked at me like I was everything right before they disappeared. Somewhere I could forget the way the scent of pine and moss made my heart race. Somewhere where someone might think I was worth sticking around for.

My wolf whined again, plaintive and desperate.

I ignored her.

The door swooshed open, interrupting my spiral. Darla slipped into the office, her eyes flicking to me briefly before she headed straight to Lucian.

He watched her approach and must have seen something in her demeanor as he said into his phone, "I need to call you back."

As he placed the receiver down, Darla leaned close to whisper something in his ear, but my enhanced hearing caught the words anyway: "Derek Shaw is here."

My heart seized in my chest, squeezing so tight I thought it might shatter. Lucian's eyes flicked to me, studying my reaction with an unnervingly calm assessment.

"You want to see him?" Lucian asked, his tone carefully neutral.

I forced my voice to remain steady, even as everything inside me trembled. "No. I don't want to see him." The words tasted like lies on my tongue, but I pushed through. I had to start somewhere if I was ever going to get over him.

Darla's pale blue eyes narrowed slightly before she moved to the side of the room, phone already in hand.

"Get rid of him," she ordered, hanging up before the person could reply.

My wolf growled at me, her claws scraping against my mind.

Mate.

We don't want to see him, I shot back.

Mate.

As if that magically made all our issues disappear.

Darla's phone rang loudly just as insanity erupted below.

Shouts. Then a deafening crash. I rushed to the window overlooking the fight club just in time to see one of Lucian's bouncers sail through the air, his massive body arcing high before crashing into the two fighters inside the ring.

What the hell?

And then I saw him.

Derek stood at the entrance to the fighter's walkway, and the world stopped turning.

Dark jeans clung to his powerful thighs like a second skin, a white button-down stretching across his broad shoulders, sleeves rolled up to expose the corded muscles of his forearms. Power radiated off him in waves, his presence filling the space even from this distance. But it was his expression that grabbed me by the throat. Pure, raw fury carved into every line of his face, every inch of his body. He was wrath personified, a wolf in barely human skin hunting for something that belonged to him.

He prowled into the club with the deliberate, fluid grace of an apex predator. Each step declared ownership of the ground beneath his feet. His gray eyes swept the room with cold calculation. He looked dangerous, determined, absolutely lethal—and so beautiful it hurt.

The crowd parted instinctively, prey animals recognizing a predator in their midst. Then whispers rippled outward as bouncers and fighters moved to intercept him. Derek's lips curved into something that wasn't quite a smile, more like a promise of violence that he would enjoy.

My heart slammed painfully against my ribs, each beat thundering in my ears. Heat flooded my body. Why now? When I'd finally convinced myself to leave, why did he have to stride in looking like every dark, dangerous fantasy I'd ever denied having?

His head snapped up suddenly—a movement so swift it blurred—his gaze cutting through the space between us like he knew exactly where I was. There was no way he could see me, not through the one-way glass, but I felt the heat and intensity of his stare burning straight through me. Hunger. Determination. Something possessive and wild that made my knees weak. Impossible—he couldn't see me—but the connection burned between us, molten and undeniable. For that suspended moment, the world disappeared: no club, no crowd, no past between us, just Derek and me locked in a gaze that scorched away every defense I'd built.

Then the spell shattered as fighters swarmed him from all sides, a tide of muscle and violence converging on a single point. He disappeared beneath them, swallowed by the mass of bodies.

Chapter Thirty-Four

DEREK

I knew she was here; would know her scent anywhere. I didn't think, my focus bypassing every rational thought and igniting something primal that obliterated everything but the need to find her.

They came at me all at once—bouncers in black tactical gear, spectators pissed I was ruining their show, fighters dripping sweat and blood or riled up with adrenaline waiting for their bouts. The first punch came from a mountain of a man with arms thicker than my thighs—all brute strength, zero finesse. His knuckles glanced off my jaw, sparks of pain fracturing my vision.

Like that, is it?

Fine.

Years of black ops missions, ambushes in Goddess-forsaken hellholes, and back-alley brawls had taught me one immutable truth: hesitation gets you killed. I didn't hesitate. I *roared*, the sound tearing from my chest as I surged upward, throwing them back. I didn't let them think, didn't let them regroup. I blocked a wrist mid-swing, twisted with surgical precision until cartilage separated and bone splintered beneath my grip. His scream—high and animal—pierced through the crowd as I yanked him forward into my rising elbow. His nose broke with a wet, pulpy crunch. Blood erupted, not dripping but spraying in a crimson arc across the floor. He dropped like a stone, still conscious enough to clutch his ruined face but no longer a threat.

The next attacker launched himself at me—a shaved-headed bruiser with prison yard tattoos crawling up his neck and fists wrapped in blood-stained gauze. The way he moved told me he was experienced, but the tremor in his hands, the unnatural dilation of his pupils, meant he was amped on something. I slipped under his jab, pivoted on the ball of my foot, and drove my fist deep into his face. Teeth scattered across the floor like bloody dice. A bouncer lunged from my peripheral, the electric crackle of a taser with him. Too slow. I dropped my shoulder, twisted past the electrodes, and drove my elbow up under his jaw with bone-shattering force. There was a sharp crack, and the taser dropped from his hand as his eyes rolled back and his body hit the ground.

The crowd's frenzy intensified, their circle tightening like wolves enraged that their Packmates had been taken down. But I'd been killing men bigger, stronger, and better trained than these for years. My training snapped into place, each movement economy in violence, no wasted motion, no hesitation, no mercy. A throat strike here, bones crushed there. A shoulder dislocated, ligaments tearing like wet paper. Bodies dropping around me in an expanding radius of groans and stillness.

But through the copper tang of blood, the stink of fear-sweat and adrenaline, the cologne and spilled liquor—one scent cut through it all. Sofia. Her scent coiled through me like smoke after fire, intoxicating with every breath. Vanilla and amber and something purely, unmistakably *her*—something I would recognize in a room of thousands, across battlefields, through fire itself.

Nothing was going to keep me from her. Not these men, not Stone, not hell itself.

I spat a mouthful of blood onto the ground. "That all you got?"

The next wave charged—leaner, faster fighters whose fluid movements would have betrayed what they were even if I hadn't already caught their wild, earthy scent. Shifters.

The first one came at me bent almost double, using the momentum of his run to slam his shoulder into my stomach with enough force to lift me off my feet. Air exploded from my lungs as he drove me backward. I brought my elbow down on the back of his neck. Once. Twice. Three times before he dropped me, stumbling to the floor. As he went down, I smashed my knee into his face, and he was out.

The second Shifter came at me fast, a broken bottle in his hand. He swiped at me. I arched back, feeling the glass whisper past my chest, close enough that my shirt parted where the edge caught it. Too close. I lashed out with a sidekick that caught him dead center in his sternum. The impact sent him flying backward into the crowd, colliding with another fighter who had been circling for an opening.

Another fighter leaped into the gap, coming at me with a barrage of kicks and punches that forced me to give ground. A fist slipped through my guard, connecting with my ribs with enough force to crack bone. Pain lanced through my side, white-hot and distracting.

Focus, idiot. She's close. She's here.

I slapped away his follow-up swing and countered, driving my knuckles into his exposed throat. Cartilage gave way. He reeled back, eyes bulging, hands clawing at his crushed windpipe as he collapsed, gasping and retching.

"Enough!"

People must have recognized the voice because more than half the remaining fighters froze instantly, their heads snapping around to locate the source. I turned to see Lucian Stone standing at the edge of the ring, arms crossed over his chest, his stance deceptively casual. I don't know if it was my heightened senses, but the air around him nearly crackled with a kind of primal power that made my wolf's hackles stand on end.

No human gave off a presence like this. This was something else.

"Where is she?" I growled.

He didn't answer my question, just raised one eyebrow, his expression unreadable. "You're far from home, Derek."

"Stop playing your fucking games. Tell me where she is, or I'm gonna rip you apart one piece at a time."

"You just tore through half my security." He gestured faintly toward the groaning bodies littering the edges of the ring. "And put on quite the show while doing it. Are you here to audition? You want in the ring, is that it?"

I was done playing. I stalked toward him, each step deliberate, promising violence. I would break him bit by bit until he told me where Sofia was.

A flicker of something—maybe amusement, maybe calculation—shadowed Lucian's face. He lifted one hand in a gesture that either meant stop or surrender.

"I assure you, she's safe."

"Not good enough. You got thirty seconds to get her here, or I'll reduce this place to rubble. And I'll enjoy the fuck out of doing it," I warned.

Lucian's lips curled into something too sharp to be a smile. "And then what?"

My wolf bristled, sensing something wrong before my human mind could process it. The air around Lucian was changing—becoming thicker, charged with energy as if the atmosphere itself bent to accommodate his presence.

"Tell me, Derek, what makes you think she wants you?"

My wolf snarled, clawing at my control. "She's my mate."

"Ah yes, your mate." He tsked softly, the sound incongruously gentle. "Kidnapping her and tying her to a bed? Really, Derek?"

Shame and fury warred in my chest. "That's between me and her."

"Do you know where I found her?" Lucian pushed. "Fighting for her life. Where were you, her *mate*, when she was being hunted?"

I narrowed my eyes at him, ignoring the way his words hit home. "That's also between me and her."

He took a step closer, and the air around him shimmered with heat. "She is under my protection now. She doesn't want to see you."

My fists clutched, blood dripping onto the floor in soft, rhythmic splashes. "Let her tell me that herself."

"Or what?" His voice was heavy with challenge. "You'll fight your way through more of my men? Try to fight me?" He chuckled, but there was no humor in it. "You're good, Derek, but you have no idea what you're dealing with."

As if to emphasize his point, the temperature around us spiked so dramatically that sweat instantly beaded across my forehead.

What. The. Fuck?

"What I'm dealing with is someone standing between me and my mate. That's all I need to know."

"You really want to do this?" Something ancient and predatory flashed behind his eyes.

I rolled my shoulders, ignoring the protest of bruised muscles. "I'm not leaving without her."

"Your choice." Lucian sighed, almost regretfully. "Just remember—you asked for this."

"Stop!"

Sofia's voice rang out from behind Lucian, and I whipped around, my heart slamming in my chest at the sound as my eyes desperately sought her out.

CHAPTER THIRTY-FIVE

SOFIA

Both Derek and Lucian froze at the sound of my voice, their heads snapping toward me in perfect unison. The intensity of their combined stares nearly made me take a step back. If these two ended up fighting, there wouldn't be a building left standing when they finished. I couldn't have them fighting, wouldn't allow it. Not over me.

"Sofia." My name on Derek's lips was a prayer, a plea, filled with such raw longing it made my chest ache. My breath hitched as I took him in—bloody but upright, his shirt torn in places to reveal tanned skin and the rippling muscles beneath. Blood spattered across his face only enhanced the dangerous angles of his features, the wild gleam in his stormy eyes. The very image of raw, untamed power. He looked every inch the lethal predator he was.

And for one wild, unbidden moment, all I could think was: *He looks like mine.*

"What the hell are you doing here?" I demanded, my voice steadier than I expected.

He frowned, as if my question made no sense whatsoever. "I'm here for you."

Maybe if I counted to ten, my head wouldn't explode. I got to three—go me!—before my hands went to my hips, and I glared at him. "Is this a joke?"

"A joke?"

"Yes, Derek, a joke." I spread my arms wide and did a slow twirl. "As you can see, I'm perfectly fine, no thanks to you. I don't need rescuing, I certainly don't need your protection, and I definitely don't need *you*."

"Sofia." His voice held more than a hint of warning, like *I* was the one being unreasonable.

"Don't 'Sofia' me, Derek Shaw. You've got some balls showing up here."

Nerve! I meant nerve! Why did I have to say *balls*?

His lips twitched into that infuriating smirk—the one that made him look like he could hear every deranged thought in my head—then he spread his hands in a placating gesture.

"Let me explain."

My head really was going to explode. Right here. Right now. Gray matter splattered across Lucian's fight club.

"No explanation necessary, Derek. You gave me a mind-blowing orgasm..." I hesitated for a heartbeat, realizing I'd just announced to the entire fight club that Derek had given me a mind-blowing orgasm, but powered on, too angry to care right now. "Then left me without explaining shit. I've got the hint. It took me long enough, I admit. And me being a slow learner is definitely something I'm going to work on," preferably somewhere hundreds of miles from him, "but while it may seem important to you right now, rehashing the most embarrassing times in my life is not what I had in mind today."

His face darkened, and he looked even more pissed off, something I didn't think was even possible.

"Most embarrassing times?"

"Ah, so you do listen when I speak. Maybe with your next..." *mate*—no, I was his only mate, damn it—*girlfriend*? that didn't sound right either, "sex bunny..." Oh Goddess, had I just called myself a *sex bunny*? I pushed through the blush I could feel scorching up my face. "When she says 'no, don't tie me up so I'm all helpless for the scary-ass hunters to find,' you might consider listening to her."

"And maybe if I thought you actually trusted me so when I told you to do something, you'd do it without making it into a five-act production with step-by-step reasoning delivered on paper, I wouldn't need to tie you up just to get you to stay in the one place I thought you'd be safe."

There was a pause, broken only by the sound of one of the men on the floor groaning. Then I stepped forward, closing the space between us in two swift strides, and swung my fist with every ounce of strength I possessed. The impact was sharp, jarring, my knuckles connecting with the hard edge of his jaw. Pain flared through my hand as the force of the punch sent Derek's head snapping back.

Derek took an audible breath in, and a long, measured breath out. Then he touched his lip with the back of his hand, studying the fresh blood there with almost clinical detachment. His eyes weren't angry when they looked back up at me. No, they were soft with something I couldn't place.

"I deserved that."

Damn fucking right he did.

"Let me... let me explain everything." His eyes searched mine. "Please, Sofia."

It was the "please" that made me hesitate. I'd never heard Derek say please to anyone. His usual idea of negotiation was a well-timed growl and a death stare that made most people in the Pack check their life insurance policies.

Lucian's eyes flickered toward me. "Your choice."

My choice. He was asking if I wanted to talk to Derek or if I wanted Lucian to throw him out. Or try to, anyway. I glanced around at the carnage scattered across the floor, men still groaning and clutching various broken parts of themselves. There'd been enough fighting for one night.

"Fine." The word came out clipped, reluctant. "You got ten minutes."

If I hadn't been watching him so closely, hadn't been so painfully attuned to every micro-expression that crossed his face, I might have missed the way Derek's shoulders softened—a fraction, no more. He straightened immediately, muscles re-engaging like armor sliding back into place, but I had felt the shift in him, anyway. He really had been ready to fight his way through everyone to reach me.

Lucian's expression was unreadable, but he gestured to the side, where Darla stood with her arms crossed.

"Take them upstairs," Lucian said simply. "I'll deal with getting this mess cleaned up."

She didn't acknowledge the order verbally, just gestured for Derek and me to follow with a sharp jerk of her chin.

I could do this. Ten minutes of Derek Shaw, then he would be out of my life for good. I could endure anything for ten minutes. No problem. None at all.

The lights flared to life, harsher than before, as I trailed after Darla and Derek across the ruined floor of the fight club. Men lay scattered in twisted shapes, some moaning quietly, others unconscious. The scent of sweat and blood, threaded through with adrenaline, pain, and fear, was strong, a metallic tang that stung the back of my throat. Derek didn't seem fazed by any of it; didn't so much as glance down at the damage he had wrought.

Darla led us up to Lucian's office, pushing open the heavy wooden door and waving us inside with a gesture that managed to be both casual and commanding. She paused in the doorway, her eyes narrowed as she took in Derek's blood-spattered form before her gaze came to rest on me.

"Want me to stay?"

Yes.

"No," I said. "I can handle him."

Darla studied me for a beat longer. "Call if you need anything." She threw a parting glare at Derek—a silent promise to inflict violence if he stepped out of line—and strode out, the door clicking softly behind her.

CHAPTER THIRTY-SIX

SOFIA

"Sofia..." Derek took a step toward me, and I hated how my body responded, instinctively wanting to lean into him. Even after everything, he felt safe, felt right; he felt like I belonged. This pull, this undeniable feeling that he was mine and I was his, made me want to launch myself into his arms.

The mate bond.

Well, fuck that. It was a physical response. That was all. I was in control. I got to decide, not the Goddess, not some predetermined cosmic bullshit telling me who to be with.

And this? This shitfest that was Derek and me? It wasn't what I wanted. No, I wanted what Mai and Ryan had, what Wally and Thomas shared, a love so deep and committed that they would always have each other's back, they would never leave the other, they trusted and made decisions *together*. I knew now that I would never have that with Derek. But I wouldn't settle. I would rather be alone than have him break my heart again and again. And he would. I had to get rid of him. Had to get as far away from him as possible. This was it. Our goodbye. A chance to get some closure before I cried my eyes out for the next year.

"Ten minutes, Derek."

He nodded, his eyes roaming around Lucian's office, cataloging everything in that hyper-vigilant way he always did when entering a new space, looking for threats, exits, advantages.

His gaze settled back on me, and my breath hitched. When he looked at me like that, it was like there was nothing else in the world. His focus was zeroed in on me, and I was the most, the only thing that mattered.

"I fucked up."

My eyebrows shot up so high they felt like they disappeared into my hairline.

"I was trying to protect you. I miscalculated."

"Protect me?" I repeated slowly. "Is that what you think I need? A big, strong wolf to keep me safe? To make all my decisions for me because I'm too weak to handle anything myself?"

Derek closed the distance between us, stopping just in front of me, so I had to look up at him. A golden sheen rolled across his eyes as they locked onto mine, his wolf close to the surface.

"You think that's what this is about? You being weak?"

"Isn't it?"

Derek moved a step closer. It was slow, deliberate, a wolf giving its prey one last chance to flee. I could feel the heat rising off his body, his scent filling my senses until it was all I could focus on. I couldn't make myself move. Couldn't force my feet to take the step back I knew I should because his eyes, with their burning, desperate longing, pinned me in place.

"You don't get it, do you?"

I opened my mouth to reply, but he beat me to it.

"You think I look at you and see what, just a barista? No, I see you. You, Sofia Miller, are the strongest person I know. When Oliver was the Alpha, when your parents and everyone at school told you that it was dangerous to be friends with Mai, you told them where to stick it. When your parents left and joined the revolution your cousin was instigating, you stepped up. You gave up your dreams of college, got a job, and worked your gorgeous ass off to provide for Jase and make sure he got to follow his dreams. You look after those in need, even though it costs you—in time, money, and your own health. You work yourself to the bone, Sofia, putting everyone else's needs above yours, especially those more vulnerable than you, and you get no thanks for it. And instead of telling people to fuck off, which you should, you keep doing it. That is not weak. That shows the most amazing strength and love and empathy."

His voice softened, becoming almost reverent. "That is who you are, Sofia. That is the person I want to take care of because she is shit at taking care of herself. That is the person I would do anything to protect."

Tears filled my eyes, and I didn't know what to say, didn't know what I felt beyond a bewildering tangle of emotions too complex to name.

"You want to know what it felt like to leave you?" Derek's voice dropped lower. "Like someone had hollowed out my chest and filled the cavity with broken glass. Like I couldn't breathe. Like I was slowly dying every single second I wasn't near you."

"But you still did it," I whispered. "You still left."

He didn't flinch. "Of course I did it. I'd do anything. I'd stand alone against an army, would wade through fire and steel and bullets, would sacrifice everything I've ever built or become if I thought it was the only way to keep you safe. I don't care about what it cost me. I only care that I hurt you by doing it."

"So why, Derek? Why did you leave me in the cabin?"

He hesitated, regret darkening his eyes. "They threatened you, and when I took you out of their reach, they threatened Sam. Said if I didn't get the USB to them, they would hurt him. I couldn't risk taking you with me. Couldn't risk handing you to them along with the USB."

My mind whirled, trying to process this. "Is Sam okay?"

He opened his mouth, then shut it. He stared at me with an odd expression on his face, then tried again. "How do you know I didn't hand them the USB?"

I rolled my eyes. "Please. I know you, Derek Shaw. Of course you didn't hand them the USB. So. Is Sam okay?"

He blinked. Once. Twice. Something flickering across his face.

"Sam's fine. But they're going to attack Three Rivers. Probably in the next twenty-four hours. Try to get the USB by force."

Well, shit.

My mind instantly went to Mai, bigger than a house and ready to drop any day. To Jase, my idiot younger brother who still refused to learn what a laundry hamper was for. To Julie and Brian, holding down the fort at the Bottley. To Mrs. Patterson and her precious tea set.

"We have to go back!" The words burst from me. "We have to help protect them."

He reached for me like he couldn't stop himself, his bloodied fingers hovering an inch from my face.

"You'll come back with me?"

With him? That was a loaded question.

He must have seen my hesitation. "With me," he repeated, his voice roughening. "I just want to keep you safe, you know that? You're precious. The only thing that is precious to me. When you're gone, it's like... like trying to navigate through smoke. Everything's muffled. Distorted. Colors fade. Food tastes like ash. I can function, sure—I'm trained to function through anything. But it's mechanical. Empty."

His fingers trembled slightly as they hovered near my face. "Then you walk into a room, and suddenly, everything snaps into focus. Sharp. Clear. Real again. Like you're this... this anchor that keeps me from drifting into some void I can't come back from."

He swallowed hard, his thumb finally making contact, tracing the outline of my cheekbone like he was committing its shape to memory.

"You help me, even when you don't know it. That night in the cabin, with you sleeping next to me, it was the only time in months, Sofia, months, that I've slept more than an hour without a nightmare. And when we're arguing, when you're challenging me, calling me out on my bullshit—it's the only time the demons in my head are quiet."

He dropped his hand but he leaned forward until his forehead pressed against mine. It was electric, the feel of his skin on mine; his breath warm against my lips.

"I know I've been doing a piss-poor job of being what you deserve. But that changes here. Right now. I'll give up everything—my job, the Pack, all of it. Every breath I take from this moment on will be dedicated to one thing: making sure you're safe and happy." His hands grasped my neck, tilting my head up. "From here on out, where you go… I go. From now on, you're stuck with me. I will never leave your side."

"You… you can't just say those words and make it better. You left, Derek." Tears ran down my face—when had they started?—so many I couldn't stop them. "You keep leaving."

His fingers gently swiped the tears from my face. "That ends today. Partners. You and me. From here on out. I promise," he vowed, his voice unwavering. "Sofia, if you'll let me, if you give me one more chance, I will never let you down again. Never. My life is yours."

He closed that final inch between us, his voice dropping lower. "No more leaving. No more cages. Just us, Sofia. Always."

My body swayed toward his without conscious thought, drawn to him like he possessed his own gravitational pull.

"I'm done. Do you hear me? Done with running, done with pretending that it doesn't kill me when I'm away from you. You want me to let you go? You want me to give up on us?"

He was so close now that the heat of his hands on me burned through my skin. His scent smothered my senses, and holy moon, it felt like home.

"Not happening," he growled, and I could feel the rumble vibrate through his chest into mine. "You can snarl and snap and show your teeth. You can mark me with every wound I've earned. You can scream at me until your voice goes raw. But you're mine, Sofia. My mate. My heart. My damn soul. The same way I'm yours. And I'm not walking away. I'll never walk away. Not again. Not ever again."

His gaze dropped to my lips, and every rational thought in my head scattered. All I could focus on was the way his breath brushed against my skin, how his rough fingers stroked my jaw, like he was afraid I'd bolt if he pressed too hard.

"I love you," he ground out, the words shaking the air between us. "Even when you yell. Even when you hate me. Even when I make the worst fucking decisions trying to protect you and you call me on all my bullshit. I love you. And if that means spending the rest of my life groveling for forgiveness, then I'll enjoy the hell out of it if it means I get to be near you."

His lips were so close I wasn't sure what was his breath and what was mine.

"You're stuck with me, Sofia. I'm not leaving you again. Ever."

I wanted to push him away. To scream at him, make him hurt a fraction as much as he'd hurt me. But all I could do was stare into those eyes, feeling his heartbeat thundering against my ribs like it belonged there.

"Say something," he pleaded quietly. "Please."

The fight drained out of me in a rush.

"I don't know if I can trust you," I whispered, the truth tearing from somewhere deep inside me.

"That's okay," he murmured, his breath hot against my lips. The first brush of his mouth against mine made my knees go weak, my body recognizing what my mind still fought. "I'll earn it. Every day, every minute. I'll earn it. Just give me the chance. Please."

CHAPTER THIRTY-SEVEN

SOFIA

Ever so slowly, his lips descended onto mine. It was careful and controlled, like he was waiting for me to shove him away. But when his mouth touched mine, hard and soft at the same time, I surrendered. My hands fisted in his hair, pulling him closer until there was no space left between us. His tongue swept into my mouth, consuming me as a low, rumbling sound vibrated through his chest.

Yes! This! I wanted, no, needed this.

He pressed me into Lucian's desk, taking control in a way that sent spikes of pleasure exploding across my body. His hands roamed my skin, erasing the memory of his absence one touch at a time—my cheekbone, the curve of my shoulder, the dip at the small of my back. He stripped me as he went, kissing and exploring all my newly exposed skin with such attention it was like there was nothing else in the world for him. Just me. Just him. Just us, together, here and now.

When I was completely naked, he looked down, his eyes cataloging every inch of me.

"Mine," he growled. "So fucking gorgeous. So fucking mine."

His shirt was gone in an instant, tossed aside as he loomed over me.

All hard lines and powerful muscle, honed from years of military and Pack duty. He was beautiful.

I surged up and kissed him again, my fingers exploring every muscle of his chest. He stilled beneath my touch, holding himself tight. But I didn't want the Derek of the cabin, the one so in control that he stopped me from touching him. I wanted him, all of him.

I pushed him back. "No."

His entire body went completely taut, as if it was taking every second of his training to hold himself there.

I tried to catch my breath, knowing this was important, that I had to get this out. "I want this, Derek. No holding back. Not from either of us."

His eyes searched mine. "You sure? There's no going back after this. I fuck you, Sofia, and this dance stops. It's me and you. Now and forever."

My eyes dropped to his lips. The thought of having those on me every day for the rest of my life sent a shiver right from my heart to my core.

I flicked my eyes back to his. "I'm sure."

"Look at me," he ordered, his voice a ragged whisper. "Every second. You understand? You're mine, Sofia; I want you to see everything."

He picked me up easily, my legs wrapping around his waist. Then his hands slipped under my ass, and he lifted me until my legs were wrapped around his head.

Okay, this was new.

He held me in place, one hand hot against my back, as he stalked over to the dance floor window. My arms flew out as my back hit the glass, and his tongue found my clit.

Holy shit!

I couldn't move without falling, could writhe or buck, no matter how much my body yearned to. All I could do was surrender to him, and it was so freaking amazing. I knew no one could see us, knew the glass was one way, but freaking hell, just the thought of all those people down there while his tongue devoured me, sucking, licking, pushing deep inside of me, nearly sent me over the edge. I was lost, helpless in the tide of his onslaught, completely under his control. One of Derek's hands reached up and stroked my breast, circling nearer and nearer to my nipple.

"Holy fucking Goddess," I gasped, knowing I was close.

His fingers stopped teasing me and found their mark, tweaking my nipple. I arched my back, panting, desperate for more. His tongue flicked against my clit as his fingers rolled against my nipple, squeezing and rolling again and again. I couldn't take any more; the orgasm exploded inside of me.

"Derek!" I gasped as my inner walls pulsed repeatedly with the force of it.

He held me in place, his tongue riding out my orgasm, until I felt like body had turned to liquid. Then he carried me over to Lucian's desk, his tongue still lightly stroking me. One hand swept across the desk, sending papers and tablet spinning to the floor.

"I want to touch you." My voice came out soft, dreamy, coming down from the high he'd given me.

"Soon," he growled as he gently placed me on the desk. Hands gripped my thighs, parting them as he knelt before me. The cool wood bit into my bare skin, but his breath was molten against my core. He kissed me there again, the sound of his mouth sucking and licking, sending a zing of pleasure searing through me.

"Derek—"

The room blurred—the shelves, the city lights winking beyond the tall windows—all of it dissolved into static. There was only his mouth, his hands pinning my hips down, his low growl vibrating against me as I shuddered.

I whimpered, strung taut and trembling. Derek lifted his head, his lips glistening, eyes molten with hunger.

"Eyes on me, Sofia."

I complied, our gazes locked as he pushed two fingers inside of me. My eyes went wide, and I inhaled sharply. Then he dragged his fingers against my inner walls as he pulled them out, and I almost came again.

Derek paused, his eyes on my face. "Not yet, Sofia."

I couldn't speak, couldn't even freaking nod. I was right on the edge, and I knew he could see it all on my face.

His fingers pushed slowly back inside, inch by inch, until they filled me.

"Derek, I can't—"

"Yes, you can. My cock is going to be inside of you when you next come, Sofia."

Just the thought of it, of his cock there instead of his fingers, brought me teetering close.

I don't know if Derek felt it or saw it on my face. "Ah. You like that idea."

"Please, Derek," I begged, knowing that I needed him. Now.

He grinned. "Don't come, Sofia. Don't come, and I'll fuck you."

Smug bastard.

He spread his fingers inside of me, running them down my walls again, and it took everything I had to hold on, to not come apart.

"Good girl," he murmured. Then he surged up, his hands dragging me to the edge of the desk.

"Wait. I want to touch you," I repeated. I needed this, needed to feel his skin under my fingers.

He dropped his hands, watching me through half-lidded eyes as I undid first his belt, then the buttons on his jeans. They hit the floor with a thud, and there he was, completely naked.

OMG!

My eyes raked over him. His cock was huge. Thick. So freaking beautiful. I was already so wet but just the sight of him had hot liquid pooling between my thighs, the anticipation of him sliding in and out of me making me squirm. I had thought I'd start with his chest, running my hands over his hard muscles but no, as soon as I saw his cock all other thoughts flew right out of my head.

I brushed my fingertips over his cock, and Derek's jaw clenched.

"Fuck!"

My hand couldn't fully close around him, he was so big, but I wrapped as much as I could around him. His cock throbbed in my grasp, a primal rhythm matching the wild hammering of my heart.

"Fucking hell, Sofia—" His curse dissolved into a groan as I tightened my grip, thumb swirling over his tip. The scent of his arousal flooded my senses, drowning me in need.

"I need to be inside of you," he panted.

Yes! Yes, freaking hell, yes!

"Yes, please!"

"Lie back. Spread your legs."

I didn't argue. I'd do anything right now if it meant getting his cock inside me. I should have felt vulnerable, bare freaking naked, legs open wide, but I didn't. In this moment, I trusted Derek completely. He aligned himself, his cock pulsing hot and insistent against my entrance. Every muscle in his body quivered with restraint, veins standing rigid along his corded forearms. I couldn't wait anymore. I bucked against him, the tip of his cock sliding inside and making me tremble with need.

"You sure?" he asked, voice shredded.

"Yes, I'm sure! I've never been surer. Now, please, shut up and fuck me!"

Derek's fingers grasped onto my hips. "Yes, ma'am." He thrust home in one devastating stroke, tearing a cry from us both. The stretch burned sweetly, but I needed more. My body arched, taking in more of him as he worked his way deeper inside me until he was in all the way to the hilt. The sensation of being so full, so wholly stretched, was so freaking delicious. His jaw clenched, sweat dripping from his temple onto my chest as he fought for control.

"Sofia—" His voice broke, a raw scrape of sound. "You're... fuck. This is..."

"Yes," I gasped my agreement, all of my nerves on fire.

He did a slow, deliberate roll of his hips that dragged every inch of him against my walls.

Holy freaking crap!

I had never felt anything like this. Every nerve inside of me was alight with need, pleasure zinging from one spot to the next.

He slid out, still controlled, and I mourned the loss. I could feel how wet I was, how desperate I was for more of him. He pushed inside again, and it felt so right, like he was exactly where he belonged.

"More," I gasped. "Please, Derek, more!"

He pumped his hips, my nails scoring his chest as I pulled him deeper, the slap of skin echoing in the room. With each thrust, the world narrowed: the bite of his fingers on my hip, holding me in place as he drove into me, the primal growl rumbling through him, the way his gaze never wavered from mine, fierce and reverent.

"Mine," he snarled, picking up pace and force. The desk shuddered beneath us, more papers scattering.

Pleasure coiled tight. He lifted one of my legs, holding it against his shoulder as he angled deeper. His hand slid between us, thumb swirling around my clit, driving me closer and closer.

"Tell me you're mine," he ordered.

I didn't hesitate. I was his. I always had been. "I'm yours. Only yours."

Derek lost control. His thrusts unforgiving, seating himself deep with each brutal stroke, each snap of his hips punching a gasping plea from my lungs.

"... Only... fucking... mine..."

His possessive growl tore through me, shattering the last fragile thread of my control. Pleasure detonated, white-hot and all-consuming.

Derek watched, eyes blazing as I unraveled beneath him. He didn't let up, kept pistoning into me wildly, the desk shaking with every thrust. It felt so freaking amazing.

Then he slid his hands down my legs and grasped my ankles. His eyes bore into mine, watching for my reaction, as he straightened my legs, placing them on his chest, and then he opened his arms, spreading my legs wide, his hands holding them there. The position meant his cock hit new parts of me, parts I never knew existed.

"Holy. Freaking... Derek!" Another orgasm tore through me. It felt like it was never-ending. I was clawing at the desk, my legs shaking, my cries pitching higher, as another orgasm chased it. Then another one. I was lost, completely and utterly lost to the feel of Derek slamming into me, of his eyes locked onto mine. Then Derek's roar shook the room as he followed, his release scalding inside me. And then—

Fire.

A golden thread seared through every single one of my veins, binding me to Derek. For one suspended breath, it felt like we were floating, our souls mixing and merging as one. I could feel what he felt, felt the staggering tide of his devotion, the jagged edges of his fear, the all-consuming need to cherish me, to protect me. His love wasn't gentle; it was a hurricane, a vow etched in blood: I was his, now and forever.

The mate bond snapped into place, thrumming with rightness, and we crashed back into our bodies. Derek collapsed over me, forehead pressed to mine, panting heavily.

"Fuck!" he whispered, his voice raw.

I couldn't speak, too consumed with the emotions I'd felt from him.

"Shit, Sofia, you okay?" His face had a look of panic on it.

I reached up, tracing a fingertip over his lips.

"You love me." I knew my voice sounded surprised, but it was the first time that I truly believed it. "You meant what you said. You're never going to leave me again."

Derek brushed a strand of hair out of my face. "You know, I can think of hella worse ways of doing this, but if the only thing that convinces you is me fucking you every day for the rest of your life, I can take that hit."

I laughed. "Really? You'd take that hit?"

"Several times a day, in fact, if that's what you need."

I shifted closer, breathing him in. The mate bond hummed between us, new and fragile yet somehow ancient and unbreakable all at once.

"Need more convincing right now?" he asked, his smirk pure sin.

Hell, yes!

Chapter Thirty-Eight

SOFIA

Sunlight cut across Lucian's office in sharp, golden blades. I blinked awake, momentarily disoriented by the unfamiliar leather couch beneath me and the quiet murmurs of the city outside. It wasn't the faint thrum of the world waking that had my focus, though.

No, it was the warmth strumming through my body—the arm slung over my waist, the solid weight pressed protectively against my back, and the soft, even breaths of the person sleeping beside me. Derek. He'd slept peacefully all night, holding me close.

I clutched the blanket—one I had no memory of finding last night when exhaustion had finally claimed us. My wolf stretched languidly beneath my skin, then settled with a contented sigh that vibrated through my chest.

Mate. Ours, she purred.

Yes, I agreed, and meant it with a fierceness that surprised me. If Derek tried to leave again, I would hunt him down and handcuff him to me. No more running. No more doubts. This was it.

Derek stirred, his arm stretching across my stomach like we'd done this a thousand times before, like his body had been crafted to fit against mine. It felt so natural. So right. Was this what Mai felt when she was with Ryan?

I turned slowly, careful not to wake him, planning to untangle myself, but the moment I moved, Derek's fingers twitched against my hip, his eyes snapping open, already alert.

"Hmm." The sound rumbled from his chest, his voice rough with sleep and something else that sent heat racing down my spine. His eyes focused, sharpening as they found mine. His lips curved into that half-smirk that had always undone me.

"Morning, gorgeous."

Goddess, did I love that. The sound of his voice first thing in the morning, the smell of him, hot and muzzy with sleep. His eyes on me like I was everything he'd dreamed of, and he'd woken to find I wasn't a dream after all.

"How are you feeling?" His hand reached up to stroke my cheek as his eyes searched mine. "No regrets?"

Did I regret what we'd done? Did I want to wind back time and stop myself from sealing our mate bond? Hell no. But words were easy. Actions were what mattered now. Starting with this whole situation with the USB.

"No regrets," I whispered softly. "But us, you and me, we start here. I want you to tell me everything."

"Everything?"

My fingers traced the hard line of his jaw, still in awe that I could touch him whenever I wanted.

"No more secrets, Derek. That was the deal. Start with why they want this USB back so badly."

He exhaled slowly, dragging a hand through his already chaotic hair. His expression shifted, all traces of sleep vanishing as he laid out the truth about Victor Kane, Simon Webster, and what Waylen had found on the USB.

"Wait." I pushed myself up on one elbow. "A decorated officer like Kane working with a witch? Why would someone so aggressively pro-human align with what he'd consider an abomination?"

Derek mirrored my position, his eyes never leaving mine as he twined a strand of my hair between his fingers.

"Because hatred makes strange bedfellows. They want the same endgame—Shifters controlled, tamed, stripped of power and freedom." His voice hardened. "Caged or eliminated."

My mind raced, connecting dots. Lucian's politician talking about segregation in the conclave cities. Mrs. Patterson's asshole son, Don, wanting her to move out of Three Rivers, a place she'd lived her entire life.

"They're manufacturing a war," I said, the realization crystallizing with sickening clarity. "Creating just enough fear, just enough chaos to turn humans against us. Frame us as dangerous, unpredictable predators." Heat burned under my skin as the full picture emerged. "And once public opinion turns..."

"It's open season," Derek finished, his hand stilling in my hair. He leaned forward, pressing his lips to my forehead, his breath warm against my skin. "Yeah."

That single word confirmed my fears. I'd wanted him to tell me I was overreacting, that it wasn't as bad as it seemed. But the grim certainty in his voice left no room for comforting lies.

"So, what's the plan?" I asked, hating the slight tremor in my voice.

"Protect you. Protect Three Rivers. Then we hit back." His jaw set in that stubborn line I knew too well.

I tilted my head. "You know, for a hot-shot intelligence guru, that's not a very detailed plan."

His smile tugged at the corner of his lips. "In my defense, I have been somewhat distracted."

My eyes traveled down his face, lingering on the fullness of his lips, the sharp cut of his jaw, the powerful expanse of his chest—his body that somehow belonged to me now.

"Mmmm." He wasn't the only one who could get distracted.

"We have to go back," I said. All thoughts of staying here or heading south were gone. Three Rivers was my home, and it needed me. "I won't let them take it from us."

Before Derek could respond, the door swung open with a slow, deliberate creak. Darla appeared, balancing an enormous silver tray piled with enough food to feed a small Pack. Her arctic-blue eyes swept the room, a knowing smirk playing at her lips.

"Well," she drawled, one perfectly shaped eyebrow arching toward her hairline, "looks like you two had an interesting night."

Heat flooded my face as I finally registered the devastation surrounding us. Lucian's meticulously organized office resembled a war zone. Papers carpeted the floor like snow. His imposing desk listed to one side, a jagged crack splitting one leg. A shattered tablet lay discarded against the far wall.

Even the leather couch beneath us hadn't escaped—cushions askew, frame slightly off-kilter, the blanket barely preserving our modesty. My stomach dropped as I imagined Lucian—obsessively orderly, pathologically precise Lucian—seeing what we'd done to his sanctuary.

A pulse of amusement radiated through me that wasn't mine. I whipped my head toward Derek, narrowing my eyes. I couldn't tell if he found the destruction hilarious or my mortification entertaining, but the fact that I could feel his emotions coursing through me like they were my own was unsettling. This bond thing was going to require serious adjustment.

Derek shot me a quick grin, laughter dancing in his eyes, making me think he knew precisely what I was feeling, too.

Damn it.

He stretched with feline grace, entirely unconcerned by the destruction or our audience.

"Worth it," he murmured, pressing his lips to my forehead. "Lucian can bill me for the damages."

"Bill you?" Darla snorted, setting the tray down on the only stable corner of a side table. "That's adorable. Lucian doesn't bill—he murders. Slowly. Artistically."

Derek shrugged, clearly unfazed.

"So," she said, eyeing a painting hanging at a precarious angle, "I take it you won't be staying with us. You made your decision, yes?"

I lifted my chin and smiled, but before I could reply, Derek's phone buzzed. His face was grim as he snatched the phone off the floor.

"Derek, you got incoming!" Sam's voice blared through the line, tight with urgency. "You have to move. Now!"

Chapter Thirty-Nine

DEREK

Darla was already out the door, barking orders into her own phone.

I tossed Sofia her clothes while yanking my shirt over my head. A thunderous crash echoed from downstairs, the door shuddering in its frame.

"Sofia." I held my hand out as she skimmed into her jeans. She looked up at me, her eyes wide and fearful.

Before she could take my hand, I pivoted, shielding her body with mine as the door burst open and Lucian strode in.

His gaze swept the room in a single, razor-sharp assessment. "We're under attack. You two need to go." His voice remained ice-cold, not a hint of panic. Good to know he could handle pressure.

"They're here for us," explained Sofia.

Lucian dismissed this with a flick of his wrist. "I know who they are and what they want. We'll hold them off."

I hesitated, torn between getting Sofia to safety and wanting to rip apart anyone who thought they could attack my mate.

Lucian's eyes locked on mine. "I'll take care of them. Your job is to look after her."

Sofia's hand slipped into mine, warm and certain.

Another explosion rocked the building, closer this time. I felt Sofia flinch against me, and my wolf surged forward, hackles raised. The sounds of battle spilled up the stairway as one of Lucian's bouncers staggered through the doorway, clutching his temple. Blood painted half his face crimson.

"Boss!" the man choked out.

Darla materialized behind him, her sharp features tight with fury. She ignored the bouncer, zeroing in on Lucian. "I need to get you to a secure location."

"And miss all the fun?" Lucian replied coolly. "Not a chance."

"For fuck's sake, Lucian! Why can't you be the easy brother to guard? You got any idea how sick I am of this shit?" Darla's eyes swept over Sofia and landed on me. "You still here?"

"No," I said, already moving, pulling Sofia after me, her hand still in mine. We sprinted down the stairs, walls vibrating faintly with each new sound of impact from outside.

"When we get out of this," I ordered, glancing back at her, "you're going to tell me exactly what Stone is."

Her fiery eyes narrowed on the edge of a challenge I could almost taste. Good. I wanted her angry, not scared.

"Focus on getting us out, Shaw."

Right.

At the bottom of the stairs, I signaled Sofia to hang back. I cracked open the door, nostrils flaring.

The stairwell door opened onto a dance club floor. In the dim emergency lighting, I could make out a figure heading toward us, rifle ready.

I struck before he could react, my hand clamping over his mouth as I dragged him back up the steps. A quick, precise twist, and he crumpled silently to the floor.

"This way," Sofia whispered, tugging my hand as I lifted her over the body. "Through the dance floor—there's an exit at the far left wall."

We ran across the dance floor as more soldiers swept in from the right.

"Stay behind me," I breathed, then launched forward.

The first soldier spotted us, his rifle snapping up. Too slow. I clamped down on the barrel, wrenching it sideways while driving my palm into his throat. He dropped without a sound.

Another flash of movement—Sofia ducking as a soldier lunged. Her instincts were sharp, her foot lashing out to shatter his kneecap. As he fell, I grabbed his vest and slammed him against a column hard enough to crack plaster.

The next two went down before they could raise their weapons—a throat strike for one, an arm lock and a head slam for the other. The fifth managed a wild shot before my elbow connected with his temple. Six and seven came together. I dropped low, sweeping one's legs while using the other's tactical vest to hurl him into a nearby table.

Gunfire erupted from across the club. Bullets shattered the mirrored wall panels, sending shards cascading onto the dance floor. Shouts and screams pierced through the silence.

Sofia cursed, grabbing my wrist. "Exit's blocked!"

I scanned the room. More soldiers piled in, fanning out in a disciplined formation, cutting off every direct route.

"Back through the fight club!" I ordered, already maneuvering us toward the western archway.

We sprinted down the hallway as another round of gunfire burst behind us. I yanked Sofia against a pillar, shielding us both with my body as bullets ricocheted off the concrete walls.

"Go!" I shoved her ahead, turning just in time to intercept another soldier vaulting over the club railing above. He landed in a low roll, fluid as hell. I met him mid-motion, driving my knee into his ribs and twisting his rifle free while my elbow cracked into his nose. Blood spattered the floor. Another soldier reached for his radio, but Sofia snagged a liquor bottle from a nearby ledge and smashed it against his skull.

She grinned breathlessly at me. "Not just a pretty face, Shaw."

I grabbed her hand, dragging her through the maze of hallways toward the fight club entrance.

Almost there.

Then, from the far end of the corridor, another wave of soldiers surged forward. No more than ten feet between us.

Shit.

Men. Dozens of them. Streaming into the room in steady, measured movements. Their tactical uniforms were darker than the shadows they emerged from, their weapons gleaming with lethal promise. They swarmed forward, spreading into a formation that boxed us into the center of the room.

I heard Sofia's sharp inhale, felt the edge of her panic through the bond. She pressed against my side. I adjusted instantly, moving to shield her.

"Stay close."

The first man stepped forward, his rifle raised.

Lucian strode onto the aerial balcony, his figure bathed in the dim light.

"Welcome to my club, gentlemen. Unfortunately, we are closed, so I'm going to have to insist you leave."

Half the guns snapped up to target him.

"No? Oh, well." A ripple moved beneath his skin.

Sofia stiffened beside me. "Oh, boy..."

What the hell?

"Er, there was something I meant to tell you—" Sofia's whisper died in her throat as her eyes widened.

The nearest soldier fired at him. The bullet never landed. Before it could hit, Lucian *Shifted*.

His limbs lengthened. Scales—fuck off, steel-colored scales—erupted across his body in a metallic wave, muscles stretching as massive wings unfurled from his back, cracking the air with raw power. The moment his talons scraped the metal rail, flames spewed from his maw, curling through the air in a violent inferno.

Pure, unrestrained destruction.

The soldiers scrambled back, but it was too late. Lucian's fire slammed into them, incinerating the front line before they could so much as scream. The heat seared against my skin even from across the room.

Fucking. Hell.

"We need to go. Now!" I grabbed Sofia's arm, pulling her through the chaos, dodging flaming debris as Lucian tore through the room from above.

Gunshots rang out, but they were drowned by the roar of the fire.

Smoke filled the air, cutting visibility to almost nothing.

Somewhere above, the dragon unleashed another roar, the sound shaking the walls and my bones alike.

We dove through the nearest exit just as a section of ceiling collapsed. Sofia stumbled, but I caught her, holding her tight until we broke free into the cool morning air.

We didn't stop until we were clear of the building, our breaths ragged and mingling with the city's faint hum. Sofia stood beside me, hand pressed to her chest, her wide eyes staring back at the inferno Lucian had made of his sanctuary.

I turned to her and raised an eyebrow. "A dragon, Sofia? A fuck-off dragon?"

CHAPTER FORTY

SOFIA

We'd torn out of the city, Derek's SUV swallowing the highway while fire engines and police cars screamed past in the opposite direction.

I couldn't believe Lucian had torched his entire club. A successful business. One of many, but still.

"Lucian and Darla," I said, my voice calmer than I felt. "Do you think they're—?"

Derek glanced at me. "Oh, I'm sure they're fine. Lucian's a dragon. Darla's with him. She's mean enough to make the devil apologize. They're not the ones I'm worried about."

Okay. He was probably right. The guilt gnawed at me, anyway.

"You're handling the whole 'dragon Shifters are real' revelation remarkably well," I ventured carefully.

"I just watched a man turn into a goddamned dragon. And burn down a building. 'Well' isn't in my emotional vocabulary right now."

"Well, you haven't driven us into a ditch yet, so that's something."

"Exactly how long have you known?"

I hesitated, my fingers curling against the seatbelt. "About Lucian and Darla?"

"Yeah."

"Since the night before they left Three Rivers."

He blew air out through his lips. "That's over a year."

"Mmm," I agreed. Small noises seemed safest right now.

"And you didn't think the Pack's intelligence officer deserved this information because...?"

"Well..."

"Don't stop, Sofia. I really want to hear this."

"I... Look, Lucian posed zero threat to the Pack. He saved my life. It was need-to-know, and you didn't, um..."

Derek's face darkened. "Need to know?" His voice had dropped dangerously low.

Warning bells clanged in my head.

"Er, no."

"Is there anything else that you didn't think I needed to know? If there is, now is the time to spill."

Hmmm. I twisted in my seat so I could get a good look at him.

His eyes flicked to me. "What?"

"Just waiting to see if your head explodes."

"Seriously?"

"Not so fun being kept in the dark, is it?"

He shot me a quizzical look.

"Not knowing the whole story."

"Sofia—" The growl in his voice vibrated through me.

I held up my hands in a peace gesture. "No, there's nothing else I've been hiding. What about you? Anything else you want to tell me? If there is, now is the time to spill."

"You're impossible, you know that, right?"

"And yet you still haven't pulled over and left me on the side of the road. Fascinating."

"Don't tempt me," he muttered, but there was no heat behind it.

Derek's phone buzzed on the console. His eyes flicked toward the phone, then to me for a brief second before he put it on speaker.

"Sam," he said curtly, his voice gruff. No pleasantries. No hesitation.

"You clear?"

"Yes."

"Sofia with you?"

"I'm here, Sam." I leaned toward the phone. "I'm okay."

"Thank the Goddess." Sam exhaled audibly. "I would say welcome to the family, Sofia, but let's be honest, you've always been family."

I blinked. What was he going on about? "Family?"

"Your mate bond with Derek. It sealed. Congratulations, although I hope you know what you're getting into. You do know he leaves his smelly socks just lying around the house, right?"

I glanced at Derek, momentarily stunned. "How did he—?"

Derek gave a casual shrug, his eyes fixed on the road. "He's my twin. He knows stuff."

"He's not wrong," Sam said. "I know everything. But I'm serious, Sofia. You've always been part of this family. I don't know what he did to finally persuade you to give him a chance, but he's one lucky bastard, and I know he'll do anything to make you happy."

What did that mean? Did he know when Derek and I fooled around? Did he *feel* what we felt?

Heat blazed up my neck. "When you say 'know everything'…"

Derek caught my eye and grinned, shaking his head slightly.

"Any updates on Kane?" Derek pivoted smoothly.

"Waylen's got a contingent of Kane's forces tracked to a location about an hour north of Cornwall on an old airfield. He's been hacking into their comms, but he's treading lightly. Looks like they're mobilizing."

"For an attack?"

Sam hesitated. "Yeah. We've got six hours, Derek. Maybe less. They're set to move just before dusk. Their target is Three Rivers."

The words punched the air from my lungs. My hand shot to the armrest, gripping it like it would keep me grounded.

Sam continued, "We've got a strike team assembling to intercept, but we'll need everyone we can get. The location's about three hours from where you are. Can you get there?"

"Send me the coordinates," Derek said without hesitation.

"Sure," Sam replied. "Sofia, you want to head back to Three Rivers? Ryan's staying put. He'll protect the Pack if we fail. I can arrange for a car to meet you and bring you back."

Derek's response was instant. "She goes where I go."

My mouth clicked shut as a warm feeling spread across my chest. He really did mean it when he said he wasn't going to leave me.

"Well," Sam replied, his tone laced with amusement, "I guess that's sorted. I'll see you both soon. Try not to do anything that makes Sofia want to unseal the bond on the way, bro."

Derek's eyes flicked to mine. "I'll see what I can do. Later."

Derek touched the red button, leaving just me and him.

"You know," I teased, "when I said I didn't want you to leave me again, I think I could make an exception if you're heading into high-risk situations where we might end up, oh, I don't know—dead."

Derek's lips twitched, the ghost of a smirk threatening to break through his otherwise stern expression. "You're mine, Sofia," he said. "I'm not letting you out of my sight again."

The simplicity of his words, the raw conviction behind them, made something that had been held tight in my chest unfurl. He really meant it. Maybe I could trust him. Maybe I was worth staying for.

CHAPTER FORTY-ONE

SOFIA

The car jolted to a stop, waking me from an uneasy sleep. We'd pulled into a mall parking lot, its fluorescent sign buzzing faintly.

"What are we doing here?"

Derek killed the engine, one arm draped casually over the steering wheel. "We need supplies. And you need clothes."

Supplies. Right. I opened my mouth to argue, to insist that we didn't have time for detours, but then I caught sight of my reflection in the side mirror. My shirt was smeared with soot from the club, my jeans had a tear near the knee—I had no idea how that had happened—and my shoes... well, one of them had a burn mark near the toe. Not exactly the outfit of someone ready to take on the world—or Kane's army.

I sighed. "I don't have my cards on me, and you got rid of my phone, remember?"

Derek's lips twitched, the barest hint of a smirk playing at the corner of his mouth. "You weren't gonna pay for any of it."

"Derek—"

"Come on, we don't have time to argue about it."

He was right. Annoyingly. I unclipped my seatbelt and slid out of the car. The mall was quiet; the early hour meant it was mostly empty except for the occasional jogger or those grabbing coffee.

Derek guided me into a clothing shop, the kind with racks of overpriced items and soft ambient lighting. I made a beeline for a shelf of plain black T-shirts, determined to get in and out as quickly as possible, but Derek's hand on my elbow stopped me before I could start picking through sizes.

"Let me," he said simply, with the kind of confidence that didn't leave room for debate.

I watched, half-amused and half-bewildered, as Derek walked the aisles with the efficiency of a soldier on a mission. He didn't ask me my size. He didn't consult me on colors or styles. He just started grabbing things—jeans, T-shirts, a cute waist-cut jacket.

"You know, I'm perfectly capable of dressing myself," I said, crossing my arms as he tossed a pair of combat boots into the growing pile in his arms.

He didn't pause, just glanced at me over his shoulder, one brow raised. "I noticed. But you've been rocking the post-apocalypse look for hours now, and if we are going to do this, you're going to need the right clothes."

I scowled. He remained infuriatingly unaffected.

"Besides, you'll argue with me if I ask your opinion on every item, and we'll be here all day. This is faster."

My eyes narrowed. He wasn't wrong, and that was part of what made him so annoying.

I trailed after him, my arms itching to wrest the pile of clothes away from him and do things my way, but there was something calculating about the way he moved through the store that piqued my curiosity. He wasn't just guessing, wasn't just grabbing things at random—he was choosing items deliberately, like he'd memorized my entire body.

"How do you even know my size?"

Derek paused, holding up a pair of dark-wash jeans as if to confirm his choice. He didn't look at me when he answered. "I pay attention. Especially if it has anything to do with you."

And there was that unfurling feeling again. I wasn't entirely sure I liked it. I'd held tight to my rock, to the belief that I could only count on myself. It was scary to think of someone else knowing me so well.

"Here, try these on," Derek said as we passed a changing room. He opened the door, hung up the clothes, and gestured for me to go inside. I hesitated for a second. Derek grinned.

"Not convinced I know your measurements, huh? How about we make this interesting?" His voice dropped to that register that made my skin tingle. "If I got it right on every single item in there, you have to tell me one fantasy. Something you've always wanted to do sexually but never admitted to anyone."

I froze, the possibilities flashing through my mind. Heat bloomed in my chest, spreading up my neck. "A fantasy?"

His eyes darkened. "The kind that keeps you up at night. The kind you think about when you're alone."

My mouth went dry. The look in his eyes told me exactly what he'd do with that information.

"And if you get even one thing wrong?" I managed to ask.

"Then I'll tell you mine." His gaze traveled slowly down my body and back up. "In explicit detail."

The thought of confessing the things I imagined him doing to me made my heart pound wildly. I wasn't sure I could say those things out loud, but I absolutely wanted to know his fantasies.

"Deal," I said, surprised at how steady my voice sounded.

I slipped into the changing room and shut the door in his wolfish face. We didn't have much time, so I flew through the clothes as quickly as a girl could, getting more and more annoyed. The clothes fit me perfectly. Every single fucking one of them. How did he do it? Was this some sort of previously unknown werewolf superpower? Derek could make a fortune as a personal shopper. The image of him striding around a department store, pointing at items and saying, "That one!" to a long line of assistants who hurried after him, arms full of clothes, popped into my head, and I had to stifle a laugh.

"All good in there?" His voice was smug. He knew he had everything right.

Damn it.

By the time I came out wearing dark blue jeans that clung to my hips like they were custom made, Derek was leaning against the opposite wall, typing into his phone.

He looked me up and down as I came out, then did a twirl motion with his finger. I obliged.

"You look beautiful."

I smiled.

"So?"

"You got everything right."

His grin turned smug.

"Except the white T-shirt. It was too small."

Derek's eyes flickered to the shirt in my hands.

"Show me," he ordered.

"We don't have time, Derek." I went to walk past him, but he caught my arm gently.

"I got a lot riding on this. We have time."

"Fine." I stomped back into the changing room and swapped T-shirts. The white one fit perfectly. I examined myself in the mirror. Was there any way to make it look smaller?

Nope. Damn it!

Alright then, there was only one thing for it. I flung open the door and twirled faster than a ballerina on her sixth coffee of the morning.

"You see? Too small, Derek! Just admit it, you lose. I win. Now I get to hear your fantasy in all its glory."

His eyebrows shot up. "That eager to know what I think about late at night?"

"Yes. I need all the details."

"As much as I would enjoy sharing that, I don't think so. Turn around and look in the mirror, gorgeous. The T-shirt is a perfect fit for your perfect body."

Mmmm. I did like it when he said that.

He moved up behind me, close enough that if he breathed, his body would touch mine. His voice, when he spoke, was all deep and growly, and it sent a pulse of pleasure right to my core.

"Looks like I win, Sofia. I know exactly how that body of yours fits in clothes. Now I want to know exactly what you imagine me doing to it when no one's watching."

I felt my panties get wet. Okay, maybe it wouldn't be so bad if I lost.

"Fine," I said, crossing my arms.

In the mirror, I saw his grin widen. "You don't have to tell me now. But when I ask—and I will—I expect the truth. Every. Delicious. Detail."

Chapter Forty-Two

SOFIA

The meeting point was an old fishing dock, fifteen minutes from where Waylen thought Kane was amassing his troops. The dock was long abandoned and slowly being reclaimed by nature. Wooden planks were warped from years of rain and neglect, while a handful of crooked shacks sat further back from the river, their peeling paint blending into the marshland like forgotten ghosts. The river itself stretched out in front of us, dark and steady, its surface smooth as glass.

It felt like the kind of place where things disappeared.

I cracked open my window, and a cold wind rolled off the water, carrying the scent of mud and reeds.

"They're late."

Sam had texted the coordinates and let us know that my brother was coming with him. I wasn't sure how I felt about that. No matter how quickly Jase climbed the enforcer ranks, I would always worry about him.

"I'm sure they're fine. Sam's with Jase, along with twenty of our best enforcers."

I looked at him out of the side of my eye. Did he know what I was thinking because he felt my worry along the mate bond?

"No, I just know you."

Derek saw my expression and grinned. "I don't need the mate bond to know you love your brother and will always be looking out for him."

Okay, point taken.

Waiting wasn't my strong suit. I paced along the dock, eyes constantly scanning the access road. My muscles ached, my body still running high on adrenaline, but exhaustion was creeping in at the edges.

"Here." Derek pulled out a slim black phone from his back pocket and handed it to me. "Something to distract you."

I blinked at it before taking it, turning it over in my hands. "What's this?"

"Replacement for the one I got rid of."

I unlocked the screen. The basics were already set up—contacts loaded, settings adjusted. Just like my old phone. I swallowed past the sudden tightness in my throat and tapped Mai's name. The line barely rang once before her voice came through, exasperated and sharp.

"Where the hell have you been? I need my pickled jalapeños! Ryan is refusing to buy them; some bullshit about spicy foods being bad for acid reflux in pregnancy. I need them, Sofia!"

Despite everything, I grinned. "Ah-ha! I knew you kept me around for something."

"Sofia, seriously, where the hell have you been? I'm going insane stuck in this bed, and Ryan won't tell me anything."

"Ryan's just trying to keep you from stressing out," I hedged, twirling a loose thread in my sleeve. "Things got a little complicated, but I'm okay."

There was a long, tired sigh. "Yeah, you not telling me anything either doesn't make me feel any better."

I bit back a laugh. "I promise I'm fine."

"Are you at least gonna come over with my jalapeños?"

I hesitated, my eyes flicking to Derek.

"Not yet," I admitted. "I have to handle something first."

Mai made an irritated sound. "That's vague and incredibly unhelpful."

I sighed, wishing I could give her more. "Just focus on resting, okay? You've got two little pups to think about."

"If I don't give birth soon, I'm murdering someone. Probably Ryan." She groaned. "Do you know how ridiculous he's being?"

"Oh, I can imagine."

"No, Sofia. You can't. He tried to stop me from going to the bathroom by myself yesterday. Said it was too risky."

I snorted. "Well, you did faint mid—"

"Do *not* finish that sentence!"

Laughter bubbled up in me, warm and easy. "That kind of trauma sticks with a man, chickie. At least you've got Wally keeping you sane."

As if summoned, Wally's voice came through the phone. "If by keeping her sane, you mean providing endless entertainment with my superior gossiping abilities, then yes, I am an absolute delight."

"Between him, Thomas, and Ryan, they've basically turned my bedrest into a three-man babysitting operation."

"That's because you don't listen, darling," Wally drawled. "Do you have any idea how hard it is to keep someone in bed when they've got the attention span of a caffeinated squirrel?"

"I do not have the attention span of a squirrel!"

"Mm-hmm," Thomas' deep voice finally chimed in, full of quiet amusement. "That's why you tried to sneak out the window yesterday?"

I nearly choked on my laugh. "Mai, you didn't!"

"It wasn't that high up!" she insisted.

I could sense the waves of amusement rolling off Derek at our conversation.

"Mai, you're pregnant!"

"As I keep telling everyone, that doesn't make me an invalid all of a sudden. I'm a werewolf. The babies are werewolves. Besides, I needed out of here to get some jalapeños and peanut butter, and Ryan has enforcers stationed at every door in the house."

"Ryan is going to lose his mind," I muttered.

"Oh, he already has," Wally said cheerfully. "Thomas spent two full hours last night talking him down from locking Mai in the safe room. He even wanted her to deliver in there!"

"And I'm still not convinced it isn't a fucking awesome idea!" Ryan shouted from somewhere in the background.

I shook my head, warmth and longing tangling together in my chest. This was home. This chaos, this family we'd built in Three Rivers.

"I really do miss you, Sof," Mai's voice whispered.

"I miss you too," I admitted, gripping the phone a little tighter.

"Promise you'll be back soon?"

"I'll try," I said, and we both knew it wasn't the same as a promise.

I hit *end* on the call as Derek's warm arms pulled me close.

"I'll get you back before the pups are born," his voice rumbled against my cheek.

I nodded against his chest and let myself sink into him. He smelled of home, of safety, of Derek.

"You hungry?" I asked.

"I could eat."

I walked to the SUV and opened the passenger door, rummaging through supplies we'd picked up earlier. My fingers brushed against something small and plastic, and I pulled it out.

A Darth Vader USB.

I turned slowly, raising an eyebrow at Derek, who was watching me with a carefully neutral expression. "Is this the same one you stole from Sam? I thought it was back in Three Rivers?"

Derek crossed his arms. "Waylen commandeered the one I borrowed. He's still working on it. Figured I'd get Sam a replacement."

I smirked, turning the USB over in my fingers. "My new phone. Now this. You do realize this is an apology gift, right?"

Derek frowned. "It's a replacement."

"For the one you stole."

"The one I borrowed."

I arched an eyebrow again. "Oh, this is rich. Derek Shaw, international man of mystery, combat expert, Pack spy master... incapable of just saying sorry."

His scowl deepened, but there was the slightest twitch at the corner of his mouth. "He doesn't need an apology. He needs a working USB."

"You even got him the same one. That's basically the werewolf equivalent of flowers and a hug."

Derek exhaled sharply, staring out at the water as if willing the conversation to end. "It's his favorite. Ever since we were seventeen, whenever he's bought a USB, it's always had to be a Darth Vader one. I figured... I don't know. Whatever."

I tilted my head. "You really miss him, don't you?"

Derek didn't answer.

Something in my chest tightened. "I know you haven't been getting on, but he's still your twin, still your brother."

Derek let out a soft scoff.

I nudged his arm with my elbow. "Maybe you two should just sit down and talk. Use your words. You remember words, right?"

He glared at me. "You're enjoying this."

"A little." I grinned. "But only because it's adorable watching you struggle with emotional vulnerability when I'm not on the other end of it."

"I should've left you locked in the car," Derek muttered, rubbing a hand over his face.

I smirked, popping the USB into his hand before stepping back toward the SUV. I grabbed a protein bar for Derek and an apple for me, then hopped up onto the hood of the car, stretching my legs out as I bit into the crisp fruit.

Derek's phone buzzed, and he pulled it out, glancing at the screen. He answered and put it on speaker, even though he knew I could hear the conversation perfectly well without it.

"You're late."

"No shit," Sam's voice crackled over the line, frustration laced in his tone. "We hit a snag. We're about an hour out."

"Cuts it close, but we should still have time to stop Kane before he moves."

Derek's phone buzzed again, and he sighed. "Hold on." He pressed a few buttons, merging the calls. "Waylen, you're on speaker with me and Sam."

"Wow, look at that. Shaw's finally picking up my calls. Must be a special occasion."

"Waylen." Derek's voice held a hint of exasperation.

"Yeah, yeah, get to it, I know." I could hear Waylen tapping on his keyboard. "Kane's people just moved up their departure. New ETD is twenty minutes."

Derek swore under his breath. I stiffened, my grip tightening around the apple in my hand.

Sam exhaled sharply on the other end. "Shit. We're still an hour out."

"Yeah, well, Kane didn't get the memo. And it gets better." Waylen's voice carried that particular edge it got when he was delivering bad news with a side of sarcasm. "They're splitting up. Sending squads in different directions, hitting Three Rivers from multiple angles."

"How many squads?" Derek asked.

"Latest intel suggests at least six."

"Can you track them?"

"Of course I can track them." Waylen said it the same way an Olympic butterfly gold medalist would say, 'Of course I can swim.' "That's not the point. The point, gentlemen, is that Sam does not have enough people with him to set up six different roadblocks and hit them all before they reach us. You have to stop them *before* they leave."

"We're too far out. Derek, you'll need to stall them."

Derek turned to me, his eyes sharp with calculations. I knew he was going to ask me to hide, to wait for Sam while he went in there. Alone.

"Don't," I warned him.

"Sofia," Sam cut in, knowing in that eerie twin way exactly what was going on with his brother. "You're a barista."

"Yeah, and?"

"You make coffee." His tone wasn't condescending, but it was firm. "I know you fought during the battle with Brock's army. I know you held your own. But this? This is different. All of them are military-trained, and they'll have weapons. This isn't the place for you. Let Derek handle this so he can concentrate on what needs to be done and not on protecting you."

I took a slow breath, then pushed it out.

"These people are coming to attack my Pack, my home. Mai is there, Mrs. Patterson is there, Julie and Brian are there. From what I've seen, they will do anything to stop the information on the USB from getting out. And if they do, then what? They want the world to think we're dangerous animals. We will be killed, caged, or kept as pets. They're dividing our communities, destroying our homes, and turning our neighbors against us. They're coming for us. It may not be open warfare yet, but it's warfare, all the same."

I stared at Derek as I continued, needing him to hear me on this. "We let this happen when we stand by and do nothing. I'm done feeling helpless. I'm done feeling like I have no power, that I have no control over the events that shape my life, my Pack. I will not stand by and watch them tear apart everything I believe in. I fight."

Sam was silent on the phone. Derek reached out with one hand, hooked his fingers around my neck, and pulled me to him. He placed a kiss on my temple, and I knew I'd won this one. Sam knew it too.

He exhaled sharply. "Goddess, you're a pain in the ass."

I grinned. "That's the spirit."

"Alright, then. I've got plans to make."

Waylen sighed. "Don't die, be careful, all that crap. I'll keep monitoring their comms and send you updates. Just... don't get yourselves killed. I like Sofia. The Shaw twins? You guys are growing on me. Kinda."

The line clicked as Waylen disconnected.

"We'll be coming in hot," Sam said. "Stall them. Don't die, or I'll be extremely pissed off."

"I'll do my best," Derek replied.

He hung up and looked at me, a muscle in his jaw twitching.

"We go together," I said, my voice firm. I knew he wasn't done trying to persuade me. He didn't have to like it, but if this was going to work, he couldn't tie me up and leave me behind anymore.

"Sofia—"

"We go together," I repeated.

"Fuck!"

I grinned. I knew I'd won.

"I don't know what you're smiling about. We're probably both gonna die."

The smile slid off my face. Oh. Right.

Chapter Forty-Three

DEREK

The abandoned airfield loomed ahead, a skeletal remnant of a time long past. Rusted fences lined the perimeter, curling in places where nature had begun to reclaim its territory. Cracked asphalt stretched in long, jagged lines, leading toward the hulking remains of hangars and the control tower standing like a silent sentinel against the dusk sky.

There was no time for tactical planning; we just had to get in there and see if Kane would talk to us. He always did like to talk, and if I baited him enough, maybe we could stall them.

Sofia sat rigidly beside me, hands knotted in her lap. She hadn't spoken in the last five minutes, but I could feel the tension radiating off her in waves.

"Sofia—"

"Don't even think about pulling over and asking me to get out here. I'm coming with you. I might be a barista, I might not be the best fighter, my instincts might stink, but we're all that's standing between Three Rivers and an army that wants to eliminate us from the face of the earth. You stop me from fighting for my home, my Pack, and I'll never forgive you, Derek. Never."

Alright, then.

"If things go south, you run, Sofia. Promise me this. I give you the signal, you get the hell out of there."

She studied my face for a moment, then nodded. "Okay. I promise."

Thank fuck for that.

"So, do you at least have a plan?"

I rolled my shoulders, my fingers tightening around the steering wheel. "Maybe."

Her sharp green eyes narrowed. "Maybe?"

I glanced at the Darth Vader USB sitting in the console between us. "Depends on how much Kane likes surprises."

"So we're winging it?"

"We're adapting."

"Adapting sounds a lot like making shit up as we go."

I smirked. "That's what I said."

The headlights illuminated the chain-link gate ahead, where two guards stood, assault rifles slung across their chests. They straightened as we approached, one raising a hand to signal us to stop.

I killed the engine and exhaled, letting my wolf settle beneath my skin. He wanted out—wanted to tear these men apart before they could threaten our mate, our Pack. But not yet. Not now.

One guard stepped up to my window. He was built like a brick wall, his dark tactical vest straining over his shoulders. A recent sunburn peeled across his nose, suggesting he'd been stationed outside for days. When he leaned in, I caught the scent of energy drinks and cinnamon gum. He was probably fighting to stay alert at the end of his shift.

"State your business."

I kept my expression neutral. "We're here to see Kane."

"You think you can just roll up and get an audience with the boss?"

I held up the USB. Light from the dying sun caught the black plastic, making Vader's helmet gleam.

"I have information he's going to want. And he's not going to be happy if you waste time by keeping us out here."

He hesitated, then nodded. "Step out of the car. Both of you."

Sofia and I moved in unison, both getting out with slow, measured movements. I could smell her nervousness, though she kept her face carefully composed.

The other guard was leaner, wiry, with sharp eyes that flicked between Sofia and me. His scent was filled with coffee and stale cigarettes, his deodorant failing to mask either. He kept his gun trained on us; it looked like a standard SIG Sauer M18 but with a slightly wider barrel. We'd used something similar in Echo Command, and my guess was it had been modified for tranquilizer bullets. If so, the magazine would be able to hold ten rounds before he would have to replace it. Was this standard issue for Kane's men? Ten rounds would down even the biggest Shifter.

The bigger guard, who I mentally nicknamed Brick, reached into a pouch on his belt, rummaging around with a frown. "You got any silver ties?"

The wiry guard grimaced. "We're out. They all got used on the others."

Others?

Silver was only used on Shifters.

Sofia picked up on it, too, and stiffened beside me.

"You'll have to use the plastic ones."

Brick snapped, "Hands out."

Every instinct screamed against letting them restrain me, but plastic wouldn't hold a werewolf for long. Despite knowing this, my wolf thrashed inside of me. It was Sofia. The thought of her bound, vulnerable to the humans here, made both him and me furious. Her lips pressed into a thin line, but she stepped forward and offered her wrists without hesitation. I looked at her, silently asking if she was sure, and she gave a barely perceptible nod.

I let them tighten the restraints around my own wrists. As soon as they were on, Brick radioed in, asking for an escort. Thirty seconds later, two more guards appeared: a tall woman with close-cropped blonde hair and hard eyes, and a stocky man with a ginger beard and burn scars along his neck. Both carried themselves with the alert readiness of seasoned veterans.

They led us through the gate and into the compound. The old airfield swarmed with activity, a war machine in motion. Barracks emptied in disciplined waves, soldiers moving with lethal efficiency. The scent of gun oil, sweat, and pre-battle adrenaline thickened the air.

I counted quickly. Thirty, maybe forty per squadron. Six squadrons visible, with more movement behind the massive hangar. Too many. Way more than expected.

"Five minutes to roll out!" a voice cut through the controlled chaos. "Gear check and load up!"

The guards steered us toward one of the hangars, its towering doors yawning open. Inside, the cavernous space had been stripped and repurposed. The high ceiling vanished into shadows, steel beams crisscrossing above, industrial lights buzzing with a harsh fluorescent glare. The concrete floor bore scuff marks from constant movement. Makeshift partitions carved the space into briefing areas, comms stations, and weapons racks.

We passed desk after desk, one with a half-eaten protein bar left on the keyboard. Another had a mug of coffee and a photo taped to a monitor of a golden retriever in a party hat. Cables snaked across the floor, bundled with zip ties. A trash bin overflowed with energy drink cans and ration wrappers.

Twenty men in this room alone. Another dozen in the corridor beyond. All armed. All ready.

The guards herded us deeper, through the nerve center of the operation. Here, officers were barking coordinates into headsets. A man clicked his pen against his teeth, eyes locked on a tablet. A woman with dark circles under her eyes blinked in quick succession, then applied eyedrops without missing a keystroke. There was a clear tang of gun oil mixed with printer toner and someone's too-strong cologne.

Analysts pounded keyboards, pulling up satellite feeds and terrain overlays. A printer spat out freshly marked maps, snapped up as fast as they appeared. And then, a screen.

Three Rivers. My territory. My Pack.

Bottley's glowed on the display, its entry points marked in red. Then, the enforcers' building and Alpha Compound. Finally, the Alpha House, where Mai was on bed rest, appeared.

Rage burned through me with every new image.

Sofia paused, her eyes wide as she stared at the screen. The stocky, ginger-bearded guard shoved her forward.

"Keep moving."

The contact was brief, just enough to make her stumble, but my vision went red.

Instantly, Sofia turned her head and gave it a quick shake in warning.

Not yet.

I forced down the urge to tear the guard apart, but I knew his scent. The way his boots scuffed against the floor. Later. I'd find him later.

The blonde guard stopped us at a reinforced door. "You wanted to see the boss?"

I nodded, steeling myself to see Kane again. I wanted to look that motherfucker in the eyes. I had to stall him long enough to let Sam get here, but then I could tear him apart.

Two quick knocks, then the guard pulled the door open.

I froze in the doorway, catching a scent I thought I would never smell again.

No.

The ghost of every nightmare I'd had for years stood there, flesh and blood and impossible. Same military stance. Same sharp eyes. Same scar above his left brow.

Not Kane.

Harris.

My wolf howled, the sound echoing through my skull until I couldn't think. Memories slammed into me: *Harris's blood on my hands, his last breath rattling in his chest, the weight of his body as life drained away.*

But he was here. Alive. Standing. Smirking.

The room spun. Was this part of my PTSD? Was I hallucinating Harris here? Fuck, I needed to be clear-headed right now. I couldn't let this happen. Couldn't let my mind betray me, not when Sofia's life was on the line. My legs locked to keep me upright as reality cracked around the edges.

Sofia shifted beside me, anchoring me to the present. She must have picked up that something was very wrong. Her fingers twitched against her restraints—ready to move, to fight. To protect me, even now.

Harris grinned, slow and easy.

"Derek Shaw." His voice was exactly as I remembered. "It's been a while."

He tilted his head, studying me with those calculating eyes. Not a memory. Not a hallucination. He was real.

"You look like you've seen a ghost." His smirk widened. "What's wrong, brother? Surprised to see me?"

Brother.

The word twisted in my gut.

I forced air into my lungs. Forced my voice steady. Forced everything down—the rage, the betrayal, the accumulation of years spent drowning in guilt.

"Harris."

One word. That's all I could manage without ripping his fucking head off.

Chapter Forty-Four

SOFIA

The man Derek had called Harris stood behind a steel desk. Six men stood around it, tablets and papers scattered across its surface like they'd been planning an invasion. Which, I supposed, they had been. Broad-shouldered with the solid build of someone who could probably open pickle jars without that little grunt most people make, he carried himself with the easy confidence of a man who rarely heard the word "no." He wore authority like other men wore cologne—too much and hoping you'd notice.

I recognized his type immediately—the same kind who'd order complicated drinks at Bottley Bar, then critique my technique while checking out my ass. But this couldn't be right. Derek had told me Harris was dead. He'd died trying to protect Derek.

"Aren't you supposed to be dead?"

Harris's attention snapped to me, his assessment clinical and cold. A muscle twitched in his jaw before his lips curved into something that wasn't quite a smile.

"Sorry to disappoint, sweetheart, but as you can see, I'm very much alive."

So, he was the man Derek had thought of as a brother. What the fuck was going on?

"Kane never blackmailed you, did he?" Derek was laser-focused on Harris. "He never had photos of your sister. It was a lie. You were working with Kane willingly. All along."

"And he finally catches on." Harris circled around the front of the desk and then leaned his ass on it. A radio crackled somewhere outside; orders being relayed, troops moving into position. Time slipping away from us.

"Yes, I was working with Kane. You were getting too close. When you found evidence linking me to him, I had to spin a tale you'd believe, buy us time to organize my exit. We had a witch in place for just that eventuality. And they earned their keep; they did a damn fine job of making it seem like I was dead."

Harris tapped his temple with two fingers. "You know, I had a bet with Kane that you'd work it out months ago. He insisted your brutish little brain wouldn't be able to connect the dots. Looks like he was right. That's one of the reasons I follow him, Derek. He sees how things really are."

Through our bond, I felt Derek's pain twist into something darker, more primal. The sensation crawled up my spine like icy fingers. Behind us, I heard the soft swish of one of the guard's weapons shifting against their side, readying.

"Why, brother?" Derek's voice was rough, like he had to force each word past his teeth. "Tell me why."

"Why? You really need to ask?" Harris's expression hardened, the facade of amusement falling away like a discarded mask. "The military was everything to me. I had no family, no friends where I came from.

No one except the brothers in our unit. I gave everything for them, for you. You were my family. And I worked twice as hard, trained twice as long, to show you what I could do, to prove I belonged there. But you got promoted to Captain over me. And then," he shook his head as if in disbelief, "it turns out you didn't even want it. I heard you on the phone, Derek. You'd submitted a request for an unqualified resignation just because the little bitch had run off her own parents. You were going to leave, to go back to her!"

I looked sharply at Derek, my heart stuttering. I had never known he'd asked to come home early when my parents left. He had tried to get back to me.

"It didn't matter that you got turned down," Harris continued. "You chose her over us. Everything I worked for, everything I ever wanted, and you were just going to throw it away. For what? A bit of Shifter pussy?

"So, no, Kane didn't have to recruit me; I went to him. He showed me your kind only have loyalty to each other. It's not your fault. It's in your DNA to betray anyone outside of your Pack. That's why you can't be trusted. Why you shouldn't be allowed to hold positions of power. You will always put Shifters first."

"Humans don't win if Shifters lose, Harris." Derek's voice dropped to a dangerous timbre. "We're not enemies competing for the same scraps. We're neighbors who've built something together worth protecting. We work together side-by-side, we shop in the same stores, attend the same schools." His eyes darkened. "The world you're talking about—where one side must dominate the other—that's not protection. That's you wanting people to live in fear just so you can have power over them all."

Derek took a step forward. "This war you and Kane are starting, it will result in the massacre of innocent people. Do you understand that? Not just Shifters—human families, too. People who trust you to protect them."

Harris shrugged, spreading his hands wide. "For the greater good. Disruption now benefits humanity in the long term. If you're strong enough, you'll survive, and you'll deserve to survive. If not? Well, if you're too weak to make it, you don't belong in the new order that's coming."

Through our bond, I felt Derek's anger building.

Harris must have sensed it, too, because his smile widened, as if Derek's rage was somehow invigorating him.

"I'm going to enjoy making you watch as we raze Three Rivers to the ground. The Pack you chose over me. I'm going to make sure not one person will be left alive."

He picked up one of the tablets on his desk, tapped it a few times, and the screen behind him powered up. I frowned, not sure what I was seeing, then my heart stopped.

A live feed from the airfield filled the screen, with the two guards who brought us here walking back to the gate in the lower left corner. Harris tapped his tablet again, and a new feed appeared. Steel cages were being wheeled out of another hangar. Inside each was a person, hands secured with zip ties. The camera feeds flickered, shifting perspectives.

More cages lined the airfield, row upon row of them. The picture zoomed in, and my breath hitched. They weren't human. Werewolves, their bodies trembling with violent spasms, their skin slick with sweat. Their eyes—Goddess, their eyes—burned red with fever, the whites bloodshot and ringed with deep, dark bruises.

Some of them were bent over, trying to Shift, their mouths open in silent screams. Others curled up, rocking back and forth, arms wrapped around themselves. One man slammed his head against the bars over and over. Blood streaked down his forehead, but he didn't seem to notice.

"Beautiful, aren't they?" Harris said, studying our reactions. "Fifty of our finest specimens. We've been dosing them with ripple for weeks, pushing the limits of what their bodies can handle. They're completely feral now—nothing of their old selves left at all."

Along our bond, I felt Derek's horror mirror my own as we watched soldiers securing the cages to flatbed trucks.

"You're going to release them in Three Rivers." My voice came out as a whisper.

"Of course. And when they're done with your precious Pack, we'll swoop in, the human heroes eliminating the threat." Harris leaned forward, eyes bright with purpose. "This is just a correction. Shifters seem to think they are part of some evolutionary process when, in fact, you're simply a chromosomal mistake. A genetic aberration that we are rectifying. Humans created civilization—laws, medicine, technology. Shifters have been wearing its benefits like borrowed clothes. In reality, though, you're still brutish animals. We're just showing the world what's always been there."

He gestured at the screen with casual pride. "Imagine the headlines: 'Werewolf Rampage Decimates Town.' Your interference actually came at the perfect moment. We needed somewhere to release them, and where better than a predominately Shifter town? If they kill everyone there, imagine what they'll do to a human town. We'll film it, of course, then release it across social media. The public will finally see what you really are—what you're capable of becoming. After that, they'll be begging us to put you down."

"They're sick," I protested, my eyes fixed on the screens. One of the werewolves caught my attention—a man who couldn't have been more than thirty. Wire-rimmed glasses lay broken on the cage floor, and his dirty, sweat-soaked dress shirt had the emblem Hedge End High School. A teacher, maybe. Someone who'd once stood in front of a classroom full of kids teaching them literature or algebra, who'd stayed late to help struggling students, who'd written college recommendation letters and chaperoned proms.

Now, he threw himself against the bars, howling in mindless rage. His muscles bulged unnaturally beneath his torn shirt, veins black and prominent against his too-pale skin. But it was his eyes that haunted me—bloodshot and wild, yet somewhere in their depths, I caught a flicker of awareness. Of terror. He was still in there, trapped in his own body as the ripple turned him into something else.

Bile rose in my throat as I watched him slam against the bars again. "You made them like this. This isn't natural—"

"Natural?" Harris cut me off. "Nothing about you is natural. You're abominations. This?" He pointed to the screen. "This is just showing the world your true faces."

"You piece of shit." Derek moved wolf-fast, his fists, still tied together, slamming into Harris's cheek.

Before Derek could do anything else, everyone in that room, all six men, had their guns out and aimed at him.

Harris held up a hand, gesturing for them to hold. He touched his cheek with his fingers as he said, "I want you alive, Derek. I want you to watch what I do with your Pack. And I want you to know that I will personally see to it that no one who has connections to Three Rivers is left alive."

His gaze settled on me, trailing over my body in a way that made my skin crawl. "Well, almost no one. I might keep this one as a pet. You chose her over your brothers-in-arms, Derek, and I'm curious to see what's so fucking special about her pussy that made you throw everything away."

"Touch her," Derek's voice was pure wolf now, deep and deadly, "and I will fucking rip you apart."

"There it is," Harris said, his voice almost gentle. "The animal underneath. That's what Kane wanted me to show you, brother. What you really are when all civilization is stripped away."

Chapter Forty-Five

SOFIA

"Tell me, Derek," Harris said, his voice casual as he undid the strap on his side holster and took out his gun. "Why did you come here? What did you hope to achieve?"

Derek didn't answer. Our bond pulsed hot and violent between us, thrumming with his desire to tear Harris apart piece by piece.

I swallowed hard. We needed a way out of this. My eyes darted to the USB still clutched in Derek's hand. It was a flimsy bargaining chip, but our only play.

"We came to negotiate," I said quickly.

Harris arched a brow, clearly amused. "Negotiate?"

"The USB," I pressed on. "That's what you want, isn't it? There's information on there you don't want getting out. We're offering you a deal. We give you the USB. You call off the attack on Three Rivers."

"You really don't get it, do you?"

A flick of his wrist, and one of his men stepped forward. Derek glanced at me. He knew I was trying to stall, buying time, giving him a chance to rein in his fury and formulate a plan. I gave a slight nod, and he released the USB. The soldier tossed it to Harris, who twirled it between his fingers before casually dropping it in the trash bin.

"The USB is nothing. Once we realized Derek wasn't playing our game, we took measures to mitigate the damage. We're currently shutting down your servers so no one in Three Rivers can disseminate the intelligence. No one in your Pack will have time to find a workaround. We're about to attack, and then they'll be too busy being dead."

My stomach dropped.

"In two hours, everyone in Three Rivers—everyone you love, everyone you have ever known—will be culled."

A sharp, ringing silence filled my head, blocking out everything else. Two hours. Two hours before they wiped out my home. Mai. The pups. Wally. Thomas. Mrs. Patterson. The Bottley Bar. All of it, gone.

I struggled to keep my breathing steady, but Harris must have seen the flicker of panic in my eyes because his smile widened.

"You came here thinking you had leverage," he continued, shaking his head. "Thinking you could outmaneuver us. But we don't negotiate with animals, sweetheart."

Footsteps echoed in the hallway. The door swung open, and three more soldiers entered, guns out but pointed at the ground. I hoped the weapons were just for show; there were too many soldiers in here now for them to use the guns without the risk of hitting each other. The new soldiers positioned themselves in a loose semi-circle around us, relaxed but alert. I flicked my gaze to Derek, knew he was ahead of me and had already come to the realization that we were done. There was no more stalling. They were going to take us and then attack our Pack. His fury burned white hot through our bond, and I knew he was going to fight, going to try to kill Harris.

My pulse spiked. If Derek moved now, they'd shoot him before he got within arm's reach of Harris.

I had to do something. We needed a distraction, something to take the focus off Derek.

I dropped my shoulders slightly, let my breath hitch just enough to make it seem like I was panicking. I widened my eyes, staring at Harris like I was terrified, letting my body language scream helpless, fragile, subservient.

It worked.

Harris smirked, satisfied. I wasn't a threat; I was a scared barista, nothing more. He turned his full attention back to Derek.

"I have to admit, brother, I was expecting more from you. This has all been too easy."

Derek stood perfectly still, his expression neutral, almost detached. Anyone looking at him would see resignation, maybe even defeat. But through our mate bond, I felt the coiled tension, the deadly focus sharpening to a razor's edge.

We were out of time. I had to strike first, had to distract them.

I spun, fast and precise, driving my heel into the kneecap of the guard closest to me. Bone popped under the force of the blow, and he crumpled with a strangled cry. Before he hit the floor, I pivoted again, twisting my bound wrists up and over the man's falling body, ramming the sharp edge of my elbow into another guard's throat.

The soldier gagged, fingers scrabbling at his crushed windpipe as he staggered backward.

Chaos erupted.

Derek had lunged the second I moved, his sheer force sending two guards flying. He ripped through his hand-ties like they were paper as

Harris cursed, shoving himself back as his soldiers swarmed us.

I twisted as a rifle butt cracked against my ribs, pain blooming deep in my side.

Damn it, I had to be faster!

I slammed my shoulder into the soldier's gut. He stumbled, thrown off balance, and I wrenched my hands forward. The plastic ties broke with a satisfying snap.

Should have used the silver ones.

Free.

Another man grabbed me from behind, his arm locking around my throat. I brought my foot down hard on his instep, twisting at the same time, and drove my elbow into his solar plexus. He wheezed, his grip loosening just enough for me to throw him over my hip. He crashed into two other soldiers advancing toward me, sending them all sprawling across the floor.

Holy shit, that felt good!

Across the room, Derek was a force of nature, his movements fluid and lethal as he cut through their ranks with terrifying efficiency.

Movement to my left—Harris.

He brought his gun up and trained it on Derek.

I didn't think. I just moved. Diving toward Harris, I stretched my hands out, trying to knock the gun from his hand.

There was a pffff sound as a dart whizzed past my ear and punched into Derek's shoulder. He staggered, a vicious snarl tearing from his throat as he ripped the dart free.

What the hell?

It was a sleek, narrow syringe, its needle dripping with something thick and clear.

Not a bullet. A tranquilizer.

"Derek—!" I shouted, but another dart slammed into his thigh.

Derek stumbled again and ripped it out, but a third one hit him in his ribs.

"NO!" My scream sounded like it came from someone else as I watched darts fly from all directions at Derek. I rolled up and sprinted toward him.

A fist slammed into my stomach, stealing my breath.

Hands yanked my hair, dragging me back.

Harris.

I twisted, trying to break his grip, but he wrenched my head down as his knee rocketed up, connecting with my face with a sickening crack. Pain exploded across my cheekbone. The world tilted, bright spots dancing across my vision as I sagged in his grip.

His fingers twisted in my curls, wrenching my head back painfully, forcing me to watch through a haze of tears and pain.

Derek gave up trying to rip the darts out. He fought like a demon, tearing through their ranks even as the drugs slowed him down, even as his movements became sluggish. He grabbed one of the guards by the throat and lifted him clean off his feet, his grip so tight his knuckles went white—but then his legs buckled.

He dropped to one knee, shaking his head like he was trying to fight through the haze. His eyes found mine, wild and desperate.

Heat flared across our mate bond, furious and primal. Derek's wolf, trying to fight through the sedation, trying to reach me, protect me.

Harris dragged me over to Derek. I tried to claw his hands off my hair, my head still spinning from the blow. With a sudden jerk, he grabbed my throat, lifted me into the air, and then slammed me into the ground.

I couldn't breathe. There was no air, none in the world, that was getting to my lungs. It felt like I was drowning. Harris pressed one knee heavily on my sternum, pinning me in place as I gasped desperately for breath, each attempt sending sharp pain through my chest.

"I want you alive, Derek, for a while, anyway. I want you to wake up and see what I've done to your precious home. I want you to know that you failed to protect it. And when you do next wake, know this, my brother: your mate, your precious fucking mate, will be broken." Harris's voice was soft, calm, the kind of voice you'd use on a child reading a bedtime story. "My creations are about to set off for Three Rivers, and that gives me and my men a couple of hours to play with. We're going to fill it having fun with your mate. By the time we're done, she won't just smell of me, she'll taste of me. You won't be able to look at her without seeing all the marks I'm going to leave on her. And she'll be nothing but my caged little pet, panting in heat, waiting for my next command to bend over and spread her legs for me."

A guttural, inhuman sound tore from Derek's throat. His body convulsed, his muscles straining against the drugs, his teeth bared in a final, desperate snarl. He tried to move, tried to lurch toward us, but even he couldn't fight off the sheer volume of tranquilizers they had pumped into him. His head lolled forward, his breathing uneven.

"No!" I gasped the word, tearing it from my throat. I thrashed wildly against Harris's knee, not caring that it felt like he was breaking all the bones in my ribs. The pain didn't matter. Nothing mattered except getting to Derek. I reached for him, for our bond, pouring every ounce of strength I had toward him, trying to will him to stay awake, to fight. He kept his eyes on me and the look that was in them almost broke me. He knew he had lost. Knew what that meant for me, for our Pack. The anguish in them was unbearable; the look of a man watching his worst nightmare unfold before him, powerless to stop it. He was still trying, still fighting to get up.

I wanted to look away, but I wouldn't do that to him. I held his gaze, tears streaming down my face as his body collapsed, his eyes rolled, and unconsciousness claimed him.

Chapter Forty-Six

SOFIA

Harris chuckled, his grip tight in my hair as he dragged me away from Derek's unmoving form. He yanked me upright.

"You see, sweetheart? Even the strongest of you can be put down."

Then he threw me toward the far side of the room. The impact sent pain lancing up my spine. I didn't care. I needed to get to Derek; that was all I could think about.

I pushed myself up just as I heard the pfff of a gun going off. A sharp prick stung my arm.

A tranquilizer dart. I jerked it out.

"Don't worry, it's not enough to send you under. I want you awake for the next part. It's just a little something to keep you docile."

My legs wobbled. The room tilted and swayed, the edges of my vision growing fuzzy. I staggered, trying to stay upright, but my muscles felt like lead and I hit the ground hard.

"You…" The word came out slurred.

I looked up as Harris stalked toward me, his belt undone, his hands moving for the zipper.

A small, detached part of my brain cataloged every detail—the acrid bite of compressed CO_2 from the tranquilizer guns mixed with the sharp, chemical smell of the sedative itself. The concrete floor reeked of industrial cleaners and soil, layered with the metallic scent of fresh blood from the fight. Harris's men, even in victory, carried the bitter edge of fear—the unmistakable stink of someone who'd faced down an apex predator and barely survived. The scents filled my nostrils, warring with Harris's sickly sweet stink of excitement and arousal—a nauseating cocktail of testosterone and anticipation that made me want to retch.

My heart hammered against my ribs, a frantic drumbeat. My breath came in short, uncontrolled gasps. My wolf clawed desperately inside me, demanding I Shift. I bit my cheek hard, the taste and smell of my own blood cutting through the fog, clearing my mind a bit. But even my thoughts were slow, sluggish. They seemed to take forever to form. The tranquilizer made everything feel distant, dreamlike.

No Shifting; they'd put more tranquilizers in me. When I woke, I'd be in a cage. Three Rivers gone.

Needed to be smart. Needed to survive. Needed to protect Derek.

Harris thought I was weak. Had to use that.

I could do this. I could get us out of this.

Harris yanked down his pants, and I knew—I *knew*—he was going to rape me.

A new wave of panic crashed over me, but I forced it down, locked it away. My limbs were heavy, my thoughts getting more and more scattered.

No! I couldn't be scared. Had to think!

Fingers curled into the concrete, nails scraping against the rough texture as I fought to hold on to any sensation that might help me focus.

Boots scuffed against the floor as Harris crouched by me, the sound echoing strangely in my drugged state.

"Look at you," he murmured, almost like he was admiring a piece of art. His fingers traced a slow, taunting line down my arm before tightening around my wrist. His grip was bruising, the pain cutting through the fog in my head.

Dickhead.

I snapped my hand out, the movement clumsy and delayed. He jerked back, easily missing my swing.

"You put up a good fight, I'll give you that." His grin widened as his face swam in and out of focus. "But we both know how this ends. Don't fight it, Sofia. This is what you were made for. Be content that you are finally fulfilling your true potential."

"Fuck you!" The words came out slurred, my tongue feeling thick and uncooperative.

I yanked against him, but his fingers clamped down harder. Pain shot up my arm.

"Ow!"

"You might think you should fight, but deep down? You're just another little bitch wanting to be broken. Trust me, Sofia, you'll be happy when you break. Because you'll finally be who you are supposed to be. A pet who'll do anything to please her master."

I spat blood at him. It splattered across his cheek, dark against his skin.

His expression darkened. And then the punch came.

It was like being hit with a sledgehammer. My head snapped to the side, vision fragmenting into kaleidoscope patterns before the pain finally registered. My cheekbone flared with agony, the impact ringing through my skull and making the room spin even more.

Another blow landed—this time, a jab to my ribs. I gasped, my breath whooshing out of me as fire shot through my torso. He was deliberately targeting my injuries. I lashed out blindly, aiming a kick at his knee, but it went wide, my depth perception shot. His hand caught my ankle in a vise grip. With a sharp yank, he flipped me onto my stomach, my chest slamming against the cold concrete.

His knee pressed down between my shoulder blades, keeping me pinned, the pressure sending new waves of nausea crashing through me.

"Stay down."

I bucked against his hold, my wolf howling inside me, frantic and desperate.

He leaned forward, putting his full weight on my back. "Submit." Harris's breath was hot against my ear. "Or I'll have my men put a bullet in Derek's head right now."

I blinked over at Derek, trying to force my eyes to focus. Two, then three Dereks swam in my vision before merging back into one.

Bound, drugged, unconscious. Helpless. A soldier stood above him, a handgun pointing at Derek's head.

Fuck. Fuck. Fuck!

Harris knew he had me. Knew I'd do anything for Derek.

I forced myself to go limp beneath him. Wanted to fight, to Shift, to rip him apart with my hands. But I couldn't. Not while Derek was unconscious, vulnerable.

"That's it," he murmured, the sound distant, like it was coming from underwater. "Knew you'd come around."

Rage burned through some more of the haze.

"Please," I whispered. "Just… don't hurt him."

He rolled me onto my back. "See? Was that so hard?"

I forced myself to shake my head and drop my gaze, though the movement made the room spin sickeningly. My wolf snarled inside me, fighting against both the drugs and my forced submission.

"You're gonna be surprised at how easy it is for you to be compliant, Sofia, at how much you'll want to please me when I'm done with you. Now, take off your pants."

"Sir?" One of the soldiers moved forward. "Convoy rolling out in two minutes."

Harris snapped his head around to the soldier, frowning. "Let them wait. This first time won't take long."

I almost giggled. I'd done it; I'd stalled him.

By possibly getting raped.

The hysterical giggle in my head went silent.

This was not the plan. This was so not the fucking plan. My eyes flickered over to Derek. There was no movement except the small rise and fall of his chest. I felt along the mate bond. Nothing. He was completely out.

Fuck!

"I said, take off your pants."

"What?" My tongue felt swollen, clumsy.

"I don't know how you werewolves do it, but you're about to get fucked by me and then by as many of my men who want a go. So, take off your pants. I want you to remember that you were actively involved in your own submission."

"I…" My voice trembled, and I hated myself for it.

"Sergeant Hill!" Harris barked.

The soldier pointing the gun at Derek didn't take his eyes off of him when he answered. "Yes, sir?"

"Shoot him."

"No! Please, no! I'll do what you say. Look..." I fumbled with the zipper on my jeans, then shoved them down my legs.

"Better. I like it when you say please, Sofia. After I'm done, you're going to ask nicely to let each of my men fuck you. I might even wake Derek up so he can watch."

Harris yanked his pants down and lay down on top of me, his hands bracketing my wrists against the cold concrete. The stench of him filled my nose, the sickening mix of excitement and sweat making the room spin faster. I could feel the head of his cock against my entrance, and bile rose in my throat. My wolf thrashed against the tranquilizer's hold, each surge of adrenaline burning away tiny fragments of the fog in my mind.

"You know," he mused, brushing hair roughly away from my face, "I'm really going to enjoy fucking Derek's little bitch."

Something inside me snapped as a tsunami of rage flooded along my mate bond, the sheer force of it cutting through the chemical haze like a blade. My wolf seized that moment of clarity, that flash of pure fury, and used it to tear through another layer of sedation.

Through numb lips, I forced out the words, "It's like the Captain's job."

Harris froze. "What the fuck did you say?"

"You always come second to Derek, don't you? That's all you're ever good for: his sloppy seconds."

Anger twisted his features.

I lunged upward, sinking my teeth into his throat, tearing into flesh and muscle. Hot, coppery blood flooded my mouth. Harris roared in pain, his entire body seizing, his hands scrabbling to shove me off.

I held on, biting down harder, my jaw locking as I tore deeper.

He punched me, his fist slamming into my ribs with sickening force. Once. Twice. The third blow nearly made me black out as pain exploded through my torso.

But I didn't let go.

Harris screamed, wrenching back, tearing himself free. Blood poured down his neck, soaking into his shirt. His hands clamped over the wound, his eyes wide with shock and fury.

I braced, waiting for the tranquilizer darts I was sure would come. His men didn't shoot me, though. They were frozen in place, staring at something behind Harris.

And then the growl came.

Low. Deep. Dark.

A sound that rumbled through the walls, through the floor, through my very bones.

A sound I knew.

Slowly, Harris turned.

Derek in, wolf form, loomed behind him.

Massive. Snarling. Eyes glowing with pure, unfiltered rage.

I barely had time to roll out of the way before Derek lunged, his fangs cutting into what was left of Harris's throat and ripping it out.

Chapter Forty-Seven

SOFIA

Derek dropped Harris's body, a wet, meaty thud that echoed around the room. Behind Derek, the guard who had been pointing the gun at him lay lifeless in a pool of red.

The scent of fear from the surrounding soldiers flooded my senses. Derek took one step forward, his muzzle dripping with blood.

Whatever shock the soldiers felt broke. Chaos erupted as some dove for cover while others swung their weapons up.

Derek leaped.

A scream cut short as Derek's fangs sliced into an arm, and blood sprayed against the walls. Tranquilizer darts pfffed in an almost constant sound, but Derek kept moving, a whirlwind of claws and fury. He was an unstoppable force of nature, pure instinct and vengeance. One soldier got a shot off, the bullet hitting Derek's right leg. He didn't slow down, didn't hesitate, just swiped a massive paw across the soldier's chest, claws ripping through his vest like it was paper.

The soldier crumpled, gurgling, one hand trying to stem the blood pouring from the deep gashes across his chest, the other reaching desperately for his fallen gun. I forced myself to move through the drug-induced haze, ignoring the throbbing pain in my ribs, to kick the weapon beyond his reach. His eyes locked onto mine, filled with hatred.

I stared back, unflinching. These men thought they could cage us, experiment on us, wipe out my entire Pack. They'd looked at me and seen nothing but a scared female to be controlled. A pet, Harris had called me.

Rage that I'd kept leashed unfurled in my chest.

The soldier dragged himself forward, one hand over the other, trying to get to me. It was them or us. I brought my foot up and stomped down hard on his head. He lay still, unconscious or dead; I wasn't sure.

I spun around, ready for the next soldier, and sucked in a sharp breath. Everyone in the room was on the floor with gaping, bloody wounds to their bodies and heads.

Holy fucking Goddess!

Derek's eyes, mad with rage, focused on me.

Every hair on my body stood on end as he took a deliberate step toward me, his huge paw leaving a bloody print on the concrete.

"Derek?"

He growled, showing no sign of recognizing me.

"Derek!" I tried again.

He took another step, lowering his head as he stalked closer.

I held still as shock coursed through me.

Bloodlust. Derek was in bloodlust. There was no coming back from that.

No! I wouldn't allow it. Wouldn't let this be the end. I held up my arm and slashed at it with my nails. Blood bloomed, my scent filling the air. Derek would never hurt me, no matter how far gone in the bloodlust he was. It wasn't something I believed. It was something I knew. I watched his nostrils flare. His ears flattened. His lips curled back, revealing fangs slick with blood.

Oh, shit.

I don't know if he recognized me but he did recognize the scent that was on me. Harris.

A howl ripped from Derek's throat—primal, ancient, terrifying. The sound vibrated through my bones, making my teeth ache and my skin prickle. It wasn't just a howl; it was a promise of violence, a declaration of war. Every instinct I had screamed at me to run, to hide, to get as far away as possible from the predator before me.

This wasn't the controlled power of an enforcer or even the dominance of an Alpha. This was something darker, more primitive. The sound echoed off the walls, building and building, until it felt like the whole room would shake apart from the force of his rage. In that moment, I understood why humans once huddled in caves, terrified of what lurked in the darkness. This was the howl that haunted their nightmares, that lived on in their oldest stories—the call of a hunter that would not stop until everything in its path was dead.

My heart slammed against my ribs. The rest of Kane's men would hear us. The airstrip was crawling with them; there was no way we could fight our way out of here.

But the sound resonated within me, too, awakening something ancient and untamed. Part of me—a part I'd always tried to contain—wanted to throw back my head and join him. To let the world hear our fury, to make them tremble at what they'd awakened in us.

I surged forward, placing my hands on either side of Derek's broad head.

I think it was only pure surprise at my move that kept him from attacking me.

"Enough, Derek," I whispered fiercely, my forehead pressing against his. "They'll hear you. We need to be smart. We need to live. We need to find a way out of here." My voice dropped lower, a dangerous edge to it. "And then we're going to make every last one of them pay for what they've done."

His ears flicked toward my voice, but he showed no other sign that he recognized me as he snarled. For a moment, I thought he would attack me, but then a loud metallic bang sounded behind me. I looked over my shoulder as the door was kicked open.

Gunfire erupted.

Not tranquilizers this time.

Derek was already moving, launching himself in front of me at the wave of soldiers spilling into the room. His front paws hit the first soldier, tearing at his jugular as he rode him down. The soldier was dead before he touched the floor, and Derek exploded into motion, jumping from one soldier to the next. They went down one after the other as Derek tore through them, his form a blur of muscle and fury.

I sprinted toward the fallen soldiers, my feet sliding in the blood. I grabbed a tranquilizer gun as a soldier stumbled backward, trying to escape Derek's wrath.

I took aim and fired.

A dart hit his neck, and he collapsed.

Derek leaped over the fallen man without a glance, his focus already on his next target as he sped out the door.

My eyes locked on a combat knife strapped to one of the fallen soldiers' thighs. Without hesitating, my fingers closed around the familiar weight, and something inside me steadied. This—this I knew.

There was no sign of Derek in the corridor, just more bodies littering the way. I checked their pulses as I went past, but Derek hadn't left any alive.

The bloodlust had to be fueling him.

An alarm blared through the hangar, followed by shouts and screams ahead of me. They knew we were loose.

I rounded the corner to see Derek on the other side of the space by the hangar doors, his massive form silhouetted against the dying sun.

More bodies sprawled across the room, some bent over desks and chairs, others on the ground gurgling their last breaths. The air had the acrid stink of adrenaline, gunpowder, and fresh blood.

I picked my way around the bodies, scanning for signs of life. The few who were still alive had weak, irregular heartbeats; I knew there was no saving them.

There was so much carnage, so much damage. How had Derek managed to do this in such a short amount of time? I struggled to take it all in. Rapid gunfire came from outside, and I sprinted to the hangar doors.

Outside, on the airstrip, soldiers were scrambling, trying to form defensive lines. The scent of fear was thick, curling under my skin. They knew what was coming for them, and even if I could stop him, I wouldn't. These soldiers were ready to murder every single member of my Pack. They had signed up to Kane's ideology willingly, happy to carry out genocide. My only thoughts were for Derek. For how much damage the bloodlust was doing. I had to pull him back from this.

To my left, a soldier broke away from the chaos, spotting me as I moved through the doors. He raised his weapon, but I was already sprinting, closing the distance between us in an instant. The Caldera sequence flowed through my muscles—duck, pivot, strike. The knife became an extension of my arm as I slashed upward, catching him beneath his body armor. He staggered back. I followed through with the second movement, blade dancing across his wrist. His gun clattered to the floor as I completed the sequence with a precise strike to his shoulder. He screamed as I stabbed him twice more, then collapsed at my feet.

I turned as bullets sprayed across the tarmac. Derek charged the defensive line; blood matted his dark fur where rounds had already found their mark, but he moved like he couldn't feel them. A soldier screamed as Derek's giant jaws closed around his throat, the sound cutting off in a wet gurgle. Without pausing, Derek whirled toward his next target, a spray of crimson arcing through the air.

A bullet punched through Derek's left haunch. My heart leaped into my throat as he stumbled, fresh blood running down his leg.

"No!" I screamed, sprinting toward him. Rage surged through me, hot and electric. They would not take him from me.

But if anything, his injury only seemed to fuel his fury. He spun toward the shooter, moving faster than any wolf his size should be able to, and tore the man's arm off at the shoulder.

More bullets zinged past him, some finding their mark, adding new wounds to his already bleeding body. But he seemed beyond pain now, beyond any normal limits. The bloodlust had taken him somewhere primal, where injury meant nothing compared to the drive to kill.

A grenade bounced across the tarmac. I dove flat, hands over my head, as the explosion rocked the ground.

Derek!

I jumped up, ears ringing, to see Derek emerge from the smoke like a demon, his fur singed, blood dripping from a dozen wounds. He snarled, then crashed into another soldier, his claws raking across the woman's chest. She didn't even have time to react before Derek tore her apart.

A soldier took aim at Derek's exposed flank, his finger tightening on the trigger. Time slowed. I was too far for hand-to-hand, too far to tackle him. Without thinking, I spun my knife so I was holding it by its blade and then released it. The knife tumbled end over end, a perfect arc through the air. It struck the soldier's throat. His shot went wild as he fell to the ground. Derek's head whipped around at the sound, his eyes meeting mine for just a moment. Recognition flickered there, then was gone as he turned back to his rampage.

The remaining soldiers, seeing there was no stopping Derek, began to panic, scattering like prey. Some fired wildly, their bullets ricocheting off metal crates and abandoned vehicles. Others tried to run, but there was no outrunning my mate.

A bullet grazed my left arm. I whirled, spying the shooter: an Hispanic man, late twenties, straight black hair and ears that were slightly too big for his head. I charged. He had time to get off one more shot just as I twisted right, the bullet whizzing past my shoulder. Then I was on him, knocking the gun out of his hands and driving my knee into his chest. He fell back. I rode him down, slamming his head into the ground, then fired two darts from his own gun into his leg.

Derek's snarl ripped through the air, loud and feral.

I jumped up just in time to see him launch himself at the last cluster of soldiers, who were using the trucks with the cages on them for cover.

The werewolves inside the cages were thrashing wildly, their eyes locked onto the bloodbath before them.

I ran, weaving between bodies and debris. My breathing was ragged, my hands shaking from the adrenaline, but I couldn't stop now.

I saw the moment the soldiers realized the people in the cages might be their only chance against Derek.

One of them—a short man with a bloodied face and desperation in his eyes—lunged toward the nearest cage. The other soldiers urged him on, his trembling hands fumbling with the keypad on the side of the cage.

"No!" I yelled, urging my legs to move faster.

Derek charged alongside me, muscles rippling, blood dripping from his fangs.

The keypad beeped, and the lock hissed open.

Shit!

The cage door swung outward, and a man flew out. Medium-height, broad-shoulders, with arms covered in bruises and cuts. His dark eyes were wild, darting between the soldier and Derek, unsure of who to attack first.

The soldier took a step back. "Kill! Kill that!" he shouted, pointing to Derek.

The man didn't listen, so far gone on ripple. With a guttural roar, he lunged at the nearest target. The soldier tried to raise his rifle, but the Shifter swiped at it, and the gun clattered to the ground. Then he was on him, ramming the soldier into the cage, his fists pummeling against him. Blood splattered across the metal bars, the soldier's screams cutting off as the Shifter crushed his throat with a savage punch. The others, frozen in shock until now, turned and ran. The man howled, the noise wrong for his human throat, then he sped after his fleeing comrades.

Derek leaped, landing on the Shifter and ripping into his neck before they hit the ground. Then he jumped again; a blur of motion, a shadow flowing from one soldier to the next. Three bodies fell in rapid succession, torn open with savage efficiency. The last soldier managed five steps before Derek clamped down on his head with a sickening crunch.

The soldier fell as Derek skidded to a halt, his ears flattening. He turned his head and growled low in his throat. His eyes snapped to mine, wild and dangerous. Blood matted his fur and dripped down his side; I couldn't tell what was from his wounds and what was from the soldiers he'd killed. I felt his wolf pulse through our bond, a tidal wave of fury and bloodlust. He didn't recognize me. He was too deep in the hunt, too lost in the primal need to eliminate everything around him.

I froze, my heart feeling like it was shattering into pieces inside of me—there was no getting Derek back. He was lost, completely and utterly lost to me.

Chapter Forty-Eight

DEREK

Time stuttered around me. Fragments of moments spliced together. My teeth sinking into flesh. The sweet release of violence.

Blood.

Thick. Metallic. Everywhere. Clinging to my fur. Filling my lungs. Coating my tongue in copper.

The world looked wrong. Colors bled into each other at the edges, then sharpened to painful clarity when I focused. Sounds arrived distorted—heartbeats thundered like war drums, whispers screamed like sirens. Time stretched and compressed. A man falling took an eternity; my teeth ripping through his throat happened between one heartbeat and the next.

A face flickered through the crimson haze. Harris. His name floated up from the depths of my mind. His blood. His death. Wanted him to suffer more. But dead all the same.

Harris touching her. His hands on her body. The rage exploding through me like a supernova.

The memory seared through me, then disappeared. Where was I?

What had happened between that moment and now? Bodies littered the floor. My doing? Yes. Mine.

Good.

The others. Men who tried to hurt her.

Her. No name surfaced this time, just a single thought.

Mine.

Pain burned along my ribs. A bullet graze. A knife wound. A deep tear in my shoulder.

Didn't matter. None of it mattered. Only her. But I didn't know what she looked like, didn't know where she was. Just a faint memory of a smile. Of green eyes. Of warmth.

Kill. Hunt. Protect.

The thoughts crashed against each other, contradictory yet somehow the same. I wanted blood. Needed it like oxygen.

Concrete, the killer of soil, stretched before me, strangely distorted. Colors muted, edges sharper. Bodies on the ground, some still pumping out blood, heartbeats fading. The air, thick with gunpowder, sweat, and fear, was a cocktail that made a savage delight surge within me.

I smelled their terror. It lingered even after death, sweet and sharp. It drove me onward, demanding more.

I turned, my breath ragged. Chest heaving. Vision tunneling. Maybe damaged worse than we thought.

I longed to chase, to hunt, to kill. My eyes focused, locking in my next target; my breathing steadied. Now—

Hunt them down. Leave nothing breathing. Threatened what is ours.

Ours? The word jarred something loose. Pack. Something about Pack. About home. But the thought slipped away before I could grasp it.

Something brushed against my consciousness, a tugging sensation, like a half-forgotten song. I growled low, shaking it off. Nothing mattered except finishing this. Except spilling more blood.

A scent cut through the miasma of death. Coffee. Honey. Something else, something that made me pause.

Female.

I turned, snarling, hackles rising as I faced this new presence. Her body was rigid, eyes fixed on mine. Blood trickled down her arm. Her scent—not right, not entirely. Tainted. A male's stink lingered on her skin.

Harris.

The rage returned tenfold, a crimson tide that threatened to drown whatever fragments of me still clung to my consciousness. I threw back my head and howled—not the controlled sound of a call to Pack, but something ancient and terrible, the promise of vengeance and death.

She didn't run. Didn't cower.

Instead, she moved toward me with deliberate steps, her heart racing but her gaze steady. Not afraid. Not prey.

What was she?

Something about her sparked recognition—a brief flash, like lightning illuminating a night landscape before plunging it back into darkness. I knew her. Didn't I? The thought felt foreign, human, weak. I snarled it away.

Female. Threat. Kill.

But another voice, deeper, more primal: *No! Not this one. Never this one.*

The conflict tore through me, my muscles bunching, then relaxing, caught between attack and restraint. Her scent called to something beyond the hunt, beyond the kill.

Blood stained her shirt—some hers, most not. She was hurt. I could smell it now, beneath the adrenaline and battle-rage.

Protect.

The imperative overrode everything else. Why? Why this one? All were prey before me.

I moved toward her, tracking her reactions. She tensed but didn't retreat. Her pulse quickened—not with fear but with something else. Hope? The subtle change in her scent tugged at memories buried deep.

For a heartbeat, a name hovered at the edge of consciousness. I shook it away.

Motion caught my eye—a soldier, half-hidden beneath bodies, still breathing. Still a threat. I growled, lowering my head as I stalked toward him. His blood seeped between his fingers, where he clutched at a stomach wound. Easy kill. Finish it.

A hand touched my fur, gentle but firm. Her scent surrounded me, cutting through the bloodlust.

"Enough, Derek. It's enough. He's not a threat. There's no one left who is a threat."

Derek. Me? Yes. But also not me. Not now. Now, there was only death.

A flash of memory—her smile, her laugh, her body beneath mine.

I bared my teeth, resistant. The need to kill still pulsed through me, demanding satisfaction.

Her fingers threaded through my fur, finding skin beneath the matted blood.

"Come back to me, Derek. Come back."

Something inside me shifted, the red haze thinning at the edges. I leaned into her touch, her warmth seeping into me, anchoring me. For a moment, her features sharpened—green eyes, fiery curls, skin that I knew better than my own.

Sofia.

The name rose from the depths like a bubble breaking the surface—there and gone in an instant, but leaving ripples. Who was Sofia? What was she to me?

Everything. She is everything.

A noise cut through my focus—not the dying man, not Sofia. My head snapped up, ears swiveling toward the sound.

Cages. The men inside them watched us, some snarling and throwing themselves against the bars, others simply staring. One caught my attention—skeletal, his eyes sunken but clear. His hands gripped the bars, knuckles white with the effort.

He wasn't raging like the others. He was watching. Waiting. Hoping I would end it for him.

Something about him—about all of them—called to me. They were wrong. Broken. Their scent corrupted by chemicals and pain. They should be free. They should be running beneath the moon, not trapped in metal cages with poison in their veins.

Her fingers tightened in my fur. "Stay with me," she whispered.

I breathed her in, letting her scent wash through me, letting it settle inside me. For a moment, the need to kill receded.

Then—engines. Tires screeching. Doors slamming. Footsteps approaching fast.

The rage returned instantly, my muscles coiling as I positioned myself between the female and the new threat. A snarl ripped from my throat, the sound echoing across the blood-soaked tarmac.

Scents hit me—familiar ones, ones of my Pack, but I had no names for them.

A man approached slowly, his hands visible, his movements careful. His eyes moved from the bodies to me, assessing, cautious. Didn't matter. He would die like the rest.

I bared my fangs, hackles rising. Behind me, the female's hand found my flank, her touch gentle but insistent.

"Don't come closer."

The man stopped, maintaining distance. Smart, but it wouldn't save him.

"Sofia?"

"He's in bloodlust."

A spike of something in his scent. Fear?

Good. He was right to be afraid of me.

He lowered his eyes, not meeting mine. He knew he was prey. "Derek. It's me. It's Sam."

The name meant nothing to me. Blood. I needed more blood. More death. That was what I was for. I was a predator. A hunter. There was only now. Only the hunt. Only the next throat to tear out.

I shook off the female's hand and attacked.

Chapter Forty-Nine

SOFIA

I felt Derek's muscles bunch, knew what he was going to do a split second before he attacked. Derek didn't recognize his own twin. He would kill him.

My body moved before my brain could catch up. I threw myself between them, arms outstretched, facing Derek's charge head-on. He skidded to a halt just inches from me, claws gouging trenches in the concrete. His snarl vibrated through my bones, spittle flying from his jaws as he bared his teeth, but he didn't attack.

"Sofia, what the fuck are you doing?" Sam hissed, stepping up behind me. "When I say move, you're going to run to the cars, okay?"

I kept my eyes locked on Derek, not daring to look away. "No."

"The bloodlust has taken him," Sam whispered, his voice cracking. "He doesn't know who we are. He doesn't know who you are."

"He knows exactly who I am. He won't hurt me."

Derek began to pace, his head lowered, stalking first to our left, then to our right. Testing. Assessing. Looking for an opening.

"Sofia, please." There was such raw anguish in Sam's voice. "My job now, and always, is to make sure you are safe, protected. Even from

Derek. Please. If Derek attacks, if he hurts you…"

"He won't—"

"Look at him! That's not Derek anymore. He's gone, Sofia."

I knew that bloodlust was a death sentence. I knew that no werewolf had ever come back from it, but I refused to accept it.

"He's still in there. I can reach him."

Derek stalked closer, muscles rippling beneath his blood-matted fur. A low, continuous growl rumbled from his chest.

"Sam…" Jase's voice came from somewhere behind us, tense with warning.

"I know."

I felt Sam shift behind me.

"Sam, don't do this—"

"I'm sorry, Sofia." His arm wrapped around my waist. "He's my twin. I have to do what he would want. You are all that matters."

"Sam—"

In one swift movement, he lifted me off my feet, spun, and threw me. I flew through the air, too surprised to even call out, straight into Jase's arms.

"Get her out of here!" Sam roared just as Derek lunged.

The brothers collided. Derek's immense wolf form against Sam's human one. I lost it. Screaming, I struggled wildly against Jase's iron grip as he picked me up and pulled me backward.

"Let go!" I thrashed, but Jase just tightened his hold.

"I can't, Sofia. I'm so sorry, but I can't."

Derek's jaws snapped an inch from Sam's throat as Sam barely rolled clear, coming up in a defensive crouch. Blood streaked Sam's forearm where Derek's claws had caught him. Sam's expression hardened, the last traces of hesitation vanishing.

I saw his lips move, whispering something. I wasn't sure, but I thought he'd said, "I'm sorry, brother."

When Derek lunged again, Sam dropped and rolled beneath him, a flash of silver slicing into Derek. As Sam came up on the other side, I glimpsed what he held—a combat knife I hadn't even realized he was carrying. Derek howled, blood pouring from a deep gash in his underbelly.

Neither brother was holding back. They were going to keep at this until one or both of them were dead.

Derek spun with frightening speed. He didn't retreat or try to protect his wound; he charged, more ferocious than before, driving Sam back with the sheer force of his fury.

Sam hurled himself to one side, his hand swiping upwards as he went, the blade slashing along Derek's shoulder.

"No!" I scream. I would not let them do this. No matter who won, it would devastate the other, and I was sure, I knew it in my soul, that Derek could be saved.

Sam's knife flashed again, catching the fading light as he narrowly avoided Derek's jaws. Blood—too much blood—splattered across the concrete.

"Stop! Please, just stop!" I begged, tears now streaming down my face as I fought Jase.

The mate bond pulsed in my chest. Yes! Derek was still there. Still fighting to come back to us.

I went limp in Jase's arms as if I had fainted.

"Shit, Sofia, are you—"

I drove my elbow into his solar plexus. The air left his lungs in a sharp whoosh. As he doubled over, I hooked my foot behind his ankle and shoved with all my strength. He toppled backward, and I tore away from him.

"STOP!" I screamed as I jumped between the brothers.

Sam's eyes widened in horror, his body twisting mid-strike as he fought against his own momentum. The knife disappeared from his hand, his boots skidding across the concrete as he desperately tried to abort his attack.

Derek was already mid-leap. A sound I'd never heard before—half roar, half whine—came from his throat. He contorted unnaturally, his back legs scrambling to change direction while still airborne. Then he crashed down barely a foot from where I stood.

"Sofia, don't make any sudden moves," Sam panted, out of breath; his words were steady and low, but edged with panic. "I want you to back away slowly."

I stood my ground, heart hammering violently in my chest. This had to work. It had to. Derek growled, his eyes flicking from me to Sam and back again, as if he couldn't decide which of us to attack first.

"Sofia—"

"No, Sam. I know you think you're protecting me, and I love you for it. But I'm not the one who needs protection right now." I took a deliberate step toward Derek. "He does."

Derek's growl deepened, his ears flattening against his skull as I closed the gap between us. But he didn't lunge. Didn't attack. That had to mean something.

"Sofia, please," Sam begged. "Don't do this. This isn't what Derek would have wanted."

I ignored him, focusing entirely on Derek. On my mate.

"I know you're in there," I whispered, extending my hand slowly. "I know you can hear me."

Derek's lips peeled back, but he backed up a step, then two. His eyes—wild, feral, pupils blown wide—locked onto mine with predatory focus. There was no recognition there, just the calculating stare of a hunter.

"Fight it, Derek," I urged, taking another cautious step. The mate bond in my chest fluttered painfully, like a bird trapped in a cage. I pushed against it mentally, trying to force my presence through whatever darkness had swallowed him.

Derek's head snapped up, nostrils flaring. A low, threatening rumble built in his chest as his muscles bunched beneath his fur.

"Sofia, he's going to attack," Sam warned. I could hear him shifting his weight, ready to dive in front of me.

"Stay back!" I ordered, not daring to look away from Derek. "This is between me and my mate."

I reached deeper into our bond, throwing everything I had into it—every memory, every touch, every moment that had forged us together. The first time he'd kissed me. How he made me feel when he touched me. The way he looked at me when he thought I wasn't watching. His smile in the morning light.

Derek's snarl intensified, his front paw scraping at the concrete. He took a step toward me.

"Derek, I know you would never hurt me."

He snapped at the air between us, a warning.

"I love you," I said, the words raw and desperate. "Do you hear me? I won't let you leave me again. You're stuck with me, Derek Shaw. Now and forever. So snap the fuck out of this, and come back to me!"

He crouched, ready to spring, and time seemed to stop. Behind me, I heard Sam's sharp intake of breath.

Fine.

I opened my arms wide and dropped to my knees. I was showing him my belly, showing submission. He could kill me with one swipe of his paw, and I was completely and utterly vulnerable. But I believed in Derek.

He darted forward fast, too fast for even Sam to reach us. His jaws opened, and teeth scraped against the skin on my stomach. There was no blood, though, no pain.

Out of the corner of my eye, I saw Sam leap high, knife out, about to plunge his knife into his brother's neck.

"NO!"

Sam had a split second to decide, then he dropped the knife and crashed to the ground.

"Stay down, Sam," I ordered, hoping I hadn't just signed his death warrant.

Derek inhaled deeply. Scenting me.

"That's it," I whispered. "Remember me. Remember us."

I placed my hands on either side of his face, forcing him to look at me.

"Come back to me, Derek. I need you."

Derek's body went rigid beneath my touch. The bond between us flared suddenly, a blazing connection that made me gasp at the intensity. His agony, his confusion, his desperate struggle against the bloodlust that had consumed him flooded into me. His entire frame shuddered violently. I held on, fingers digging into his fur, refusing to let go.

He whined. I watched as recognition seeped back into his eyes. He shuffled forward slowly, nostrils flaring. Then his tongue darted out, licking at the cuts on my arms.

Tears flowed down my face, and I did nothing to stop them. Derek was back. He was back, and he was mine.

He whined again, looking up at me. Then pain crashed along our mate bond.

Fuck! Derek was hurt. Really hurt. His eyes focused on me for a moment, so full of guilt and love, then they rolled back in his head as he passed out.

Chapter Fifty

SOFIA

I had to hand it to Harris's soldiers; they knew how to stock a medical bay. As soon as Derek passed out, I started screaming for a phone to call Thomas. He took one look at Derek through the video camera and ordered us to search for any medical supplies that might be on site.

Evelyn and Jase raced off, taking some of the other enforcers with them. The others guarded us as I cradled Derek's unconscious body. Sam sat next to us, unable to take his eyes off his brother, not saying a word.

By the time Jase returned with news that he'd found a fully stocked medical room, Derek had Shifted back into his human form. An unconscious Shift like this sometimes happens when we're badly injured. A Shift will heal a lot of injuries, but this one barely made a dent in his wounds. Blood gushed from at least six bullet holes that I could see.

Sam moved, lifting his brother into his arms and running after Jase. I followed, and by the time I made it to the medical room in one of the side hangars, Derek was already hooked up to an IV. Sam had a scalpel in one hand, slicing into him as Thomas talked him through removing bullets.

I paused at the entrance, too shocked at the sight of all of Derek's injuries to move. Jase appeared at my side, his face pale as he surveyed Derek's wounds. Then his eyes shifted to me.

"Sofia," he said quietly, a new note in his voice I'd never heard before. "What happened out there..."

I glanced up. My little brother was looking at me differently—not with his usual protective concern, but with something like awe, and I wasn't sure how I felt about that.

"All those soldiers," he continued, shaking his head. "You and Derek did that?"

I nodded once, not having words to explain what had happened, then stumbled to the head of the bed, stroked Derek's hair, and told him he was never leaving me. Finally, after what felt like hours, Thomas declared we'd done all we could with his major injuries and to get Derek back to Three Rivers so he could treat the rest.

We bundled Derek into one of the cars, Sam catching my arm as I went to follow him.

"Call me with any news. He's not out of the woods yet."

"You're not coming with us?"

Sam shook his head. "I need to be here. Sort out the dead. Deal with the others."

It took me a moment to realize he meant not just the tranquilized soldiers, but the ripple-infected werewolves.

"What will happen to them?"

Sam snaked one hand behind his neck. "Mason's on his way. They've been doing some research into those affected by ripple at

Bridgetown. Depends on what he says; we might be able to take some back to Bridgetown, see what we can do. If not, though…"

He left it unsaid, but I knew he meant they might have to kill them. It was a horrifying thought and I got the feeling that this wouldn't be the first time Sam had had to do something like this.

"Oh, Sam." I hugged him, wanting to take this from him, wanting the world to be different, for ripple to never have been created.

"Be careful with Derek. I've never heard of anyone coming back from bloodlust. We don't know how it might change him."

"It doesn't matter. He's alive. Anything else we'll deal with together."

Sam kissed my forehead. "I know you will. Sofia Miller is one bad-ass motherfucker. I have no doubt that you can handle anything."

Tears welled as I got in the truck beside Derek. Then Sam closed the door behind me, rapping on the roof twice to tell Jase to go.

When we reached Thomas's house, Jase carried Derek inside to a waiting Thomas. I tried to follow, but Wally stood in my way.

"Nuh-uh, darling. You're half-naked and covered in blood. We need to get you cleaned up and have a good look at your injuries."

"After. I need to be with Derek."

He crossed his arms. "You need to make sure you're okay. Sam called. We have no idea who or what is going to wake up in there. You're no good to Derek if you collapse from blood loss. So you, girlie, are going to let me sort you out. Then you can go to him. You know he's in good hands. The best. Thomas and Jase will look after him. Let me take care of you."

I opened my mouth to refuse, but Wally pulled out his phone and held it up to me.

"You leave me no choice. So if the next words uttered out of your mouth are not 'Yes, Wally,' I'm going to call Mai and tell her everything. It will probably put her into labor. Do you want to be the person who has to explain to Ryan why his pups are arriving before they're ready and his mate is screaming at her best friend for being an idiot?"

I clicked my mouth shut.

"Smart choice."

I fell asleep while Wally was patching me up, listening to the sporadic pulses throbbing along my mate bond. Derek was alive. He was there, just next door. Derek. Not a bloodlust werewolf. Derek.

I woke briefly when Wally lay me down next to Derek. He was still out, bandages over... well, most of his body. I put my arm around him, snuggling in as close as I could without touching any of them, and went back to sleep.

The next time I woke, it was slowly, drifting through layers of sleep, aware first of warmth, then pain, then the gentle rhythm of fingers combing through my hair. For a moment, I kept my eyes closed, savoring the sensation, afraid that if I opened them, it might disappear, that it might be a dream.

"You're awake." Derek's voice was little more than a whisper.

"Am I? Or is this just the best dream?" I felt a tear leak out of my eye and run down my cheek.

Warm lips kissed the tear away.

"You can open your eyes, gorgeous. I'm here. I'm really here."

My eyes flew open. Moonlight spilled through the window, casting the room in silver shadows. Derek lay beside me, his eyes—clear and focused—fixed on my face.

"Derek." His name came out as a half-sob, half-whisper. I reached up, catching his hand and pressing it against my cheek. "How do you feel?"

"Like I've been hit by a truck. Then backed over. Then hit again." He winced as he shifted slightly. "Thomas says I'll live. Apparently, I'm not allowed to die because that would mean leaving you."

I smiled. "Damn right."

His thumb traced the curve of my cheekbone, so gently I might have imagined it. "Sofia... I remember everything."

My heart clenched. Of course he did.

"It wasn't you," I said fiercely. "It was the bloodlust."

"But it was me. I felt it, Sofia. The rage, the hunger—it didn't come from nowhere. It came from inside me." His voice caught. "I wanted to kill. And I did. I enjoyed it."

I pushed myself up onto my elbow, ignoring the stab of pain from my shoulder. "Listen to me. You fought it. You came back to us. No one has ever done that before, but you did."

"Because of you." His fingers trailed down to my throat, resting against my pulse. "I was gone, completely gone. And then I heard you. Felt you. It was like... like drowning in darkness and then seeing a single light." His voice broke. "You called me back."

He shook his head, his expression so vulnerable it made my chest ache. "I almost killed Sam. My own brother. And you—" His hand began to tremble against my skin. "You put yourself between us. Do you have any idea what would have happened if I'd—"

"But you didn't."

"I could have."

"No." I took his face between my hands, careful of the cut along his jaw. "You wouldn't. Not ever."

"How can you be so sure? How can you trust me after what I did?"

I leaned forward until our foreheads touched.

"Because I know you, Derek Shaw. Better than anyone. Better than you know yourself." I brushed my lips against his, feather-light. "You will always protect me, no matter what."

"I don't deserve you."

"Too bad. You're stuck with me. Now and forever, remember?"

He made a sound that was half laugh, half something else. "I remember."

CHAPTER FIFTY-ONE

SOFIA

The bedroom door clicked shut with finality, sealing us in a cocoon of muted gold lamplight. Derek didn't turn on the lights. He didn't need to. Moonlight streamed through the windows of his bedroom, gilding the hard planes of his face as he leaned back against the door, watching me with a predator's stillness.

Ripple was still spreading through our communities. Kane was still out there, and none of us was under any delusion that this was the end of it. Sam had shared the information they found on the USB with those he trusted on the Council, which, it turned out, was only five others. We couldn't be sure just how far Kane and Webster's operations had spread inside the Council, but it didn't look good.

I had no doubt that there were more warehouses or hangars with werewolves being forced to take ripple. That Victor Kane would be looking for another town to release them into. We were onto them now, though. We knew their plans; we knew their end goal. It was going to be brutal and bloody, but we would stop them.

Most of Derek's injuries had healed through Thomas's help and Shifting several times a day. He hadn't had any nightmares since we got back, and it had been three days since Thomas had declared Derek as fit enough to go home. Three days of Derek not leaving my side, of debriefs, of assuring Jase I was okay—while he sat and glared at Derek just in case he spontaneously sprouted fur and fangs and tried to eat me—of us drinking tea with Mrs. Patterson after Derek carried her shopping up to her apartment, checking in with Julie and Brian, Derek holding his phone out to me and telling me either I was going to fire Shannon or he would, and finally sitting with Mai for three hours as I explained everything. Mai had not been happy, but she hadn't gone into labor either, so I was taking that as a win.

Derek seemed to be on a mission to take care of me. Yesterday, he'd cornered me in my kitchen. "Either you fire Shannon, or I will," he'd said flatly. "Not negotiable. She's unreliable as fuck. She's gotta go. I'll find you someone else, someone you can count on."

And then this morning, he'd informed me—not asked—that I was moving in with him. When I raised the issue of Jase, Derek had simply shrugged. "Your brother's a grown-ass man. He can learn to cook and clean just like everyone else."

When I'd pointed out that I wasn't sure Derek *had* learned to cook, not if his attempts at the cabin were anything to go by, he'd stared at me for a beat and then said, "I'll learn too."

It gave me a warm feeling inside, one I was coming to associate with Derek. Especially when he then brought out rectangular box all wrapped up in blue paper.

"What's this?" I asked, my fingers already reaching for it.

"Open it and see."

I carefully unwrapped the paper, lifting the lid off the black leather case inside. Nestled in velvet lay a Damascus steel throwing knife with intricate swirling patterns etched into the blade. My eyes widened as I lifted it up. The handle was wrapped in dark leather that felt like it had been made specifically for my grip. It wasn't just beautiful—it was perfectly balanced, the kind of weapon that becomes an extension of yourself.

"This is a Katsumoto original," I whispered, recognizing the maker's distinctive style. The Japanese bladesmith made fewer than a dozen knives a year, each one crafted by hand using techniques passed down through fifteen generations. "How did you even—"

"I ordered it months ago," Derek admitted.

It was everything I'd dreamed of—the perfect pivot point, the seamless balance between blade and handle, the edge that could split a hair. But it was more than that. It was Derek seeing me—truly seeing me—when I thought I'd been invisible.

"Derek..." My voice cracked. I couldn't find words for the constellation of emotions expanding in my chest—gratitude, joy, and something deeper that terrified and thrilled me in equal measure.

When I finally looked up at him, his expression was unguarded. There was a vulnerability there, a question in his eyes that made my heart stutter.

"You like it?" he asked softly.

I laughed, a sound caught between a sob and pure delight. "No. I freaking love it!"

I placed the knife carefully back in its box, then launched myself into his arms. Because some feelings couldn't be expressed with words—they needed to be shown.

The Pack was still worried about Derek, though. He wasn't showing signs of bloodlust, but everyone was on edge, as if waiting for him to turn again. I knew, through the mate bond, that it was pissing Derek off. But I also knew he wasn't entirely sure it wouldn't happen, either. He felt guilty about Harris, about not realizing he was still alive. He was second-guessing his every decision since he'd left the army. He was worried he would succumb to bloodlust again and hurt me. I'd noticed today he was getting grimmer by the hour, drawing into himself, reminding me more and more of Sam.

I wouldn't let that happen. Wouldn't let both Shaw twins get lost in the darkness. So I'd told him he had a window of one hour to collect on his bet, or it would be gone for good. It was the first time I'd seen him smile today. He needed this. I needed this. Needed to feel alive, to know that Harris hadn't won.

"You sure about this?" he asked, his eyes searching my face. "After everything that happened, after Har—"

"I'm sure," I cut him off. I wanted Derek to erase Harris's touch on me. I wanted to prove to myself that he hadn't damaged us, hadn't put an end to Derek and me, hadn't had any effect on us whatsoever.

"Say the word, Sofia; tell me to stop, and I will. You're in control here, you understand?"

Warmth spread through me that had nothing to do with how close Derek was standing to me. "You want to collect on your bet?"

The tension in his shoulders eased slightly, a glint of wickedness lighting his eyes. "I did win. Time to pay up."

I took a deep breath. I could do this. I'd faced down Harris. I'd brought Derek back from bloodlust. I could tell Derek about one of my fantasies.

"Well..."

"Yes?"

"I have a few. You only earned the right to hear about one of them."

He raised an eyebrow; a look of surprise was quickly replaced by calculation. "So, this is just the first one?"

"First one." I nodded.

Okay, I could do this. Given that Derek was still recovering from his injuries, I had chosen one that wouldn't require too much physical effort. "I want... I want to have sex in the shower."

"The shower? That's it? Not getting dressed up as Little Red Riding Hood while I chase you through the forest?"

I laughed. "Not today. Today, the shower. But..."

"But?"

"I don't know if I want a hot or a cold shower."

He got a speculative look in his eye, then grinned. "Shower it is, then." He scooped me up without warning, making me yelp.

"Derek!"

"What?" he said, already striding toward the bathroom. "We've got work to do. I want to see you wet and slippery, flushed from the heat. I want your cold, perky nipples begging for my hot mouth. I want to make you come so hard you forget everything but my name."

Okay, then.

The shower stall was large, with a rainfall showerhead and a handheld sprayer. The sleek glass stall took up the entire far corner of Derek's bathroom. Dark slate tiles covered the floor and climbed halfway up the walls, meeting crisp white paint that brightened the space despite the lack of windows. The double vanity with matte black fixtures and marble countertop and the oversized tub built into an alcove were already giving me new fantasies.

He set me down gently, his hands lingering on my hips before he reached into the shower to turn the water on. The chill of the bathroom tiles seeped into my bare feet as I watched steam begin to rise, fogging the glass door and the wide mirror that ran the length of the vanity.

"Hot it is," he murmured, his voice a low rumble that made my core clench with anticipation.

Steam began to fill the room, obscuring the mirror and fogging the glass doors of the shower.

"Strip," Derek ordered.

The command rolled through me like thunder, low and inevitable. My pulse spiked. His eyes, molten with desire, never left mine as he pushed off the door and prowled closer.

"Now, Sofia."

A shiver raced through my body, pooling heat in my core. I dropped my pants, then my panties, then pulled off my vest and bra.

"There she is. So. Fucking. Gorgeous."

It was an emotion I wasn't used to, but I smiled, feeling safe and loved and treasured.

"Your turn."

He peeled off his shirt, revealing the hard lines and defined muscles of his chest and abs. I couldn't help but stare, my fingers itching to trace every contour. My eyes lingered on the fresh scars from our battle with Harris—raw pink lines and healing punctures that marred his skin. A reminder of how close I'd come to losing him.

Shower forgotten for the moment, I traced my fingertip lightly along a jagged wound on his ribs.

"Does it hurt?" I asked softly.

"Not when you touch it."

I leaned forward and pressed my lips against the scar, feeling his breath catch. I moved to another mark on his shoulder, a deep gash that had nearly reached bone.

"I almost lost you," I whispered against his skin, unable to keep the tremor from my voice.

Derek's hand came up to lift my chin, forcing me to meet his gaze.

"But you didn't." His thumb stroked my lower lip. "I won't leave you, Sofia. No matter what."

I rose on my tiptoes, pressing a kiss to a smaller scar near his collarbone. Derek stood perfectly still, his breathing shallow as I worked my way across his injuries, kissing them when I found them. The slash across his pectoral. The bruising along his side that was still fading from yellow to normal. The bullet wound on his forearm.

My fingers found his belt, undoing it slowly, never breaking eye contact as I slid his jeans down powerful legs, and then he was standing before me in all his glory, his cock thick and hard. My mouth went dry. I couldn't believe he was mine, all mine.

My nipples hardened into peaks. Derek's eyes lingered on them, then he smiled, all pleased and predatory, his eyes devouring my body.

"Me fucking you in the shower? Gotta say, Sofia, I'm loving your fantasy."

There it was again, that feeling of being treasured and safe. A girl could definitely get used to this.

He guided me into the shower; the hot water sluiced over my skin, just shy of scalding. My heart beat faster as Derek's hands followed the rivulets that trailed down my body. He cupped my breasts, his thumbs circling my nipples, sending jolts of pleasure straight to my core. I gasped.

"Fuck, yeah," he groaned, then bent down to take one into his mouth. He sucked hard, his tongue flicking against the sensitive bud as I moaned and arched into his touch as he worked first one nipple, then the other.

The sensation of the hot water on my skin, the steam in my lungs, the heat of Derek against me, was taking me there already.

Derek released my nipple with a wet pop. "Ready for more?"

Freaking hell, yes, I was ready!

I nodded. Derek trailed his hand down my stomach, going straight for my clit. He swirled his finger once, twice, three times.

"Holy crap!"

His finger paused. "Is that a good holy crap or a bad holy crap?"

I looked into his eyes, at the wicked glint in them; he knew exactly what kind of holy crap it was.

"I want to hear you say it, Sofia."

"Good," I gasped through the almost overwhelming need for him to touch me again. "Good. Holy. Crap."

He smirked, then spun me, so my back was flush against his chest.

"Put your hands on the tiles, Sofia."

I did, and he kicked my legs apart, hands tilting my hips so my ass pointed up.

I glanced over my shoulder at him, watched as his eyes followed his fingers down my back, over my cheeks and dipped inside. My legs went weak, and I locked them in place, not wanting to move, not wanting this to stop. My head dropped and I panted, trying to keep myself in control of the sensations flooding through me.

Derek moved to my side, his free hand grasping my throat, forcing me to look at him, as his fingers kept pumping in and out.

Okay, wow. Just freaking wow.

It was so hot, him holding me here, the water running off us both. My skin felt on fire, every nerve open and alive, my breathing short and shallow.

"You're fucking drenched, Sofia. And I ain't talking about the water. You want me inside you? Want to feel me fucking you?"

Freaking hell, yes!

"Derek." That one word was all I could manage.

He grinned, a smug grin, as if knowing exactly what he was doing to me. He turned me again, pressing me back against the cool tile wall. The cold against my back made me gasp in surprise, but I didn't have time to savor it before he lifted my leg, hooked it around his hip, and thrust inside me, all in one swift motion. I cried out, the fullness of him buried inside me almost too much to bear with all the other sensations.

He growled in response, a primal sound that resonated within my chest.

He began to move, slowly at first, each thrust deliberate and deep, hitting a spot inside me that lit up my entire body. The sound of our bodies coming together, slick and fervent, echoed around the shower.

He drove into me again and again, methodically driving me higher and higher. I loved it, loved the feel of him stretching me to my limits, the feel of the water cascading down our bodies, a scalding curtain that heightened everything.

I wanted more, needed more. He was holding himself back. Too afraid of losing control, of what might happen if he let loose. I had to reach him, had to show him that he wouldn't hurt me. That he was safe, that he wasn't going to slip back into bloodlust, that I had him.

I trailed my fingers over his abs, his chest, my nails lightly scraping against his skin. Then I found his nipples and pinched them.

"Holy crap!" he gasped.

I grinned. "Is that a good holy crap or a bad holy crap?"

"Good, definitely fucking good, Sofia!"

I pinched his nipples again, getting his attention. "Then I need you to let go, Derek. Stop holding back."

Water ran off his face. He flicked it away with a shake of his head. "I—"

"This is my fantasy, right?"

He paused, his eyes searching my face, before he nodded.

"So, I want the whole of you. The bloodlust is not going to take you again. And if it does, I've got you. I'll bring you back."

I cupped his face, my fingers tracing the rough stubble along his jaw. "I trust you, Derek Shaw. I trust us."

He leaned into my touch, his eyes closing briefly. When he opened them again, his eyes were filled with fire.

"You might regret asking for this; you know that?"

Derek didn't wait for an answer. He hiked my other leg around his waist, his hands going under my ass as he lifted me up. He held me in place, with just the tip of his cock inside me. I squirmed, desperate for him to be inside again, to fill me completely.

"Derek!"

He slammed me down on his cock.

Yes! Freaking hell, yes! Holy crap, yes!

He lifted me up again, and I struggled to catch my breath as he drove his beautiful, huge cock inside of me. This was too much, all of the different feelings overwhelming me, but especially the feel of him bucking into me, over and over again, completely out of control. It was fast and furious, and I could feel my inner walls contracting.

"I..."

"Not yet, gorgeous," Derek panted, then reached behind me and turned the heating switch to cold.

The sudden blast of cold water against my heated skin was a shock to my system, a jolt that had me gasping for breath. I didn't know what I thought it would feel like, but this... this was freaking amazing. Like all of my nerves, inside and out, were switched on and alert. My skin was so freaking sensitive from the sudden, drastic change in temperature. The cold water on me, pouring over my nipples. Derek's heat, his hot skin on mine, his cock buried deep inside me, heightened the pleasure tenfold. Every inch of my body was being caressed, being stimulated. I wrapped my arms around his neck, holding on as he drove into me again and again.

My back arched, pressing my breasts against his chest, the contact sending little shocks of electricity through me. I could feel the tension building inside me, a tight coil of need.

"Derek, I'm...," I gasped, the words torn from me. Then, with a cry that echoed off the tile walls, I shattered around him, my body convulsing with the force of my orgasm. Stars exploded behind my eyelids as wave after wave of pleasure washed over me. With a final, powerful thrust, I felt his cock pulse as he came, filling me with new warmth as the cool water cascaded over us.

It felt like it took forever to come down, Derek's breath mingling with mine as our breathing eventually slowed.

"Fucking hell, Sofia."

I nodded, not able to speak yet.

"I'm thinking we're going to be doing more fucking bets. I'm going to find out your fantasies, gorgeous, and we're going to do all of them." He kissed me softly. "Every last one."

My inner walls pulsed. That sounded so freaking awesome.

CHAPTER FIFTY-TWO

EPILOGUE - SAM

The secured wing of the Bridgetown medical facility smelled like antiseptic and sickness—the sharp tang of disinfectant barely masking the underlying scent of sweat, fear, and something worse. Something... wrong.

The werewolves we'd brought from the airfield lined were in the reinforced containment cells, most strapped to their beds or restrained by silver-laced cuffs. Some barely moved, their bodies twitching in restless, fevered sleep. Others thrashed against their restraints, their eyes red-rimmed and wild, lips curled in silent snarls, trapped in an endless cycle of rage and violence.

A low, broken moan echoed from cell three, where a woman—once someone's daughter, someone's Packmate—curled into herself, rocking back and forth. The scent of ripple clung to her like poison, warping everything about her into something unnatural.

I exhaled sharply. "This place is a goddamn nightmare."

Mason stood beside me, jaw tight, arms crossed. His eyes swept the cells with clinical detachment. "We're doing what we can."

I let out a frustrated breath, running a hand down my face. "How many of them do you think you can save?"

Mason hesitated, his broad shoulders rising and falling in a slow breath. "Some. Maybe." His gaze flicked toward cell six. A kid, who couldn't have been more than nineteen, was trying to gnaw through the cuffs securing his wrists, his blood-streaked teeth bared in a feral grimace.

"Not all of them," Mason finished grimly.

I hated this. Hated that I had to be the one to point out the obvious. They were beyond saving; it was kinder to put them down than to have them suffer like this.

"You know what we have to do."

"We're not there yet." Mason's voice hardened.

I got it. I really did. When I started working for the Council, I'd been the same. Desperate to save as many as I could on the chance that we'd develop a cure.

"How many more secure wings can you build? The number of werewolves who are addicted to ripple is increasing by the day. Where are you gonna keep them all? How are you gonna feed them?" I leaned closer. "There's no cure. No going back. You need to think about what we're doing here. At some point, you need to ask if we're saving them or just dragging out the inevitable. What would they want?"

Mason's hands curled into fists before he relaxed them. "I refuse to accept that they can't be saved."

"Yeah? And what happens when one of them breaks free?" I'd seen it happen. Had been there to clean up the bloody aftermath. "What happens when they take out an entire Pack, your Pack, before we can stop them?"

"I won't let that happen."

Yeah, I'd thought the same thing once, but it had ended with so much fucking death, if I lived to be a thousand, I wouldn't be able to forget the faces of the children who'd been killed because of my arrogance.

"Mason, listen to m—"

"Enough." His tone slammed the door on the conversation. "Shya and I decided. We keep as many as we can, as long as we can, while we research a cure."

Fuck! There was no arguing with Mason when he dug in like this. I'd run Shaw Investigations with him and had learned the hard way when to back off. I'd try again in a few days—assuming none of the werewolves broke free before then.

"You talked to Derek?"

My jaw clenched before I answered. "He's got Sofia with him. He doesn't need me checking in."

That wasn't entirely true, but I didn't want to think too much about why I hadn't called Derek. Why I couldn't. I'd nearly killed him, for fuck's sake. My own brother. My twin, the one who knew me better than I knew myself. I'd made that decision. Was having nightmares about it because I hadn't hesitated. Derek was in bloodlust. There was no coming back from that. I knew he would have wanted me to kill him, to protect Sofia at all costs. And I tried.

How did I face him after that? How did I explain? What made it worse was that I wasn't sure what I should apologize for—trying to kill him or not succeeding? If it was me, if I was a danger to my mate and my Pack, I'd want someone I trusted to get the job done.

And now I didn't know if Derek turned again whether I'd be able to finish what I started. And if I couldn't, I'd have failed him when he needed me most.

"Sam." Mason's voice was quieter now, more measured. "You need to talk to him. You guys have to fix this, whatever the fuck *this* is."

My phone buzzed.

I glanced at the screen, saw the name, and immediately regretted every life choice that had led me to this moment.

Gideon Calloway. Enforcer to the Wolf Council. His official job was to support and protect Council members. His unofficial job was to make my eyebrow twitch with annoyance whenever he was nearby.

With a sigh, I swiped to accept. "I'm busy, Calloway; what do you want?"

"Aw, Sammy-boy, is that any way to greet your favorite Wolf Council enforcer?"

"You're not my favorite anything."

"That hurts, Sammy. That genuinely wounds me to my core. And here I am, about to make your day. I should hang up just to teach you manners."

I pinched the bridge of my nose. "Just get to it."

"You know, you're no fun these days. I thought you might want a heads up on not one but two delightful tidbits of intel."

If Gideon was calling them delightful, it meant it was bad fucking news. Why did he never call me with good news?

"First up, Talia Johnson has been locked away in her hotel room studying the documents you sent over."

I frowned, wondering why she was in a hotel and not back at the Council when I remembered she was one of the delegation in Philadelphia meeting with the human governments. I was supposed to be there, but Derek was more important.

"She is pissed, man. Like, the woman never smiles, but this, this is a whole new level of ice-queen fury."

Talia was one of the few I trusted outside of my old Pack. She'd been the one who'd trained me when I'd first joined the Council.

"But it has, apparently, given her a plan.

"Plan?" I asked, immediately wary.

"The undercover, probably-gonna-get-you-killed kind." Gideon's voice was practically gleeful. "You know Simon Webster's little coven of psychopaths? She needs someone in his organization to feed us intel on it."

"Why me?"

"Apparently, you've got an in. Or rather, you know someone on the inside."

I frowned. "Who?"

"Half-witch, half-werewolf disaster named Annabella McGrath."

Why did that name sound familiar?

My eyebrows shot up when it hit me. "Sofia's cousin?"

"Bingo! Give the man a prize. Annabella is indeed a cousin to a Sofia and Jase Miller, who I believe are members of the Three Rivers Pack, no?"

"And she's working with Webster."

"Oh, yes. He's bankrolling her group of fanatical insurgents, according to a report that just came in."

Fuck! Well, this day was just getting better and better.

"And the second piece of news? I'm guessing it's an update on the meeting in Philly."

"Aw, you know me so well. We just wrapped a delightful little meeting with some human government types. Great people—if you enjoy humans in bad suits looking terrified of their own shadows."

"They agree to our demands?"

"Well, they've agreed to stop working on their little 'anti-werewolf vaccine' for now."

"For now?"

"For now," he echoed, voice mocking. "But in exchange, they had a teensy request. One that our fearless leaders jumped to accept."

I felt the headache forming behind my eyes. This had to be bad. Gideon only drew things out when it was bad news. "Just say it, Gideon."

"They're putting a human rep on the Council. Full voting rights, full authority. Congratulations, Sammy, we're officially letting the humans sit at the grown-ups' table."

A human on the Council? Making decisions that affected Shifters, with Webster and Kane running around trying to start a war between us? That was a seriously bad fucking idea.

"Who?" I demanded.

"I have a feeling you've heard of him. Some ex-military type who disappeared for years but is now back making nice with the human governments, and apparently is super passionate about 'containing the werewolf threat.'"

I froze, wondering if our luck could really be this shit, if the forces against us were really this organized.

"Name?" I demanded.

"Er, let me see, Kane. Victor Kane."

⁂

The Relentless Mate, Book 6 in the Shifters of the Three Rivers series

Half-witch, half-wolf, fully deceived—until her greatest enemy awakens her true self...

A steamy paranormal romance featuring enemies-to-lovers, fated mates, undercover identities, and finding family in unexpected places. Perfect for fans of werewolf romances with strong heroines and possessive heroes who will do anything for their mates.

You've seen them get their HEA, but see how it started! Sign up to my newsletter at www.kiranightingale.com and get Fairground Fling, a free prequel short story about Derek and Sofia's first date!

FREE BOOK! COME JOIN US IN THE SHIFTER REALM!

Kira Nightingale
Mystically Dark, Wildly Romantic...

You've seen them get their HEA, but do you want to read about how it started? Sign up to my newsletter and get Fairground Fling, a free prequel short story about Derek and Sofia's first date!

As an author, I write paranormal romance books that are full of hot Shifters with action-packed plots and small-town vibes. I send out my newsletter every week, and in it you can get exclusive content and snippets from my current work-in-progress, fun memes and polls, and sometimes even photos of my beast of a cat, Scout. You can sign up to my newsletter at www.kiranightingale.com

Fairground Fling, Shifters of the Three Rivers 0.5

No way will I let fate decide my destiny, but Derek Shaw is back and proving impossible to resist...

Sofia

All I wanted was to run my coffee shop in peace, avoid my fated mate, and forget about our Shifter bond. Is that too much to ask for?

Apparently it is, because Derek Shaw just walked back into my life, all rippling muscles and piercing eyes. The man sets my blood on fire, but there's no way I'm giving in. I've seen what happens when "fated mates" are torn apart, and I won't let that happen to me.

Derek left to join the military, turning his back on our bond. Now he's back in the Three Rivers Pack, determined to win me over. But I've built walls around my heart that even an Alpha wolf can't break through. At least, that's what I keep telling myself...

Derek

I left Three Rivers to serve my country, but I never forgot Sofia. Every day, her fiery hair and captivating scent haunted my thoughts.

Now I'm back, and the pull towards Sofia is stronger than ever. My wolf won't rest until I claim what's mine. But Sofia's determined to keep her distance. That's okay, though. I'm a Shaw, and we never back down from a challenge.

ALSO BY KIRA NIGHTINGALE

Shifters of the Three Rivers series

The Runaway Mate

The Renegade Mate

The Resolute Mate

The Rescued Mate

The Reluctant Mate

The Relentless Mate (coming 2025)

A Three Rivers Holiday Tale: A Shifters of the Three Rivers Novella

Boxsets

Shifters of the Three Rivers, Omnibus of Books 1-3 (ebook only)

Mai and Ryan's story with ***an exclusive epilogue!***

Audiobooks (available on Audible and Amazon)

The Runaway Mate

The Renegade Mate

The Resolute Mate

ABOUT KIRA NIGHTINGALE

Kira Nightingale is a Scot living in Canada. She has always wanted to be a writer, and can't believe how lucky she is to finally be able to write romance stories all day long. She lives with her husband, her two children and a massive cat called Scout. Kira loves to drink tea (her favorite is Long Island Iced Tea, but unfortunately she only gets to drink this occasionally) and likes to dunk cookies in it (yes, even the Long Island kind.)

ACKNOWLEDGEMENTS

This book would not have been possible without the unwavering support of some truly incredible people.

First and foremost, to Mr. Nightingale—thank you for being my constant source of strength, encouragement, and inspiration. Your patience, humor, and love have been my anchor throughout this journey.

To Kid 1 and Kid 2, my amazing children, thank you for filling my life with endless joy, laughter, and perspective. You remind me every day what truly matters, and your belief in me means the world.

A huge thank you to my phenomenal PAs, Martinique and Seth. Your dedication, organization, and ability to anticipate what I need before I even know I need it have been nothing short of miraculous. You've kept me grounded and focused, and for that, I am endlessly grateful.

Once again, I have to give special thanks to my wonderful editor, Brigitte Billings. Brigitte, your keen eye, unwavering patience, and insightful suggestions have elevated this book in ways I could never have imagined. Any mistakes that remain are entirely my own.

To Jamie Ty and the talented team at 100 Covers, thank you for creating such a stunning cover. Your creativity, vision, and support brought this book to life in a way that perfectly reflects its heart and soul.

Finally, to you—the readers—thank you for picking up this book and spending your precious time with my words. Your support means everything, and I hope this story resonates with you as much as it does with me.